"WARE!"

Mondragon heard the kid's voice shout, close, and muscles jumped, dropped him into a deep crouch and had his hands going for his sword as a cloaked figure rushed him, up the arch of the bridge, sword glittering.

He came up on guard, met the attack, flung his cloak out of the way, attacked and parried, pushing the cloaked man back and back. Attack and parry and attack, a scratch on his opponent, a second scratch, a third, and the man backing and backing.

But the kid was screaming murder, there was something else, *someone* else—

Diversion cost him a scratch of his own, blade slipping past the quillon and the half-guard, and he came back in quarte, back again and back again with a triple disengage and a plain feint to terce, then attack, straight in past the too-extreme reaction, hardly a shock as the point went in and his opponent ran up on him, still trying to defend himself when Mondragon spun and freed his blade and kicked his opponent off the bank into the raging Grand.

—facing a second swordsman and a third, holding Denny Takahashi with a gun to his head. . . .

C.J. CHERRYH

THE ALLIANCE-UNION UNIVERSE

The Company Wars
DOWNBELOW STATION
The Era of Rapprochement
FORTY THOUSAND IN GEHENNA
MERCHANTER'S LUCK
The Chanur Novels
THE PRIDE OF CHANUR
CHANUR'S VENTURE
THE KIF STRIKE BACK
CHANUR'S HOMECOMING
VOYAGER IN NIGHT
PORT ETERNITY
The Mri Wars
THE FADED SUN: KESRITH
THE FADED SUN: SHON'JIR
THE FADED SUN: KUTATH
SERPENT'S REACH
Merovingen Nights (Mri Wars period)
ANGEL WITH THE SWORD
Merovingen Nights—Anthologies
FESTIVAL MOON (#1)
FEVER SEASON (#2)
TROUBLED WATERS (#3)
SMUGGLER'S GOLD (#4)
The Age of Exploration
CUCKOO'S EGG
The Hanan Rebellion
BROTHERS OF EARTH
HUNTER OF WORLDS

C.J. CHERRYH invites you to enter the world of MEROVINGEN NIGHTS!

ANGEL WITH THE SWORD *by C.J. Cherryh*
A Merovingen Nights Novel

FESTIVAL MOON *edited by C.J. Cherryh*
(stories by C.J. Cherryh, Leslie Fish, Robert Lynn Asprin, Nancy Asire, Mercedes Lackey, Janet and Chris Morris, Lynn Abbey)

FEVER SEASON *edited by C.J. Cherryh*
(stories by C.J. Cherryh, Chris Morris, Mercedes Lackey, Leslie Fish, Nancy Asire, Lynn Abbey, Janet Morris)

TROUBLED WATERS *edited by C.J. Cherryh*
(stories by C.J. Cherryh, Mercedes Lackey, Nancy Asire, Janet Morris, Lynn Abbey, Chris Morris, Roberta Rogow, Leslie Fish)

SMUGGLER'S GOLD *edited by C.J. Cherryh*
(stories by Mercedes Lackey, Roberta Rogow, Nancy Asire, Robert Lynn Asprin, Chris and Janet Morris, C.J. Cherryh, Lynn Abbey, Leslie Fish)

MEROVINGEN NIGHTS

SMUGGLER'S GOLD

C.J. CHERRYH

DAW BOOKS, INC.
DONALD A. WOLLHEIM, PUBLISHER

1633 Broadway, New York, NY 10019

Cover art by Tim Hildebrandt.

Maps by Pat Tobin.

DAW Book Collectors No. 759.

First Printing, October 1988

1 2 3 4 5 6 7 8 9

PRINTED IN THE U.S.A.

CONTENTS

MEROVIN

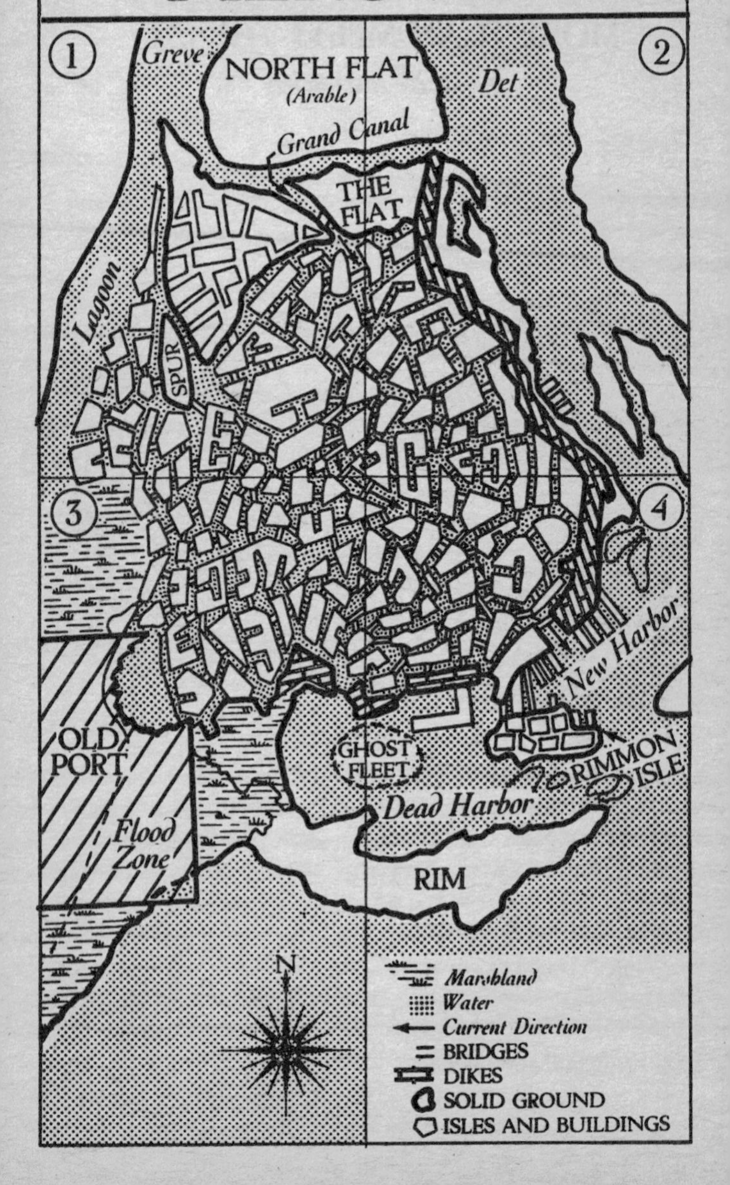

1
Greve
NORTH FLAT
(Arable)
Det
2
Grand Canal
THE FLAT
Lagoon
SPUR
3
4
New Harbor
OLD PORT
Flood Zone
GHOST FLEET
RIMMON ISLE
Dead Harbor
RIM
N
Marshland
Water
Current Direction
BRIDGES
DIKES
SOLID GROUND
ISLES AND BUILDINGS

MORE THAN MEETS THE EYE

by Mercedes Lackey

It was dark, and it was dangerous, and Denny was so happy he could hardly stand himself. If it hadn't been too risky to chance *any* sound, he'd have been singing. Or humming, anyway.

He was upside-down, suspended by his knees from one of the dozens of timbers supporting Megary's leaky, half-rotten roof—the kind of position he'd held enough times in the past that he was almost as comfortable upside-down as he was on his feet. Hidden by the darkness, two stories beneath him, the canal-water lapped quietly against the foundations of Megary, but there was not much else in the way of sound. There wasn't even so much as a breeze to make the timbers of the building sway and creak, which made it all the more imperative that *he* keep silent.

And what he was doing up here—oh, Lord and Ancestors, what a *glorious* stunt! If *only* he could tell somebody besides Rat and Rif and Tom Mondragon! This was even better than the Boregy's window!

He was sawing most of the way through the bolts that held the metal grilles and bars protecting Megary's second-story windows. *Most* of the way, not all; just enough so that somebody who was determined on a break-in had only to give a good hard pull to break the grilles free—but from inside or outside, to everything but a close inspection, all was secure.

He grinned to himself, working the cable-saw carefully, slowly, back and forth on the bolt currently under his fingers. Rat had threatened his life if he lost that *very* expensive little saw—but had been quite willing to loan Denny the tiny high-tech thief's tool when she heard *whose* place it was going to be used on. Little more than a bit of wire with two handles, it would cut through damn near any metal, and was making short work of Megary's soft iron bolts.

It was as black as the inside of a cat tonight, no Moon, no Dogs, nary a star showing through the clouds of a warm, overcast spring night. No matter; Denny hadn't ever needed to *see* to know what he was about on second-story work. Rat and Rif had taught him to work blind; it was *best* working blind in some ways, the darkest nights were a thief's best friends.

One: case the place till you know it like the inside of your mouth. Two: take it slow. Three: go by feel and know by feel.

Those were Rat's rules for nightwork. She might have added the one Denny was abiding by tonight.

Four: have you a lookout.

And Lord and Ancestors—*what* a lookout!

Down there somewhere on the canal below him, hidden in the darkest shadows and straining eyes and ears against the thick blackness, was no less a personage than Altair Jones—and a more unlikely pairing than himself and Jones was hard to imagine.

The greater wonder was that *Jones* had come to *him* to ask for his help.

Runners had lunch *after* the rest of Merovingen; not the least because runners were often sent to fetch lunches and drink for their employers. It made for a long morning and a grumbly stomach, but Denny had gotten used to it. Besides, it meant the afternoon was that much shorter.

And you could pick up some nice bits at half price from vendors anxious to unload what was left now that the noontime crowd was fed. So this afternoon Denny had been pleasing his palate with spiced fish rolls that were only slightly soggy, his hide with warm spring sunshine, and his feet with the fact that his behind was firmly planted on a Gallandry walkway. He had a good view of the canal below from here, and no one hassled a kid in Gallandry-runner colors so long as he kept his butt near enough to the edge of the walk that he didn't impede traffic.

He had been dangling his feet over the edge, and had both arms draped over the lower bar of the guard rail, watching the traffic pass in the half-light below him. He was rather pleased that he knew a good many of those passing by name—even if those good folks would hardly appreciate the "honor." He watched, feeling his back and shoulders ache in sympathy, as Del and Tommy labored against the current, poling what looked to be a nice little cargo of barrels of some kind up the canal. He noted one of the younger Bruders go by, riding in one of the family boats, and old man Fife in a hire-boat going the opposite direction. And he saw a double-handful of canalers he recognized besides Del Suleiman, and rather wished he had his brother's incredible memory. There might be valuable information there if only he could remember who he saw going where.

He was halfway through his lunch when he saw Jones tie up down below. So far as *he* knew she had no business on Gallandry today, so he wasn't much surprised when she strolled along the walkway and planted herself beside him; feet dangling, like his, over the edge, the rest of her hugging the bottom railing.

"Bite?" he said, offering her a roll to be sociable. It didn't pay to be less than polite to Jones at any time—but most especially Denny walked softly these days. What with her being short-fused, Tom Mondragon short of cash, and Denny's brother more than half the cause of both—

"Ney," she said shortly. "Et."

He shrugged. She'd say her say when she was ready; he wasn't about to push her.

He kept a watch on her out of the corner of his eye all the same. After living these many weeks with Tom Mondragon, Denny knew Altair Jones about as well as he knew anybody—and the storm-warnings were definitely out. The sleeves of her dark blue sweater were pushed up over her elbows, which she only did when nervy; her battered canaler's cap was pulled down low on her forehead, like she was trying to keep her eyes from being read. But Denny was close enough for a good view, and he could see that her square jaw was tensed, the dark eyes gone darker with brooding, the broad shoulders hunched, the fists clenching and unclenching—storm warnings for fair. Could be things hadn't been going her way of late. . . .

"Ye got the sneak's ways, Deneb Takahashi," she said at last, softly, so softly her voice hardly carried to Denny.

Denny tensed up himself; in all of Merovingen only Theta Gallandry, Altair Jones and Tom Mondragon knew his real name, his and Raj's. Only *they* knew that Raj Tai and Denny Diaz were really brothers; were *Rigel* and *Deneb* of the Nev Hettek merchant clan Takahashi. Only those three knew that the boys had fled from assassins who had killed their mother, and were still very probably under death sentence from the Sword of God for the things their dead mother Angela might have told them and the names and faces they knew.

For Altair Jones to be using his *real* name—this was *serious.*

"I ain't no sneak," he said shortly. " 'Less Tom wants it. It don't pay, 'cept t' buy a piece 'f rope. 'Less ye're *real* good." He thought of Rat, of Rif, their skills and bravado, with raw envy. "I'm good; I ain't that good."

"What if *I* wanted ye to turn sneak for a bit?" came the unexpected question.

"*Huh?*" he responded, turning to stare at her, jaw slack with surprise.

She moved her head slowly to meet his astonished gaze. "Megarys," she said tersely.

He nodded, understanding her then. *Somebody*—Sword, likely—had kidnapped the redoubtable Altair Jones; had kidnapped her, and truly, *truly,* frightened her, something Denny had never thought possible. She said that nothing else had happened; Denny believed her, mostly because she hadn't burned Megary's—which was where she'd been held—to the waterline. If she'd been molested (as half of those who plied the canals still thought might have happened) that's what Denny reckoned she *would* have done, and damn the consequences and the cost.

Instead she was pursuing a quiet little one-woman vendetta against the slavers, a vendetta that up until now had been confined to vandalism and dirty tricks. In this she was being aided and abetted by most of her canaler friends who didn't have much love for the Megarys at the best of times, and were determined to teach them a lesson about crossing the line and messing with canal-folk.

Now, though, it seemed like she might be thinking

of branching that vendetta out a little, to broaden the way she was hitting them. To—second-story work? Could fit; and not a bad thought, either. It was possible some of her friends were getting tired and dropping out of the feud; that might account for the suppressed ill-temper she was showing. Besides, to really hurt the slavers you would have to hit them where it counted most—the pocket. That meant break-*outs,* or break-*ins,* or both.

"Yey," Denny replied slowly. "Yey, Jones, ye got me. You say, how and when."

The hunched shoulders relaxed a bit; she favored him with a ghost of a smile. "Knew ye wasn't *all* bad," she said, grabbing the railing and pulling herself to her feet.

Denny wasn't all fool, either; *he* knew where his primary loyalty lay—with the man he'd privately chosen as his model and mentor, Tom Mondragon. So when Denny had found Mondragon alone that afternoon in the sitting room of his apartment on Petrescu that all four of them now called home, with no sign of Jones *or* Raj being back yet, he had felt no qualms about interrupting the man's reading with a terse report of Jones' attempt to recruit him.

The warm, comfortable sitting room seemed to turn cold as Mondragon's expression chilled. Mondragon's hands tightened a little on the sheaf of papers he was holding; the green eyes went cloudy. Denny knew *him* now, too—knew by those slight signs that Mondragon was not happy with this little piece of news.

Denny clasped his hands in front of him and tried to look older than his thirteen-nearly-fourteen years; and capable; capable enough to run with Jones. Maybe even to run a bit of control on Jones.

"M'ser," he offered, then, before Mondragon could

speak to forbid him to help, "ye *know* I ain't bad at roof-walkin'. Ye seen me; ye set me jobs yerself. Ye know if I tell 'er 'no' she's just gonna go it alone. Lemme help, yey? Happen I c'n keep 'er outa real bad trouble. Happen if she's got me 'long, she maybe won't go *lookin'* fer bad trouble so damn hard, figurin' she's gotta keep me outa it."

A good hit, that last; Jones was likely to feel at least a little bit responsible for Denny, if only because she was four, five years older. That was the line Rif had taken when he was along on one of her jobs, and she was one of the *least* responsible people Denny knew. Mondragon tilted his head to the side and looked thoughtful when Denny finished, then put the papers down on the couch to one side of him, crossing his arms over his chest and tapping his lips with one long, aristocratic finger. "How if I tell *you* to keep her out of trouble?" he asked finally.

Denny winced. *That* was nothing less than an impossibility, as Mondragon should very well know. "Ask me t' fly. I got a better chance."

Mondragon managed a quirk of the right corner of his mouth. "I'm afraid you're probably right. I should know better than to ask you to do something no one else can." He stared at Denny, then stared *through* him; thinking, and thinking hard. "All right; go ahead and give her a hand. See if you can't keep her from being totally suicidal."

Denny grinned and shrugged; so far as *he* could see, both he *and* Jones had won. He'd told Tom—and he hadn't been forbidden to help or ordered to hinder. What little conscience he had was clear, and he was free to indulge in the kind of hell-raising he adored *with* Mondragon's tacit approval—

He prepared to turn and scoot down the hall to

vanish into the downstairs bedroom he shared with Raj, when Mondragon stopped him with a lifted finger.

"But—" he said, with the tone that told Denny that disobedience would cost more than Denny would *ever* want to pay, "I expect you to keep me informed. *Completely* informed. Chapter and verse on *what* she's doing, and *when,* and *how.* And I want it *in advance;* and *well* in advance."

Denny stifled a sigh of disappointment.

"Yey, m'ser," he agreed, hoping his reluctance didn't show too much. Because he knew what *that* meant. Maybe he wasn't going to have to try to stop Jones—but now he was honor-bound to *keep* her from trying to do the kinds of things *he'd* like to pull. And what that meant, mostly, was keeping things quiet. Damn. "Quiet" wasn't half the fun.

Hey, this 'un didn't work out too bad, Denny thought, inching along the rough beam to the opposite corner of the grille (ignoring the splinters he was getting in his hands) and attacking the next bolt. *Quiet—an' nothin' t' connect me 'r Jones t' the mess when th' hell breaks out. Tom was happy 'nough 'bout* that. *An' we bin doin' good t'night; this's two more windows than I'd figured likely t' cut when we planned this.*

He had gotten this bolt nearly sawed through when the *hoop-woo* of a marsh-strider sounded down on the invisible canal below him; somewhere to his right, which meant upstream.

Jones—and she'd spotted possible trouble.

Denny coiled the cable-saw up and stowed it safely away in the buttoned pocket of his pants, making *damn* sure the button was fastened and the saw *in* there. Then he inched, still hanging upside down, back along the support beam until he met the cross-brace. He switched to it, using both hands and legs, taking it slow and careful to avoid making the wood creak, until he reached the end that met the roof, where the gutter was. The drainpipes and gutterwork on Megary Isle were sound, even if most of the rest of the building wasn't; Megary got most of its potable water from rain.

Might ask Raj if there's somethin' we c'd drop inta the roof-tank, give 'em all th' heaves an' trots. Denny grinned again in the darkness—he had a fair notion Jones would like that idea real well. It was another quiet one—which would please Tom. And it was an idea that would cost Megary money, real hard cash-money—cash for the doctors, for clean water when they figured out what the cause was, and for somebody to come clean and purge the system. That pleased Denny—and there was always a chance that the fear of plague or sickness in Megary would flush some of the Sword agents out of their safe-house and maybe into the hands of the blacklegs. Hmm—another thought; if they had any human cargo in there, they might have to find another place for the captives. And that would give the slaves a chance at escape. That pleased Denny even more; he didn't have much in the way of moral scruples, but he was flat against slaving. *Rif's mighty cozy with Black Cal—if I pull this 'un, maybe I get her word about it, she gets word t' him—*

He continued to think about this new plan as he grabbed the edge of the gutter and hauled himself up onto the roof with its aid. The metal groaned a little, and he froze, but nothing further untoward happened. He continued easing himself up over the edge. He crawled from that point along the roof edge, feeling his way and moving slowly to avoid any more noise, until he found the outside corner of the roof and the place where the gutter met a drainpipe. He stopped, taking stock with his ears, and nodded after a bit. The echoes from the water lapping against the building were right for where he thought he was; and he thought he could make out the sable pit of the old frozen Marsh Gate, blacker blot in the night-shadows ahead of him. He should be right on the point of Megary where the building fronted Tidewater Canal—and Jones should be right below him, holding her skip steady against the pull of the current.

"Hoop-wah," he called softly, and was rewarded with a *ker-whick* almost directly below. He eased himself over the edge of the roof, dangled blindly for a little until he got his legs around the pipe, then shinnied silently down the drainpipe to the narrow ledge that ran around the edge of the island.

"Ker-whick-ick," he chirped, struggling to hold his balance on the cold, slippery, slimy ledge, as he positioned himself with his back to the wall. Come high tide, this would be underwater, and it tended to collect unsavory stuff. He was having to hold to the drainpipe behind him with both hands; the ledge wasn't even wide enough to get his whole foot on it here.

Ker-whick-a, came the answer, and the soft bump of a boat-nose against the ledge beside him, black blot against the reflective water. Denny squirmed about like a cat, grabbed the skip's nose with both hands and leapfrogged aboard her before Jones had a chance to say a word.

He felt his way down off the nose, worked his way past the barrels occupying the slats of the bottom, and sat down on the worn boards of the halfdeck, knowing *she* knew he'd gotten aboard safely by the skip's movement. He heard and felt her heave with the pole, moving the skip into the current of Tidewater; there was a tense moment as they passed the bulk of Megary, but it stayed quiet, with hardly a light showing anywhere in the building. Then they were on past, down to Hafiz, where Jones had legitimate—well, sort of—business. A barrel delivery from Moghi, and not all of the barrels were empty. And, as per Denny's plans, this wasn't the first night she'd had him along on the skip to help, nor would it be the last.

Make it look like business as usual, and that's what everybody is gonna figure, was another of Rat's maxims.

When they finished this delivery, they'd head home by way of Hoh's. Denny would pass Rat her little tool under cover of buying her a drink, and that would be her signal to spread the word tonight along certain channels (that only she and Rif knew how to contact) that Megary was no longer as impregnable as Megary—or the Sword, who'd arranged for the new grillework and bars—thought. . . .

Denny grinned yet again as he picked the splinters from his climb out of his palms with his teeth. *Figure as many as ten a' Rat's buddies hit 'em—Lord an' Ancestors—I damnsure wouldn't wanta be th' feller responsible fer them grilles!* he thought, smugly.

He heard Jones start to whistle through her teeth, and guessed she was thinking the same thing.

Well, that was a little more off the tote board for what he and Raj owed to Jones and Tom. A good night's work, profitable for everybody—except Megary.

"M'ser?" Raj whispered into the dark cavern under Nayab, a cavern accessible only by a hole in the foundations that faced Petrescu. He hadn't brought a light; *he* didn't intend to go crawling around down in the tumbled remains of what had been Nayab's bottom story before time and the tide and the settling of the building into the mud made the lowest level uninhabitable and the occupants had all moved one floor up.

There was, thank the Angel, plenty of light from the windows and walkways above to let him see where he was going, and to show him the footing on the ledge that led to the hole.

The fact was he really didn't want to be here at all.

But for some reason that maybe only God knew, that strange, scarred man had followed him out of the swamp after saving himself and Denny from the Razorfin gang. And presumably for that same reason he had decided to set himself up as a kind of watchdog or bodyguard for the two of them. Raj felt a certain guilty responsibility for the man's well-being.

So here he was, clinging to the ledge above the waterline, with a bundle and a message to deliver and only the maziest notion if the man was still *in* there.

If he hadn't been so paranoid, he might never have noticed the stranger at all. But he was desperately afraid that his last escapade had drawn unwelcome attention to the entire Mondragon menage, attention that would *have* to include the Sword. And if anyone who ever knew Angela Takahashi got a good look at Raj—well, there'd be no doubt whose kid he was.

So he'd been watching every shadow, and thinking out every footstep ever since—and he'd seen the man ghosting along, fifty feet behind and one level below as he went to work one morning. And no matter how he'd changed his course, there the man was. Then he'd watched from the dirty window of the Gallandry offices as the man shadowed Denny on his first run of the morning. At that point he was ready to rush out to attack the man himself out of sheer terror when he moved into and out of a patch of sunlight—

It was at that point, when he got a brief but very good look at the man's scarred face, that he'd recognized him as the mysterious stranger who'd saved them.

It was that very night that he saw the man slipping into the foundation-hole across the canal.

And now when he watched carefully he could catch

the stranger at his comings and goings—and *very* rarely, at trailing them. He thought that after a few days the man would get tired and go away—swampies weren't known for long attention spans. But he hadn't, and Raj realized that he was going to have to do some few things about the fact that he was there, and not about to give up on his self-appointed task.

First—tell Tom, so that Mondragon didn't kill the stranger, thinking he was a threat. That was easiest done in the morning, before Mondragon was completely awake and thinking.

Raj planned his approach carefully, waiting until Mondragon had gotten his first cup of tea and was starting his second before accosting him.

"M'ser Tom," he said hesitantly, "there's something you should know."

Before Tom could do more than look apprehensive, Raj had plowed onward. "That man I told you about? The one in the swamp? The one that helped me and Denny?"

Mondragon nodded, slowly putting the mug down on the table and absently running a hand through his tangled golden mane.

"He's here." Raj said shortly. "Hiding out at Nayab. I've seen him."

Mondragon didn't move, much, but he went from sleepy and a little bored to startled awake, wary and alert. Raj continued before he had a chance to interrupt.

"He's right across the canal, holed up in the foundation under Nayab," Raj said, words tumbling over each other as he tried to get them all out. "Please, m'ser Tom, I don't think he means any harm. I think he's guarding us, me and Denny; he's been following me to work, and I saw him following Denny on his runs. I think maybe he's trying to keep us safe. He's saved us once—I don't know why he did, I don't know why he's watching us, only—only please, m'ser Tom, —please don't kill him."

Mondragon regarded Raj dubiously for a moment before replying. "You have strange choices in friends, boy," he said, his words falling like stones into the silence. He picked up his mug, and studied Raj over the rim of it.

Raj hadn't the faintest notion how to reply to that, so, in keeping with his recent decision to keep his mouth shut when he didn't know what to say, he'd remained silent.

"How sure are you of this—friend?" Mondragon had asked, when even *he* seemed to find the silence had gone on too long.

Raj had to shake his head. "I'm not, m'ser. I told you, I don't know why he helped us in the first place, I don't know why he's here now. I thought maybe—he's a crazy, sort of, I thought he'd get tired and go away, but he hasn't. I don't know what to tell you, m'ser, —but I just don't think he means *us* anything but good."

Tom relaxed back into his chair, a thought-crease between his brows. Raj remained patiently standing by the table, wishing with all his heart that he hadn't been such a great fool this winter as to destroy any trust Mondragon had in him.

"*I* didn't know this watchdog of yours was even there, boy," Tom said at last, cradling his tea mug in both hands, as if taking warmth from it. "That argues for a—certain level of expertise. That is a very bad sign."

"If he wanted us, he could'a had us a dozen times by now," Raj whispered humbly. "He could'a had us in the swamp, and nobody the wiser."

"True." Tom continued to brood over the tea. "There

would be no point in his waiting that *I* can see. If he wanted to take you to use against me he should have made his move by now. Which makes me think you might be right about him."

Raj heaved a completely internal sigh of relief.

"Now I can't for a moment imagine why this man should have decided to attach himself to you and your brother, but *since* he has, and since he seems to have some useful skills—" He paused, and raised one golden eyebrow significantly. "—and since he seems to have appointed himself as your bodyguard gratis—"

Raj flushed, and hung his head. He knew Mondragon was still desperately short of money, and he knew that the reason was that Tom had spent vast sums of money trying to find Raj when Mondragon and Jones had thought he was in trouble. Money that hadn't been his to spend. Kalugin money. Or Boregy, which amounted to the same thing.

"—well, I am not inclined to look this particular gift horse in the mouth," Mondragon concluded. "But I hope he has the sense to realize that I am inclined to strike first and ask questions like 'friend or foe' afterward. And I want you to stay out of his reach after this."

"Yes, m'ser Tom," Raj had stuttered, backing out of the kitchen hastily. "Thank you, m'ser Tom—"

But here he was. Because he felt a responsibility to warn the man—and because he had come with something besides a warning.

The canalers, ignoring Raj's vehement protests that he *did not* want to be paid for doctoring their kids, had taken to leaving things at Jones' skip or with Del. Things Raj had no earthly use for—a sweater, five sizes too big, laboriously knitted out of the tag ends of five different lots and colors of yarn, half a blanket, candle ends, a homemade oil stove of the kind used on skips, and more.

Raj couldn't use it, and Jones couldn't sell or trade the stuff without going to a world of time and effort that she couldn't spare—but if the stranger had come out of the swamp, he was even poorer than the poorest canaler. These odds and ends could mean a great deal to him. So that was the thing Raj meant to do—see that the man was in some sort of comfort. He'd gotten a few pennybits doing some odd jobs on his day off—and those had gone for a bit of food for the man, flour and salt and oil, and a bit of dried salt fish, all bundled in with the rest.

"M'ser?" Raj called again into the darkness beneath Nayab, wondering if the man could hear him—or if he was even there. He turned away for a moment to look out uneasily over the canal behind him—

"I'm no m'ser, boy," came a harsh whisper from beside him.

Raj jumped and nearly fell in the canal. A long arm snaked out of the darkness and steadied him.

"M-M-M'ser, I—" Raj stuttered.

"I told you, boy," the ragged, battered stranger said, a little less harshly, as he emerged from the darkness of the foundation-cavern, "I'm no *m'ser.* Call me—Wolfling."

He waded back into the blackness under Nayab, knowing his way even in the pitch-dark, the stale water slimy around his ankles. His name had been Ruin, once—Ruin al-Banna, in a time he would rather have forgotten, a time when he was an agent of the Sword of God.

That had been before Chance Magruder had sent him out onto the foul water of Dead Harbor on what Magruder *surely* had known was a suicide mission, a mission to frighten the citizens of Merovingen into apoplexy with a phony sharrh visitation. That "visitation" was to have been faked with crude, hastily-rigged fireworks set off from a rowboat—manned and managed by Ruin.

Wolfling—once Ruin—felt his scarred lip curling into a stiff and soundless snarl. Magruder had *known* those fireworks were faulty; he *had* to. He'd seen the opportunity to get rid of the last Romanov adherent in the Sword contingent sent to Merovingen in the guise of a trade mission, and he'd taken it.

Then Jane, Lady Jane had intervened. Blessed Be.

The Hand of Jane called Raven had found him, burned and drowning; he had rescued Ruin and nursed him back to health, and then showed him Her Light. Ruin al-Banna was reborn as Wolfling, Hand of Jane—

And in a vision-quest Jane had shown him how to expiate all the sins he'd committed in the name of the Sword. All he had to do was guard the two sons of Angela Takahashi from Sword-spawned harm. And She had *brought* those two boys to him under circumstances that enabled him to begin that task. Circumstances that made them trust him.

Dry gravel crunched under his feet. Wolfling took one of the precious matches the boy had given him, and lit the candle stub he'd taken out of the bundle. By the flickering light he surveyed the place that was now his home.

He'd lived in worse. By some freak or other, the back end of the ruined bottom story was still above water and relatively dry, a kind of rubble-floored cave. You had to get at the dry part by wading through ankle-deep, stagnant water, but it wasn't bad, certainly not as bad as the swamp.

Though it was no palace, either. Water condensed on the walls and ceiling above the sunken area, dripping down constantly, so that the air always smelled damp. And with stale canal water coming in with every tide, it often smelled of more than damp. But there were feral cats down here, which kept the place free of vermin. Ruin had always admired cats—Wolfling held them almost sacred, for cats, black cats in particular, were the special darlings of the Goddess Althea Jane Morgoth. There was a mama cat with a young litter laired up down here that Wolfling had begun luring in with patience and bits of food; he had hopes he could tame the young ones enough to stay with him.

For the rest, he had a bed of sorts, made up of a couple of blankets and armfuls of dry weeds brought in from the swamp; certainly no one ventured down here, so anything he managed to acquire was safe.

He didn't have much, although he'd augmented that little with the things he'd brought from the boy's hidey in the swamp. What young Rigel had given him tonight was very welcome. After pulling the new sweater over his chilled body, and examining each little prize with care, he began stowing it all away within reach of his pallet so that he'd be able to find the stuff if he needed it in the dark.

He remade his bed to add the new coverings to the top and the rags the boy had brought as padding underneath; then Wolfling blew out the candle stub and lay back on the pallet, staring into the darkness, thinking.

Thinking mostly about young Rigel. The boy's thoughtfulness and generosity had impressed him yet again. The kid was so unlike anyone Wolfling had ever known before; he was—kind, that was it. Compassionate in a way that Wolfling really didn't understand, and could only admire from a distance. The younger boy—*that* one he understood, but the older—never.

Rigel's type was the sort he could appreciate, but never emulate.

Well, I can't be like that, he thought somberly, *but I can do what Jane put on me; I can help that boy survive to do some good. That ought to count for something.*

He settled himself a bit more comfortably, and thought about the warning the boy had delivered. *That* was something he hadn't thought of; he hadn't considered Tom Mondragon except as a fellow guardian.

Better make sure not to ever let him get a look at me, he decided thoughtfully. *Even as scarred up as I am, he might recognize me. And he won't be seein' Wolfling—he'll be seeing Ruin al-Banna. A threat. And I know damned well how Thomas Mondragon responds to threats.*

Then he grinned in the dark, his lips curling like stiff, old leather. *No threats from me, Tommy Mondragon, we're on the same side this time. But Chance, —you bastard, you,*—his grin turned into a feral snarl. *Let's just see you try and get past Tom and me together, M'ser Chance Magruder. Let's just see you get at that boy through* me. *I* might *leave enough for Thomas Mondragon to play with, after.*

Raj had another mission tonight, besides that of dealing with the man who called himself "Wolfling." He'd had a suspicion for some time that there was something not quite right in the Gallandry books; today that suspicion had become a certainty. And it was something that might well be very valuable to one Thomas Mondragon. Maybe valuable enough to repay what Mondragon had spent for his sake.

When he unlocked the front door and listened for signs of life in the apartment beyond, he heard footsteps in the kitchen; shod footsteps with certain lightness to them. Only one of the four living in this apartment wore shoes on a regular basis; so Tom was home, and puttering about in the kitchen again. Well enough, Raj always preferred to accost him back there, it was a friendlier place (small, tiled in a cheerful yellow, and always warm) than the sitting room.

He padded down the hall to the rear of the apartment and stood, quiet as you please, in the door of the kitchen, waiting for Tom to notice him. He'd been trying to imitate the wallpaper ever since the disaster of this winter, doing his level best to become invisible whenever he was in the apartment. He'd evidently gotten quite successful at it, for Mondragon got halfway through his bowl of soup before he noticed Raj standing there, twisting his cap nervously in his hands.

"Raj, I almost didn't see you! Are you hungry? There's enough for you if—" He looked, then looked again, and frowned. "Have you got something on your mind?"

"It's—something I think you ought to know, m'ser Tom," Raj replied quietly, edging into the cone of light cast by the oil-lamp above the table.

"Lord, boy, *don't* tell me you've been writing poetry again," Mondragon groaned, putting bread and spoon down. "It's been a long day; I don't think I could handle another romantic crisis."

"M'ser Tom," Raj blushed, but took heart at the ghost of good humor in Mondragon's eye. "No, m'ser, it's—there's something funny going on at Gallandrys."

Mondragon grimaced, and shoved his chair back a bit. "Raj, I'd be very much surprised if there *wasn't* 'something funny' going on there. Half this damned town smuggles—"

"It isn't that—I mean, they *tell* us what not to see, if you catch my meaning." Raj bit his lip as he struggled to communicate what he had discovered in a way that

Mondragon would understand. "This is something else; it's different. I'd swear on my life it's something that the Gallandrys don't know is going on. It's something I sort of ran into in the books. I don't think anybody else would, 'cause nobody else remembers things like I do."

Now Tom looked serious, and very much interested. He quirked one finger at Raj. "Come over here and sit where I can see you—"

Raj obeyed, pulling out the chair next to Mondragon's and plopping down into it. Mondragon shoved his food aside and clasped his hands quietly on the table before him. Raj imitated his pose without really thinking about it.

Mondragon took a deep breath. "I've got good cause to know about that memory of yours; I don't know that I've ever seen *that* play tricks. So what is it that you've uncovered?"

"About twice a month," Raj replied, picking his words with care, "There's about three or four fewer tax stamp receipts than there are items on the bill of lading inventory, which is when things go into the warehouse. But there's exactly the same number as on the warehousing inventory, when things go out. There's no discrepancy in the bill of lading and what's been paid for, and no calls for reimbursement from clients, so there's no reason for Gallandry to go back-checking the books; so far as *they* figure, they've been paid in full, everything's okay. The way things go is this—the bill of lading gets checked off at the warehouse door when the ship gets unloaded. That's the first time they make a count. Then the priest in charge of duty fees stamps each thing when it comes back out again; that's the second time. That way nobody can swipe stuff from the warehouse with the tax stamp on it an' resell it."

"Huh." Mondragon looked *very* thoughtful. "So—somebody is bringing something *in,* paying Gallandry for it, then 'losing' it before it gets duty paid on it?"

Raj nodded. "That's what it looks like to me, m'ser."

"Do you know who—or even what?"

Raj nodded again. "Spices. About three, four little spice casks at a time. I dunno if you know, but the duty on spice to the College is a silverbit per ounce, and the same for the Governor. Total two silverbits per ounce, and each one of those little casks holds five pounds."

Mondragon chewed his lip. "Adds up to a good sum, doesn't it?" he said after a pause.

Raj's head bobbed. "Enough to make a real difference to *somebody,* I'd think."

Tom brooded for a bit. "You've been doing your damnedest to act and think like a responsible adult, lately," he said, and Raj flushed painfully, lowering his eyes to his clasped hands. "I'm minded to see if you can take an adult task. It just might be worth what you cost me."

Raj looked up at him in a flare of sudden hope.

Tom smiled sourly. "You'll be fishing in dangerous waters, Raj, I want you to know that. This might be something one of the younger Gallandrys is running without the knowledge of the Family—it's certainly something worth enough money that at least one of the parties involved is going to be willing to kill to protect it. You're going to have to be very, very cautious, and very, very smart."

"You want me to find out who's involved," Raj stated. "And you figure I've gotten enough sense beat into me to take the risk and come out on top. *If* I keep my head."

Tom nodded, and coughed a little self-consciously. "And you know why. I sell information, and I don't much care who I sell it to, or how many times I sell it. If you take care, you should be all right, but this *probably* will cost you your job, no matter what—"

Raj shrugged. "It was *you* got me the job in the first place," he pointed out. "Reckon I can scrounge another one somewhere. Maybe Jones can have a word with m'ser Moghi; maybe m'ser Moghi could use a pencil pusher, or knows who could—"

"Oh no, boy—" Mondragon got a real, unfeigned smile on his face. "No, you won't have to go hunting up another job; you're going to have enough to worry about, come summer. I had a word with m'sera Kamat this afternoon—"

Raj blushed very hotly, knowing quite well that the "word" was likely pillow-talk.

"—and it seems she's talked her formidable young brother into giving you full Kamat sponsorship into the College. Think you can handle *that* assignment, m'ser Almost-A-Doctor Tai?"

Raj's jaw dropped, and he stared at Mondragon like a brain-sick fool. Never, *never* in all his wildest dreams, had he ever thought for a moment that Marina Kamat would follow through on her half-promise once he'd revealed how he'd deceived her with his poetry, poems she'd thought came from Tom Mondragon.

"Now I want you to *listen* to me, Rigel Takahashi," Mondragon continued, staring so hard into Raj's eyes that it felt like he was trying to inscribe his words on Raj's brain directly. "This is good sense, good advice I'm going to give you. Put your dreams and idealism in your pocket for a minute and *listen* to me just as carefully as you can."

"Yes, m'ser," Raj said, dazed.

"Kamat," Tom said with force, "is going to expect you to become their House physician; that's the price you will personally be paying for their gift. You're going to become fairly well-off; you'll *have* to be, you'll be an associate of the Family. Now I know you want to help out Jones' friends; that's very nice, it's very admirable—but you *aren't* going to be able to help the poor by being poor yourself. Be smart; take what comes your way and use it. Once in the Family power structure you will be in a position to *get* that medical help to the canalers. Kamat seems to have a certain sense of social responsibility." His tone was wry; not quite cynical. "You can play on that *if* you play *their* game by *their* rules. And that's the way to get what you want in this world. So *don't* blow the chance you've been given; it's been my experience that you don't often get more than one."

Raj got his jaw back in place, swallowed, nodded. "You're right, m'ser, I know you're right. The world's like that. And you've been—real good to me an' Denny. Better than you had any reason to, and I can't say as I've done much to deserve it. I just wish—" He swallowed again. "—I just wish I could do something to give you a shot at what you've always wanted. *You* wouldn't screw it up."

Mondragon turned eyes on him that reflected both wonder and pain. "I—wouldn't count on that, Raj," he whispered. "Even the people who think they know what the world is all about can be wrong."

That strange look lasted only a second—then Mondragon was back to his old self.

"One more thing," he continued, pulling his interrupted dinner back toward him, and toying with the bread. "You've been granted two ways to prove you've learned your lessons and to pay me back for the trouble you caused. One—to find out what's going on at Gallandry. Two—to become my channel into Kamat and the College, to be my eyes and ears and keep me informed. *You* know what kind of information I'm likely to find interesting. So—"

"Don't blow it," Raj completed for him, still a little bemused by the turn in his fortunes.

Tom actually chuckled. "Right," he said, resuming his meal.

"M'ser Tom, —would it be all right if I wrote my grandfather and told him about this, do you think?" Raj asked hesitantly, as he shoved the chair away from the table and prepared to leave.

Mondragon considered the possible ramifications for a moment; Raj could almost see the thoughts behind the eyes. "I can't see where it could do any harm," he finally replied. "It might ease his mind about you. Go ahead."

Raj hesitated in the doorway. "Thank you, m'ser," he said shyly, feeling that he was likely to be glowing with gratitude and happiness.

"For what?" Tom asked, weary, but amused. "Oh, go on, Raj, —if you're not hungry, go read, or go to bed. Get out of here—you keep reminding me of how old and corrupt I am."

Raj bobbed his head awkwardly and scooted back to the room he shared with Denny. The kid wasn't back from his mysterious errand with Jones—but Raj wasn't overly worried about him. This wasn't the first time he'd been out on a night-run with Jones. It was no doubt dangerous—but less so than roof-walking with his old mentor Rat, the singer-thief. And possibly even less dangerous than what Raj was going to attempt.

So Raj undressed and climbed into bed—and for the first time in months, the dreams he dreamed were bright.

He thought out a plan of action the next morning on the way to work, grateful beyond words for the presence of Wolfling on his backtrail so that he was able to spare a bit of his mind to *make* plans. The very first thing to do was to try to find out if this was an overall scam, or limited to one particular ship—which was what he thought likeliest, given the frequency.

He waved to Del on the canal below, who waved back; the man was much friendlier now that Raj was accepting "payment" for his doctoring. There was, thank God, less of that, now that the killing season of cold was over. Raj hadn't needed his coat for weeks; the only *bad* part about the weather warming was that the canals were beginning to smell. Then would come summer; plague time. And summer would tell whether or not the Janist promise of "no plague this year" would come true.

Well—that was to come; *now* was for bare feet on the walkways, and heads bared to the spring breeze, and a general feeling of cheer all around that another winter had been lived through. And the laxness that came with spring-born laziness just might make it possible for Raj to find out his information undetected.

He was early to work, scooting in through the peeling wooden doorway literally as soon as Ned Gallandry unlocked it. The early morning sun wasn't high enough to penetrate into the lower levels yet, so he had to trot 'round the dusty, cluttered outer office, lighting all the clerks' lamps. That was usually Ned's job—but the Gallandry cousin didn't look at all displeased at the junior clerk's enthusiasm. He gave Raj an approving nod and left the outer office, to take his position at the runner's desk in the next office over.

Raj had a reason for being so early; he was early enough to make an undisturbed, though hasty, check through the import lists by ship, and discover that only one, the motorbarge *Wayfarer,* ever carried the spice shipments that had the discrepancies. And only one

Captain, Nabeel Brit, had been at her helm since the discrepancies started.

This was quickly and quietly done. By the time anyone else came in, Raj was at his desk, copying the inventories from the *Star of Suvajen* into the appropriate books. One or two of his fellow clerks jibed at him for working so hard; Raj looked up from his copying and grinned slightly. "What do you expect," he countered, "when a feller is so ugly no girl'l look at him? A feller's gotta do *something* to take his mind off—what he ain't getting."

Mustafa Jamil rolled his dark eyes expressively as he settled onto his tall stool behind his slanted desk. "Lord and Ancestors, Raj,—if you ain't gettin' nothin' it's 'cause you ain't lookin'! Half them canaler girls is makin' big eyes at you behind your back—an' the only reason the rest of 'em ain't is 'cause their daddies would tan their backsides for 'em if they did." Mustafa snorted, scratching his curly head. "Ugly! Hell, I wish *I* was as 'ugly' as you! Maybe Rosita wouldn't be givin' me such a hard time!"

Raj blushed and ducked his head. *He* knew why the canaler girls were giving him the eye—not because he was desirable; because he was notorious. The whole of the Trade had been alerted when he'd gone "missing" —and the whole of the Trade knew the outcome. He was just grateful that his fellow workers *didn't;* they were landers, and canalers didn't spill canal gossip to landers. And it seemed Raj was semi-adopted now—because the Trade *hadn't* told the Land about what a fool he'd been.

And for all of that, he *still* hadn't seen The Girl since that awful day—he'd looked, but he'd not seen her once. His only possible aid, Jones, had been unable—or unwilling—to identify her. Raj sighed, recollecting the peculiar jolting his heart had taken when he'd seen her—she'd shaken Marina Kamat clean *out* of his head, and herself in.

Well, he couldn't think about her now; he had a ticklish job ahead of him.

Mustafa chuckled at Raj's blush, not knowing what had caused it; he was about to toss another jibe in his direction when Theta Gallandry stalked through the outer office on the way to his inner sanctum, and all four clerkly heads bent quickly over their assignments.

For the next bit of information Raj had to wait until the appropriate book came into his hands legitimately—though he'd picked taking on the lengthy *Pride of Suvajen* inventory with the notion of getting at that book in mind. This seagoing ship had sprung a leak in one of the smaller holds and had as a consequence sustained a bit of spoilage to chalk off on the loss sheets. And *that* was the book Raj wanted in his hands; the "Spoilage, Refund and Salvage" book—because if *he* was a captain covering tracks, that's where *he'd* have hidden those little spice casks.

And sure enough—there they were; and no one else ever seemed to have quite as much spoilage in such a specific area as Nabeel Brit.

It *looked* legit as hell, all properly logged, and with no loss on the Gallandry ledgers. Only one thing that the captain had forgotten; the casks themselves.

The miniature barrels that spices and teas were shipped in were unlike any other such containers in that they were *not* tarred to make them waterproof. Tar ruined the delicate flavor of the spices. They were very carefully *waxed* instead; calked with hemp and coated with beeswax, inside and out.

This made them very valuable, no matter that they were so small. Cooks liked them to hold flour and sugar and salt; hightowners had a fad of using them to grow flowers in, on their balconies. For that matter—a good many used the casks, with the wax coating burnished into their wood until the wood glowed, as wastebaskets, workbaskets, and for a dozen other semiornamental purposes.

So even if the spice inside *had* somehow spoiled, through leakage, or rot, or insect contamination, the *cask* had a resale value. Yet none of those casks from the *Wayfarer* inventory ever appeared on the "Salvage" side of the blotter.

And no one seemed to be interested in claiming back part of the value from the company that imported the spice for them. And *that* was very odd indeed.

And it was in the "Spoilage, Refund and Salvage" book that Raj found out who had ordered and paid for the "spoiled" spices—and who had apparently been so careless or generous as to absorb the entire loss.

Deems Spicery on Deems Isle.

The next day and the next Raj kept strictly to legitimate business, waiting for an opportunity for him to get at the packets of tax-stamps.

The Merovingen tax-stamps, placed on an article that had had its duty paid in full, were distributed by a small army of College priests. The stamps themselves were green paper seals, signed by the officiating priest, and each was preprinted with a unique number. They were perforated to tear into two parts, each half bearing the same number. The first part was gummed, meant to be glued across the opening of the article; the second was torn off and returned after counting at the College to the appropriate importer as evidence that he had paid the tax duties to College and Governor. The stamps came in from the College in packets and were kept in the cubbyholes of the tax desk, one hole for each day of the month, until the end of the month when some luckless clerk got to check them against the warehousing inventory and file them away. Raj was too junior to be entrusted with such a task—but Mustafa wasn't.

Sure enough, at month's end Mustafa got stuck with the job. And Mustafa *never* had lunch at his desk. Raj waited until lunchtime, when Mustafa had gone off to lunch with Rosita and the office was deserted, to make his move.

He slid over to Mustafa's desk, counted the little packets, and purloined the one representing the twelfth of the month, the day the spice shipments from the *Wayfarer* had been collected by the Deems representative. He thumbed through the little slips as quickly as he could, not daring to take the packet out of the office, hovering over in a corner next to the filthy glass window where the light was best. Finally he came to the Deems slips, and got the name of the priest in charge puzzled out.

Father Jermaine Harmody.

He burned the name into his memory, and returned the slips to Mustafa's desk in the nick of time, heading out the door to his own lunch just as Ned Gallandry headed *in,* bound for Theta's office with a package.

Denny was in as cheerful a mood as he'd ever been in his life. Jones was so pleased with the way he'd been handling himself that she had decided to take him into her further confidence.

And she was damned desperate.

She'd flagged him down with the little signal they'd worked out that meant she needed to talk to him somewhere where they weren't likely to be observed. He finished his current run in double time, then, when there didn't seem to be anybody about, ducked under Nayab Bridge along the ledge at water level.

And there was Jones, holding her skip steady against the pull of the canal current.

"Ker-whick-a," Denny chirped, seeing the flash of her eyes as she looked in his direction. He skipped over to the side of the boat, keeping his balance on the ledge with careless ease. "Whatcha need, Jones?"

"I got a problem," she said in a low, strained voice. "Moghi sent me t' pick up a payment fer 'im—only after I'd got it, somethin' spooked th' blacklegs. They're all over the damned water an' they're stoppin' skips—"

"An' if they find you with a bundle of cash—" Denny didn't have to finish the sentence. "Huh. Tom'd have a helluva time prying' you outa the Signeury. Pass it over, Jones. I gotta go by Ventani anyhow."

"If there's *one penny* missin'—"

Denny pouted, hurt. "C'mon, Jones, Gallandry trusts me with cash!"

"I ain't as stupid as Gallandry," Jones replied, but with no real force. "Here."

She pulled a flat packet out of her shirt, a packet that chinked and weighed surprisingly heavy. Denny raised a surprised eyebrow. Silver at the least—maybe gold. Something *had* gone amiss if Moghi had sent Jones out to make a pickup of this much coin in broad daylight.

He slipped the package inside his own shirt. "Keep headin' up th' canal," he suggested. "If it's *you* they're lookin' fer, an' lookin' fer you t' head fer Moghi's, that oughta throw 'em off th' scent."

She snorted, and pushed off from the bank. "Tell me m'own job, lander," she replied scornfully. "Just *you* tend t' what I give ye."

"Yey, m'sera," Denny executed a mocking little bow, then danced back along the ledge to the first water-stair up to a walkway.

Behind him he heard Jones swear halfheartedly at him, and grinned.

Treevor Vasoly had been trailing that canaler Jones for hours—just as the Megarys had paid him to do. Then he saw her duck under Nayab Bridge—and a moment later, saw that bridge-brat Denny do the same.

He snickered to himself; keeping tabs on the brat after he dropped out of the bridge-gangs and into "respectability" had been well worth his while after all—

"Tree" Vasoly had graduated from bridge-brat to bullyboy in the two years since he and Denny had last tangled; he sported a sword (that he used like a club) and silk scarves and a constant sneer. There were dozens like Tree on the walkways of Merovingen, and "work" enough to keep all of them in whiskey and scarves, if you weren't too particular about who you worked for. Tree certainly wasn't. Megary coin spent like anyone else's.

No one had ever beaten Tree at anything—no one but bridge-brat Denny, that is. Denny had gotten to Tree's girl, gotten her off the walkways and out of the gang and *into* the purview of his mentor Rat—

Which wasn't what the brat had intended, but before you could say "surprise," Jessie had gotten installed in an acting group and acquired a very expensive patron. And had *no* further need or desire for Tree and his gang.

It still rankled, and Tree had never forgiven the little bastard for what Denny had done to humiliate him.

But this looked like a chance to pay Denny back *and* turn a little profit by way of a couple of Megary bonuses—

He watched Denny moving in the shadows under

Nayab Bridge; he squinted, but couldn't make out anything more than a brief exchange with someone on a skip—just a meeting of a pair of shadows within the shadows. Then Denny squirted out again and scrambled up the water-stairs to the first level, and on over to Callista.

So—Jones had transferred whatever it was she'd picked up to the boy's hands—likely because of the blacklegs stirring on the water.

He grinned with absolute satisfaction, and headed up the walkway on the brat's backtrail. In a few more moments, he'd have whatever it was Jones had been carrying, and he'd have the boy as well to sell to Megary.

Wolfling spotted the swarthy bullyboy trailing Denny with almost no effort whatsoever. The scarfaced low-life was so clumsy in his attempts to shadow the boy that Wolfing snorted in contempt. This inept brawler wouldn't have lasted five minutes in the Sword.

Once Wolfling saw that the boy was on the bridge from Callista to Ventani, Wolfling had a fairly good notion where he was bound: Moghi's. Jones must have passed something on to him.

The bullyboy evidently had a shrewd notion where Denny was going as well, as he increased his pace a trifle. It looked to Wolfling like he was planning on ambushing the boy down on the water-level walk, before he could reach Moghi's. Wolfling gave up trying to be inconspicuous—there wasn't anyone much down in this decayed slum anyway—and hastened his own steps.

He was almost too late—he hesitated a moment at the shadows under Little Ventani Bridge, his eyes momentarily unable to adjust to the darkness of the little backwater after the dazzle of sun on Fisher Canal—

Then he heard Denny shout in anger and defiance—and a second time, in pain.

He saw a bulkier shadow on the walkway ahead of him, and that was all his trained body needed to respond with precision and accuracy.

A few heartbeats later the bully was unconscious at Wolfling's feet, and Denny, huddled beyond, was peering up at the face of his rescuer with shock and stunned recognition.

Wolfling gave him no chance to say a word. "Move, boy," he said gruffly. "An' next time don't go down dark places without checking to see if someone's followin'."

The boy gulped, and scrambled to his feet, favoring his right arm. "Yessir!" he gasped, and scampered down to his destination as if someone had set his tail on fire.

Wolfling considered the body at his feet, thoughtfully prodding it with one toe. He rubbed his knuckles absently; he'd almost forgotten to pull that last punch; and if he hadn't the bullyboy wouldn't be breathing. He wasn't sure why he'd held back, now; he was mostly inclined to knife the bastard and push him into the canal—

But that wouldn't keep others of his type from dogging the boy's footsteps. On the other hand, if he made an example of the bully, he might well save Denny (and himself) some future trouble.

Some half an hour later, Tree dragged himself, aching in every bone, from the cold, foul water of Fisher Canal. He was lighter by sword, dagger, purse, cloak—at least the terrible, scarred madman had slapped him awake before tossing him in. He clung to the ledge that ran around Callista, clinging to the sun-warmed, rotting wood, not thinking much past the moment. He hadn't swallowed any of the deadly water; he was bruised all over, but the crazyman hadn't smashed bones. For now he was just grateful to be alive enough to hurt and shiver.

Never, for the rest of his life, would Tree forget that masklike face, those mad eyes. Or the carefully enunciated words, spoken in a voice like the croak of a marsh-bird.

"Touch that boy again," the lunatic had said, "and the next time you land in the canal we'll see how well you swim with both legs broken."

One casual question to two independent sources—Jep at Moghi's, and Hoh's cook Kyla, had given Raj one simple—and damning—fact. The cheapest place in town for spices was indeed Deems. The prices weren't enough different to make it worth a cook's while to go out of the way for just one item—but when you bought in bulk, nearly every tavernkeeper and restauranteur bought from Deems. That penny or two difference in the price was slowly giving the Deems family a monopoly in the retail spice market.

Justice Lee had been Raj's source on Father Harmody. Raj had plenty of reason to go visit his new friend—his good news, for one; some keep-you-awake tea-weeds for Justice to use through exam time, for another. And while Raj was visiting, he'd asked Justice if *he* could find out something about a "Father Harmody's" background.

Through the art student had been a little puzzled by the question, he agreed—especially after Raj told him that if it became *any* trouble to learn, he wasn't to bother. As things turned out, it was easy enough for him to resolve with a couple of casual questions to his own patron, carefully spaced out over several days.

It seemed that Father Jermaine Harmody could easily have claimed the hyphenated surname "Harmody-Deems" as he was a contract son of one of the younger sisters of Ivan Renfro Deems. And most interestingly, Father Harmody was one of Cardinal Ito Boregy's proteges.

Well, that sure as hell explains the Deems connection, Raj thought to himself, as he hurried to reach Ramseyhead Isle and the Ramsey Bell before the lunch crowd did. *But it doesn't explain how he's getting a Nev Hetteker captain to go along with this. So there's a connection here I'm missing, and it's a Family connection, or politics, maybe. It's not enough to give Tom—yet—*

He scampered in at the back entrance; Mikey Weeks, one of the busboys, had agreed to let Raj take his place at noon for the next several days. It hadn't been hard to convince him, not when Raj had offered to split the tips for the privilege of doing his work for him. Mikey had no notion who or what Raj was; Raj let him think he was a student with some gambling debts to pay and a short time to pay them in. And Lord and Ancestors knew that a few of the patrons of the Ramsey Bell were quite good tippers.

Raj joined the milling lot of a half dozen other boys in the shabby back hall, claiming Mikey's apron from its wooden hook and bobbing awkwardly to the burly owner. "Mike still got th' bad ankle?" the square-faced man asked gruffly.

"Yes, m'ser," Raj replied, scuffing his bare feet in the sawdust on the wooden floor. "Says he's mortal sorry, m'ser, but it's still swole up."

The man actually cracked a smile. "*I* ain't, boy. You lookin' fer a job, you check by here regular. I get an opening, you got a place."

Raj contrived to look grateful. "M-m-my thanks,

m'ser," he stammered, and slipped past him onto the floor of the tavern proper.

After that it was nothing but scurry and scramble and keep his head down so that nobody could see his face enough to recognize him later; bringing orders of food and drink to tables, clearing away the dishes after, bringing more drink when called for—and keeping his ears open and his mouth shut.

For the Ramsey Bell was where the second sons of the Families met—and where they met, there was gossip aplenty. And where there was gossip—

Lord, it was wearing him down, though. He leaned around a patron's bulk to snag the empty plates before the man could holler for them to be taken away. He was beginning to be very grateful for his sit-down job at Gallandry's. He was so tired when he got home at night that he was bolting a little dinner, going straight to bed, and sleeping like a stone. Mondragon had been worried enough at that anomalous behavior that he'd actually asked Raj if he was all right—which had surprised him. He'd explained—he thought; his mind wasn't too clear on anything after sundown anymore. At least Mondragon seemed satisfied.

Two days ago he'd learned that Deems was one of Tatiana Kalugin's supporters, and as such, was not welcome at the Ramsey Bell. Which made him fair game at the tables.

From Dao Raza yesterday, Raj overheard that Deems was getting very cozy with the new Nev Hettek Trade Mission. From Franck Wex he learned that this coziness with Nev Hettek was nothing new.

And just as Raj was hauling a load of dishes to the back, he got the final key piece from Pradesh St. John.

Somebody asked if Deems was still courting the New Hettekers. The scar-seamed merchant considered the question thoughtfully before replying with the carefully worded bit of information that, indeed, they were. And that one Father Harmody was conducting the negotiations—which presumably put the seal of College approval on the whole thing.

Raj's head buzzed, and his gut went tight with excitement. So—the *College* might be involved in this new Nev Hettek policy!

Or *part* of the College was. Raj was no longer so naive as to figure that what one priest wanted, the rest did too. Father Harmody could be working for a propeace party within the College. Or his patron, the Cardinal. Assuming, of course—which those at the Bell did—that the good Father's superiors were aware of his visits. Which might or might not have been the truth. In *either* case, it was something Tom Mondragon would find fascinating indeed.

Raj hustled the last of the dishes into the kitchen, took off his apron, and hung it up for the last time. He had what he needed; time to give Mikey back his job. Now only one thing remained: for Raj to verify with his own eyes exactly what was going on down at the Gallandry warehouse and how it was being conducted.

Mondragon was beginning to have a feeling of déjà vu every time he looked up from dinner to see Raj hovering like a shadow around the kitchen door.

"Something wrong, Raj?" he asked, beginning to have that too-familiar sinking feeling. The last time the boy had that look on his face, that—creature—had moved in across the canal. And the time before—

The time before was what had gotten them all *into* this mess.

"M'ser, —" the boy stammered, and brought his hands out from behind his back. "M'ser, —this is—for you."

Mondragon took the slim package from the boy; a long and narrow, heavy thing, wrapped in oiled silk. He unwrapped it, and nearly dropped it in surprise.

It was a fine—a *very* fine—main-gauche, the like of which Tom hadn't seen, much less owned, since Nev Hettek. Watermarked steel; plain, but elegant hilt of goldwood—balanced so well in his hand that it already felt part of him—

He was so surprised that his first thought was that the boy must have stolen it. The Lord knew it wasn't the kind of thing the boy could afford! But Raj spoke before he could voice that unworthy thought.

"It—it's from my Granther, m'ser," he said, his face and voice sounding strained. "He says it's by way of thanking you. He sent me one for m'ser Kamat too—seems he wrote an' tol' them who I really was!"

"He what?" Mondragon tightened his hand involuntarily on the knife hilt.

"He says," Raj continued, "that he figgers they oughta know, an' that I'm safer with 'em knowing 'cause they'll put me where hurtin' me would cause a big fuss, hightown. 'Hide in plain sight,' is what he says."

"The man has a point," Mondragon conceded, thinking better of the notion. Relaxing again, he checked the weapon for maker's markers, and sure enough, on the blade near the quillons found the tiny Takahashi symbol. The old man was a shrewd one, all right—he hadn't kept the clan intact through upheaval and revolution without having more than a few active brain cells and a real instinct for which way to jump. Besides, if Kamat now knew what station the boy *really* was, the obligations would be turned around. Kamat would now be in the position to negotiate favorably with the silk-and-steel family of Takahashi, Raj would no longer be the object of charity, and the Kamats would actually wind up *owing Mondragon* for bringing the boy to their attention. Altogether a nice little turn of events.

"He says," Raj continued, a little relieved looking but still plainly under strain, "it's by way of a bribe, m'ser, t' keep Denny. He says he don't think we better let Kamat know 'bout Denny at all, not that he's m'brother."

Mondragon thought about young m'ser Lightfingers loose in Kamat and shuddered. "I think he's right."

Raj had carefully calculated his day off to coincide with the day that the Deems hirelings picked up their consignment from the Gallandry warehouse. By dawn he was down at the warehouse dock, ready and willing to run just about any errand for anybody. This wasn't the first time he'd been here—he'd played runner before, when he wasn't playing busboy at the Ramsey Bell; he wanted his face to be a familiar one on the dock, so that he wouldn't stand out if Father Harmody became suspicious. He even had Gallandry permission to be out here; they thought he was strapped for cash, and he was supposedly earning the extra odd penny by running on his day off.

He'd run enough of those errands by just past noon that no one thought or looked at him twice when he settled into a bit of shade and looked to be taking a rest break. The sun was hot down here on the dock; there wasn't a bit of breeze to be had, and Raj was sweating freely. One friendly fellow offered Raj the last of his beer as he went back on shift; Raj accepted gratefully. He wasn't having to feign near-exhaustion; he *was* exhausted. He was mortally glad that the remainder of his self-imposed assignment was going to allow him to sit here, in the shade of a barrel, and pretend to get splinters out of his hands while he watched the Deems skip being loaded twenty feet away.

The Deems skip was a neat little thing; newly painted and prosperous-looking. The skipboatman who manned her did *not,* however, look like the run-of-the-mill canaler.

In point of fact, that carefully dirtied sweater looked far too new; the man's complexion was something less than weathered—and those hands pushed pencils far more often than the pole of a skip, Raj would be willing to bet money on it. This was no canaler, hired *or* permanent retainer. This was likely one of the younger members of the Family.

This notion was confirmed when Father Harmody put in his appearance. There was something very similar about the cast of the nose and the shape of the ears of both the good Father and the boatman. Even in inbred Merovingen features *that* similar usually spelled a blood relationship.

It didn't take long to load the tiny casks onto the skip; Raj didn't bother to get any closer than he was. He wasn't planning on trying to see if the articles were stamped or not. He was doing what only *he* could, with his perfect memory.

Even amid the bustle of the dock, he was keeping absolute track of *exactly* how many spice casks—and *only* the spice casks, nothing else—were going into the bottom of that skip.

Three days later, when the bundle of tax stamps came in, Raj had his answer. Three more casks had gone into the skip than there were stamps for.

That night he intended to give Tom Mondragon his

full report—but that afternoon he got an unexpected surprise.

A creamy white and carefully calligraphed note from House Kamat.

The boy Raj finished his report to Mondragon, given while he was finishing his dinner in the kitchen, and Tom was both impressed and surprised. The kid had handled himself like—

Like an adult. He'd thought out what he needed to know, he'd planned how to get it without blowing his cover, and he'd executed that plan carefully, coolly, and patiently. Mondragon pondered the boy's information, and concluded that no matter how you looked at it, it was going to be worth a great deal to *both* sides of this messy and treacherous game he was playing. He nodded to himself, then looked up to see that the boy was still standing in the doorway, looking vaguely distressed.

Mondragon's approval did nothing to ease the boy's agitation; if anything, it seemed worse. "Raj, is there something wrong?"

"Tom, —I mean, m'ser, —" the boy looked absolutely desperate. "I—got this today—"

He handed a square of creamy vellum to Mondragon; feeling a terrible foreboding, Tom opened it.

It proved to be nothing more than a simple invitation for Raj—and a friend, if he chose—to come to dinner at Kamat, to be introduced to the Family.

Mondragon heaved a sigh of relief. "One may guess," he said, handing the invitation back to Raj, "that m'ser Richard Kamat has received your Grandfather's letter." The boy's expression didn't change. "So what on earth is *wrong?*"

"It's—it's *me,* m'ser Tom," the boy blurted unhappily. "I've tried and tried—but I can't *remember*—I

can't think how to act, what to wear, what fork to use—"

He looked at Mondragon with a pleading panic he hadn't shown even when he'd known his life hung in the balance. "Please, m'ser Tom," he whispered, "I don't know what to *do!*"

Tom restrained his urge to laugh with a control he hadn't suspected he had. "You want me to help coach you, is that it?"

Raj nodded so hard Tom thought his head was going to come off. He sighed.

"All right, young m'ser, —let's see if we can create a gentleman out of you." He grinned. "You *may* wish yourself back in the swamp before this is over!"

PAPER CHASE

by Roberta Rogow

Klickett the knitting-woman glared at her two visitors and attacked her latest creation with vicious energy. "Absolutely no way!" she stated flatly.

"Come on!" Rif, the tall, muscular singer, tapped the manuscript in front of her on the square table. "It's all ready to go. . . ."

"And you want it day after tomorrow? Can't be done." Klickett unwound more yarn from the ever-present bag at her feet.

"Why not?" Rattail persisted. "You've always worked things out before."

"Ya don't believe me? Ask Miko!" Klickett bawled out, without leaving her chair, "Hey! Miko!"

From the back of the shop a tall, broadshouldered man emerged, wiping well-inked hands on a well-inked apron. His fair hair fell over his head in lank strings, mingling with a short blond beard.

"Tell 'em," Klicket said bitterly.

Miko looked from Rif to Rat. "I can't print up the book," he said apologetically. "No paper."

"That's crazy," Rif stated, just as flatly. "There's always paper."

"Not your kind," Klickett said. "Fine vellum, you said. Best quality, you said. Fit for hightowners, you

said. Well, the paper mill's been flooded out since the rains, and it's shut till the water goes down."

Rat and Rif regarded the printer and bookbinder glumly. "We've *got* to get this out by next week," Rif muttered. "It's the best damned thing we've ever done, and we want to get it into the right hands . . . that is, we want to . . ."

Klickett snorted. "I know what you want to do, all right! Greening-day coming, right? Get a nice-looking book out on the streets, where the students can pick it up, right under the noses of Their High-and-Mightinesses! Get out Mother Jane's word . . . but it can't be done. Not till the paper mill opens."

"I tried," Miko said. "They were selling off the end-rolls, and I thought I could pick one up, but some pencil pusher out of the Signeury came along with a signed order, and the whole lot went off to the Signeury warehouse."

Klickett sighed. "Sorry, Rat, Rif. The only way you're gonna get that paper out of the warehouse is steal it."

Rif looked offended. "I'm a pickpocket, not a burglar," she sniffed.

Rat said thoughtfully, "You know, there just might be something to that."

Miko gulped slightly. "You don't mean you're actually going to take the paper out of the warehouse?"

"Well . . . not all of it," Rat demurred. "Just one roll. Enough for the DeLuxe Edition of the Collected Rat and Rif Song-Book."

"Let me see if I heard you right," Klickett said. "You just walk up to the Signeury warehouse, which is guarded by the blacklegs, and pick the lock on the front door, and walk out with a roll of paper, which is about as easy to carry as a small tree, and no one sees you? Tell me another one!"

Rif's eyes began to sparkle as she thought it over. "Sounds good to me. All we need is your skip."

"My skip don't go out without me, and I don't go out," Klickett said.

"It would do you good to get a little exercise," Rif commented.

"Find someone else."

"Like who?"

"The Jones kid . . . what about her?"

Rat shook her head. "We want to save Jones for really dangerous stuff. This will be dead easy. All we have to do is get to the dock, distract the guard, and get the paper."

"Who's going to haul it?" Klickett grumbled.

Rat grinned happily at Miko. The printer blushed fiery red under his inkstains. Klickett shook her head vigorously.

"Oh, no. No way is Miko going to get himself locked into the Dungeon. You're not the only folks who need printing done around here, y'know. And that skip of mine won't hold all of us and the paper at the same time. And this guard . . . now, how am I supposed to deal with him all by my lonesome?"

Rif nodded. "What we need is a really good distraction," she murmured.

There was a tinkle from the bell above the door of the shop. "Excuse me," came the well-modulated tones of Ariadne Delaney. "I meant to come sooner, but I was distracted by . . . Oh, dear. Do I intrude?"

Rif blinked rapidly and smiled suddenly. Klickett could feel what was coming.

"I got your sweater right here, m'sera," she said, before Rif could utter a word. "All wrapped up proper for ye. Be on your way before it gets too dark for the boatman."

"Oh, I took the foot-path," Ariadne said blithely.

"No need to take the boatman from his dinner for such a small errand."

"So no one knows you're here," Rif said, her smile growing wider.

"Well, I mentioned to Farren that I would be doing some shopping," Ariadne said. "I didn't precisely say where I would be doing it. Is anything wrong?" She looked around the room, noting the expressions of disapproval on Klickett's face, the embarrassment on Mike's, and the almost palpable lamp-flares of genius over Rat's and Rif's heads.

"We have got a little problem that you can help us with," Rif said slowly."

"Of course, m'sera Rif. Anything I can do for the Cause!" Ariadne's voice took on the fervor of a New Convert.

"There's something we have to get," Rat said carefully. "But it's locked up in a warehouse."

Ariadne's eyes grew round with excitement. "Are you actually going to steal something?"

"Yeah . . . that was the general idea," Rif said, glancing at Rat.

"How very exciting!" Ariadne said cheerfully. "But I don't see what I can do to help. I'm not very good at violence," she added ruefully.

"There won't be any violence," Rat assured her. "All we have to do is get to the warehouse . . ."

"Pick the lock . . ." Rif said.

"And get the stuff out," Rat finished, glaring at her partner.

"But what do you want me to do?" Ariadne asked.

"Just keep an eye out," Rif said.

"Distract the guard," Rat added.

"And what makes you so sure we'll get away clear?" Klickett brought them all back to reality. "Going to send a message to your bedmate?" She sang out:

"Old Black Cal patrols all the bridges here,
Keeps an eye on all of the fights;
But when Rif's at play
He looks the other way
On those dark Merovingen nights!"

Rif glared in Klickett's direction. "One day someone's going to stick *you* down in the Dungeon," she gritted out.

Ariadne's tremulous soprano quavered out:

"There's a shop that's down by the Grand Canal,
Often used by literary lights;
It's where Klickett sits
And gives her comrades fits
On those dark Merovingen nights."

Rat looked approvingly at her latest disciple. "M'sera, you're catching on!"

"She's going to be caught," Klickett grumbled.

"Not if we do this right," Rif assured her. "Just get the skip started, and get us to the warehouse."

"I don't even know where it is," Klickett complained, as she pulled on a many-colored garment that looked as if it had been knitted from the tag ends of a dozen other sweaters.

They filed out of the shop to the small dock alongside the island, where the battered skip was moored. Klickett muttered angrily as the skip rode lower and lower in the water.

"This here was supposed to be a two-person skip. How'm I supposed to get through without tip-turning?"

"Just get it started," Rat hissed at her.

"And be glad we gave you the gasolhol," Rif said.

Miko's weight brought the boat dangerously close to the waterline.

"Don't nobody move," Klickett growled. The engine sputtered into life. On a bridge above them, a tall man clad in black frowned into the darkness and began to pace after them, following their progress around the canals until they came to the by-water behind Fishmarket where a young man in Militia black stood against an inconspicuous warehouse door.

"You sure this is it?" Klickett asked, as she maneuvered her battered boat around the Fishmarket piers.

"Right here," Miko said. "I've been picking up their scrap paper for years. The stuff they throw away! Perfectly good stuff, only one side written on!" He shook his head at the profligacy of bureaucrats.

Klickett let the engine die. "One lamp. One guard. What now?"

"Let us out." Rat, Rif and Miko heaved themselves onto the nearest dock. "You get the guard's attention," Rif directed them.

"How long d'ya think we can keep him off your tail?" Klickett hissed. "We're not exactly the kind to sweet-talk him!"

Rif patted her on the head. "You'll think of something."

Klickett snarled, looked at Ariadne, and said, "M'sera, I'm sorry I got you into all this mess."

Ariadne was serene as ever. "I'm finding this all quite fascinating. Only fancy, me being the lookout for a . . . a heist? Is that the correct term?"

Klickett muttered, "Mother Jane help us!" under her breath. Aloud she hailed the guard: "Hey! Wayhen there!"

The guard snapped out of a dream of long-limbed uptown maidens and rich food. "Huh?" he asked, peering into the gloom beyond the ring of light thrown by the lantern above the door of the warehouse. "Who's there?"

"Us," Klickett shouted, uninformatively. "Where are we?"

"Who wants to know?" The guard watched as the skip drifted into the glare of the lantern. Behind him, Klickett and Ariadne saw three shadowy figures converge on the door.

"My good man, can you direct me to the Delaney Residence?" Ariadne's imperious soprano cut through the guard's mental fog. In his experience, limited though it might be, persons who used that tone did not belong in front of the Signeury warehouse in the middle of the night, accompanied by what looked like a refugee from the Swamp.

"M'sera?" The guard leaned farther forward to assess the situation. The door opened with a squeal that nearly got the guard's attention. Klickett kicked at her engine, drowning out any noise the burglars might have made.

"Damn-fool thing!" she snarled. "Got some damn-fool stuff from the damn-fool students. Said it would run forever! Hah! Give out on me, it did, and no lamp, and here's m'sera Delaney to be fetched off home, and where the hell are we?"

Ariadne sniffed delicately. "It might be Fishmarket," she offered.

"It might be Dead Harbor, for all the good that does us," Klickett retorted. "Next time, m'sera, don't drag a pore ole woman out on a dark night. Get yerself a reg'lar canaler!"

"The insolence of these people!" Ariadne said haughtily. She turned to the guard. "If you please, instruct this stupid creature in the best route out of this place."

"Stupid?" Klickett's voice rose over the heavy tramping of three pairs of feet, staggering under the weight of an object the size and shape of an oaken log fit to roast a whale. "Jest who you calling stupid, m'sera?

Who told me to take the left fork, hey? Catch me takin' any more hightown custom nowheres!"

The guard turned to the more articulate of the pair. "M'sera, you should have taken the right fork," he said diffidently. "If you could turn the skip around . . ."

"Turn it around?" Klickett's voice rose to a shriek. "And how do I do that in this-here bathing pool, hey? Back her out, maybe . . . Here, give us a hand. . . ."

She reached out to the guard just as the threesome staggered into the lanternlight with the long roll of paper. Ariadne grabbed the guard's other hand. Between them, Klickett and Ariadne sent the guard headfirst into the murky waters of the canal, while Rat, Rif and Miko frantically tried to work the paper roll over the dock and into the skip.

From his perch on the bridge above them, Cal could see it all: three people and a long whatever-it-was they trotted out of the warehouse, at one end of the boat, and three more people struggling at the other end of the boat. The guard splashed, cursed, and tried to get back onto the dock, while the two women did their best to see that he didn't get there. The would-be paper thieves lay flat on the dock in their efforts to ease the heavy roll into the boat without tipping it (and the paper) over into the canal. When the guard had been ducked for the third time and the roll was safe, Cal felt it was time to bring the scene to a conclusion.

"What the hell's going on here?" he demanded, as the guard floundered up onto the dock and lay there, dripping and panting. The three others faded into the shadows of the warehouse. The roll of paper lay safely under a tarpaulin, in the skip.

The guard cursed, spat out canal water, and rolled over. From his spot on the dock he looked up the endless stretches of Cal's legs and torso to the man's grim face, now set in lines of total disbelief, disgust, and disapproval.

"I was on duty, sir," the guard sputtered. "And these . . . these . . ." He searched for a word.

"Ladies," Cal said ominously. "This is m'sera Delaney, the wife of the Under-Prefect of Waterfront and Harbors."

"What's she doing here then?" the guard wanted to know.

"I was on my way home," Ariadne answered with aplomb. "And we lost our way." She turned to Klickett for confirmation. The knitting-woman shrugged.

"Can't let a lady like m'sera Delaney go out alone," she demurred.

"This ain't no Delaney Residence," the guard insisted. "This is miles away from *any* residence!"

Cal regarded the dripping watchman with disdain. "M'sera Delaney just told you she got lost. You believe her, don't you?" *Or I'll know the reason why!* was implicit in his words.

The guard took a large gulp of air and coughed heartily. The threesome in the shadows tiptoed up the stairs and over the bridge while Ariadne solicitously patted the guard on the back, and Klickett kicked the engine into some kind of action.

"I can direct your driver out of here and back to your residence," Cal offered.

Ariadne perched on the end of the paper roll. "I think we are all right now," she said cheerily. "We get out of this by-water and take the left . . ."

"Right!" Klickett snapped.

"Left," Cal corrected her.

"Left fork," Ariadne said.

"I'd still better ride along," Cal said, easing himself into the skip. The loglike object lay in the bottom of the boat, covered by the tarpaulin. He glanced at it briefly, and looked away.

* * *

Farren Delaney himself was waiting at the Delaney residence dock, lantern in hand. He shook his head as he handed his wife out of the boat.

"Where have you been, Addie? We've had to hold dinner for you . . . and who are these people?" He took in the equipage that had carried his wife across the city.

"I'll explain it all later, after dinner, dear," Ariadne said. "But I did want you to meet Sergeant Halloran. He has been most helpful. And this is the woman who makes those lovely sweaters you admired."

"Ah." Farren took this in. "Halloran? I've heard of you. Come see me tomorrow, and I'll thank you personally for helping my wife. And . . . ah . . . you . . ."

"Klickett'll do."

"A little longer in the arms next time." He led Ariadne into the house. "Addie, —you pick up the damnedest people!" The door closed behind them.

Klickett turned to the blackleg. "Where to now? Justiciary? Archangel Bridge?"

Cal hopped out of the skip, and gave it a shove with his foot. "Take whatever it is back where it belongs," he said. "And stop singing that damned song about me!"

Klickett sang into the darkness. " 'Tis advertised in Uppertown, and in the town below . . . a hundred healthy fellers, a-blacklegging for to go. . . .' "

In the bottom of the skip the roll of paper lay, snug in its tarpaulin wrappings. It would make a lovely book.

The celebration at Hoh's was at its loudest when Ariadne and Farren Delaney walked into the room. Rat and Rif were passing out copies of the "Rat And Rif Songbook," while Klickett (in a bright orange sweater) took in the money. Miko was surrounded by several young things, attracted by his un-inked charms. In a corner, Altair Jones carefully spelled out some of the poems to herself, puzzling over the meaning.

Rif waved frantically at Ariadne, who pulled her husband with her in this invasion.

"Hey, I didn't think you'd come! How d'ya like it?" Rif waved the new book at the Delaneys.

"Most attractive," Ariadne said. "Farren, dear, look at the tooling on this cover . . . and the vellum-quality . . . and the scratch-board finish. . . ."

Farren Delaney was looking over the other guests. "I had no idea there were so many . . . interesting . . . people down here," he said, smiling at Rif. He was an athletic, jovial sort of man, with thinning hair, and an infectious smile. Rif smiled back, conscious that Ariadne could tell exactly what was going on. . . .

"Farren!" Ariadne's voice cut through any thoughts of dalliance. "The paper!"

Farren frowned slightly. "Our best vellum-weight. I thought we'd sold it all to the Signeury."

"Farren, is that cider? Would you get me a glass? Please?" Ariadne dismissed her husband and turned to Rif. "I didn't want him to know what we'd been doing, but really, you should have told me what you were up to. You didn't have to steal the paper . . . we *own* the paper-mill. All you had to do was ask."

Rat looked at Rif. Rif looked at Rat. And they both began to laugh, while Ariadne stood there with the stunned expression of one who has just made an amazingly witty remark but doesn't quite know what it means.

A FISH STORY

by Nancy Asire

Springtime in Merovingen could be summed up in one word: flirtatious. One day would dawn clear and sunny, full of warm breezes and the promise of easier times ahead; then the following day would turn dark, full of gray, scudding clouds and a north wind that would sweep down the canals as if winter had never left the land. It did no one any good to pin hopes on one fine day's weather, but everyone, from the canalers to the denizens of Merovingen above, hoped for a day of warmth and sunshine to be followed by another, and another.

Justice Lee leaned on the railing of the second level walkway on the backside of Kass, and stared across at the Pile and at the citizens who thronged it, out for a breath of spring. A junction between Kass, Bent and Spellbridge, the Pile was honeycombed with small shops, benches for sitting, and small corners for talking; today it bustled with passers-by stopping to linger a moment in what sunlight they could find, before continuing on to their business.

And since tomorrow could bring clouds and sleet, today's sunshine was doubly appreciated.

A heavy, furry body bumped into Justice: he glanced down at the large, golden cat that rubbed back and forth between his legs, and smiled. Sunny was living up to his name: the cat sought out whatever sunlight the second level of Kass afforded, to sit in the warmth, motionless as some statue, glowing as if he were made of gold.

Justice settled back into his slouch at the rail, content, full of a good lunch, and in between classes. He doubted even Krishna could spoil his mood right now, though he turned away the thought of his fellow student as a blemish on the day. Things had changed for Justice in the past few months . . . changed drastically, and he was sometimes hard put to figure out what he was doing and what was expected of him.

Ever since meeting Sonja Keisel during winter exams, Justice had found himself propelled into a world he had always wanted to enter—the rarified existence of the high and mighty of Merovingen. He smiled briefly, remembering the Governor's Winter Ball, an event attended only by those of sufficient social and financial worth. As such, he had never in his wildest imaginings thought he would or could attend. But Sonja had changed all that, had invited him to accompany her, and suddenly Justice had found himself under the eye of hightown Merovingen.

Granted that Sonja's invitation had come as a result of Father Rhajmurti's plan to shatter the blackmail hopes of Krishna Malenkov, but it had been a legitimate invitation nonetheless. Without it, Justice would have only *heard* about what had happened at the ball from his fellow students, not participated in it. And, participate in it he had.

Thanks to the Lord and his Ancestors, he had not disgraced himself or, even worse, Sonja. He had comported himself with the best of manners, had kept his mouth shut most of the time, and had left the ball with the feeling that he might have scored some points with his moneyed student companions.

Sonja Keisel was not someone to be ignored. Daughter of Nadia Keisel who held the monopoly on beef trade that came into Merovingen, Sonja was also a Borg. Her father, Vladimir Borg had married her mother *before* Sonja had been born, making her a true love child, not the issue of a contract marriage.

And for some reason Justice could not fathom, Sonja seemed to enjoy his company.

He thought back on the ball: his nervousness, his concern that his best clothes would not be good enough, or his manners refined enough. That his lack of money and family connections would be viewed as a mark against him as he moved among such exalted company.

But Sonja had dismissed his worries with a smile and a wave of her hand. When he had entered the huge ballroom, clad in his best shirt, trousers and boots, Sonja Keisel at his side, the eyes of the hightowners around him had registered only curiosity, not hostility.

But now . . . now he was having a hard time trying to figure out where he stood in the scheme of things. After the ball, his fellow students had treated him—well, if not differently, then with more respect. He had been invited to several parties later, affairs he would more than likely have been passed over for had he never met Sonja. Students not in his chosen field of art had taken more interest in what he was doing; several of them even commissioned small works, landscapes or portraits of family, paying him far more than he would have asked.

He hated to plant false hopes in his heart, but maybe Sonja *was* right . . . maybe he *did* have a brilliant career in front of him. Even Father Rhajmurti had assured him this was true.

Justice shrugged and turned his thoughts to the present. Even if he *had* been noticed by the upper crust of Merovingen society, he still had to study, to learn, to do . . . to perfect his chosen career. He dared not lose sight of his goal, or consider himself "arrived" before he got there.

So, it had been back to the books, back to classes, and back to the real world of College competitiveness. But one thing had not changed since the glorious experience of the ball . . . Sonja still sought out his company, still came to Hilda's on occasion to share a meal with him, and—more staggering to Justice's mind—periodically had him over to her house for an informal meal.

The warm breeze lifted Justice's hair from his brow and he smiled, leaning there on the railing and watching Merovingen go by. Sunny rubbed up against Justice's leg, meowed, and set off down the walkway, in search of whatever it was that cats did on such a lovely day.

Justice straightened, sighed softly and, turning his back on the warm sunlight and lazy spring breeze, returned to Hilda's and his books.

There were some days, he thought, when it would be nice to be a cat.

Father Rhajmurti stood in a shadowed corner of the wide hallway and watched the students pass him by. The second story of the College was always packed after lunch, with priests on their way to teach classes and students returning for an afternoon of instruction. Rhajmurti smiled briefly as he caught sight of his protégé, Justice Lee, on the way to his next class. Justice's height would have made him stand out in a crowd, but there was a new assurance to the way the young man walked, a certain set of Justice's shoulders, of his head, that spoke of a newly found confidence.

And it was a confidence, Rhajmurti thought, that was long overdue. Justice possessed one of the brightest artistic talents Rhajmurti had seen in years and, to be honest, one of the better minds. Not that this was merely the pride a patron felt in the student he had chosen to sponsor, it was a truth. Rhajmurti leaned back against the wall: whether he admitted it or not, it was also the pride a father had in a son who thought his parents dead long ago.

One of these days, there would be no backing down from it: Rhajmurti would have to tell Justice the truth of his parentage, that his aunt was really his mother, and that his sponsor, Alfonso Rhajmurti, was his father. But now was not the time, though he had more than once since winter exams come close to admitting his relationship to Justice. No. He would tell the young man when and if the time was ripe. Such information could unseat all the carefully nurtured confidence Rhajmurti had helped instill in Justice's life.

"Rhajmurti."

He turned and found another priest standing at his side: Father Alexiev, initiated as he was at the Third Level, and teacher of literature.

"Are you free for a while?" Alexiev asked.

"Yes. I don't have another class for two hours."

"Come with me. I've got to talk with you."

Rhajmurti nodded and followed Alexiev down the hallway toward the massive front stairs. Something seemed to be bothering Alexiev: his bushy eyebrows were drawn together in a frown, his expression enough to put off any casual approach. Though Rhajmurti did not consider his fellow priest exactly a friend, Alexiev was a member of the same Fine Arts staff as Rhajmurti, the two of them had studied for the priesthood in the same year and there was some trust between them. So it was up the stairs then, past the stair guard, and to the third story, the private apartments of the priests. The cardinals lived at one end of the College in apartments far more lavish than those the priests inhabited. Among the priests, it was a mark of importance where one's apartment was located: the closer to the cardinals' end of the hall, the higher one stood—and Alexiev's rooms sat a few doors down from Rhajmurti's, toward the cardinals' end of the third story.

"Have a chair," Alexiev said, ushering Rhajmurti into his sitting room and closing the door. "May I get you something to drink?"

Rhajmurti nodded and watched his fellow priest bustle around, pouring the wine, stopping the decanter, and returning to extend one of the glasses.

"Rama's blessing," Rhajmurti said and lifted his glass in a toast.

"Hari Rama," Alexiev returned, taking a sip of his wine and sitting down in another chair so he faced Rhajmurti. "Have you heard anything unusual lately?" he asked without preamble.

Rhajmurti studied his host over the top of his glass. "Unusual regarding what?"

For a moment, Alexiev started at Rhajmurti, then glanced around as if he feared eavesdroppers. "The cardinals."

"What about the cardinals?" Rhajmurti leaned forward in his chair. "Would you come to the point, Pytor? Quit beating around the bush."

"Cardinal Ito Boregy," Alexiev said softly.

Ah. Cardinal Boregy. And most likely his private conversion sessions with Nev Hetteker Mike Chamoun. "I've heard about the conversion classes he's giving."

Alexiev shifted his weight uneasily. "Have you heard he's using—ah, shall we say, he's helping this Chamoun fellow remember his previous life with . . . a little assistance?"

"Yes."

"Do you know what it is?"

Rhajmurti shook his head. "I haven't heard."

Alexiev moved forward until he was sitting on the edge of his chair, his face as close as possible to Rhajmurti's. "It's deathangel."

"Holy . . ." Rhajmurti settled back in his chair. "Are you sure?"

"Well—why else would the word have gone out for us to gather all the deathangel powder we can?"

"No one asked me to do that," Rhajmurti said.

"I know, I know." Alexiev waved a hand. "No one asked me in so many words either. But you *have* been asked to watch out for it among your students, haven't you?"

"Yes."

"To confiscate it and give any of the powder you find to the cardinals?"

"Yes."

"Use your head, man. I think they *want* it for some reason."

Rhajmurti narrowed his eyes and stared over Alexiev's shoulder at the wall. It could likely be true. He knew Alexiev stood higher in favor with the cardinals than he did, being far more willing to—as the old saying went—brownnose. And Alexiev was also much fonder of gossip, being a periodic gold mine of information that had not yet come to the surface of College society. But deathangel? If Cardinal Boregy was using *that* in his conversion classes . . .

"You know how dangerous it is, don't you?" Alexiev asked, settling back in his chair and taking another drink of wine.

"Gods, yes. But do you know for a fact that Boregy's using deathangel on this Chamoun?"

"No, but I'd be willing to bet on it. Why else would

the cardinals be so interested in getting their hands on whatever deathangel powder we priests can find?"

Rhajmurti frowned. No reason he could think of. Drugs were a problem among the idle rich of Merovingen, and among their children. The College had always made a point of forbidding any drug dealing or drug taking in its halls. But in the past, what drugs the priests had found had been consigned to the canals, not turned over to the cardinals.

"Is it just deathangel they're interested in?" he wondered, both of himself and Alexiev.

"That's the only one we've been told to confiscate rather than destroy."

"You're right there." Rhajmurti rubbed his chin. "Have you ever taken any?"

"Deathangel?" Alexiev glanced down at his feet. "Once. Long ago. And you?"

"That's one I avoided. I saw a friend of mine die from it."

Alexiev made an quick handsign of aversion. "My experience wasn't pleasant," he said, "or at least it wasn't at the end. At first, it was, —well, I thought I was going to see what the yogis see. Gods, Alfonso. Everything was glittering, sharper edged than usual, surrounded by its own aura. I've never seen anything like it."

"And then?"

"Then I threw up. I guess I'm allergic to deathangel." Alexiev smiled crookedly. "It's a damned strange thing to be having glimpses into the otherworld while you're puking your shoes off."

Rhajmurti grinned. "Thank you, no. I'll go after such visions by meditation. No aftereffects. Do you think the cardinals are going to start using it?"

"I don't know. I haven't been told anything different than the rest of the priests: if I find it, I'm to deliver it to the cardinals. Between you and me, if they're not going to use it, then they're damned interested in seeing what it does."

"Do *you* think it can help you remember past lives?"

"I can't say, even after having used it once. I'd be more worried about the levels of toxin ingested than my heightened mental state."

"Huhn. Well, I haven't heard anything you haven't."

"Keep your ears open. If the cardinals find some use for deathangel, I'm afraid we could be in for some interesting times."

Rhajmurti met his fellow priest's eyes. Interesting times? If deathangel *was* a key to remembering former lives, and word leaked out, not a Revenantist soul in Merovingen would pass up the chance to explore one part of the mystery of personal karma.

Neither would the smugglers, drug dealers, and worse.

When Justice arrived back at Hilda's after his last class, he found Raj waiting for him. The young man sat patiently on the edge of the walkway outside the tavern, arms crossed on his knees, a small smile on his face, staring off into nothing. Raj had not said a word to Justice about what had happened when he had disappeared during winter exams, and—after the boat ride in the dark of night, delivering Lord only knew what to Petrescu—Justice had not asked.

He had seen Raj's friend, the canaler Jones, several times since that night, and had found Jones to be warm and friendly when their paths had crossed; but Jones obviously had nothing more to say about the incident, and Justice consigned the entire delivery trip to a growing number of events he considered Mysteries of Life. Raj's brother, Denny, had turned up several times at Hilda's, usually as a messenger for his brother when Raj could not make an agreed-upon get-together.

As for Raj, Justice saw his new friend off and on, mostly after Raj got off his job at Gallandrys, though there were long stretches of time when Raj would effectively disappear. Justice had continued to mention Raj whenever he talked privately to Father Rhajmurti, telling his patron how well-qualified Raj was, and how it was a shame that he was not admitted to the College. Nothing had come of those talks, but Justice knew how long it took sometimes for things to happen.

"You off for the day?" Raj asked, standing up as Justice approached. "Want a beer?"

"Sounds good to me. Where?"

Raj shrugged one shoulder. "Hilda's is good enough for me."

Justice nodded and led the way inside. Something was up—he could not remember seeing Raj looking so happy.

"So," he said, taking his place at his favorite table and gesturing Raj to sit. "What's going on?"

Raj fairly squirmed in his chair. "I wanted you to be one of the first to know. I got accepted to the College!"

Justice sat up straighter. "You did? But— Who sponsored you?"

"House Kamat," Raj said, meeting Justice's eyes with a "don't-you-say-anything-about-the-lady" look. "I'll be starting next semester."

"Damn!" Justice grinned. "That's great news! I'm really happy for you!"

Raj beamed back, his dark eyes sparkling in the lamplight.

"When did you find out? Father Rhajmurti didn't say anything about it to me." Justice lifted two fingers in Jason's direction indicating his and Raj's order for beer.

"It's not really news yet," Raj said. "You know how those things are . . . certain people have to talk with certain people, and then other people talk with the higher-ups, and—"

"Spare me the details." Jason arrived with the beer and, after he left with the tab, Justice toasted Raj with a high-held mug. "Here's to your new career! You're going in as a student doctor?"

"Yes." Raj took a long drink, then set his mug down. He reached inside his sweater and drew out a large packet. "And before we get much further here, this is for you."

Justice took the packet and hefted it in his hand. "What it is this time?"

"More herb tea for your exams. It's the same stuff I gave you earlier, only this batch is a bit stronger. When it comes time to study, a cupful of this will keep you up far into the night." A sly look crossed Raj's face. "I suspect you might be able to sell some, too."

"This is good news and bad news, you know. Now I won't have any excuse for not getting high marks on my tests. Oh, well. If Krishna gets on my nerves, I can always sell some to him, and tell him to use twice what he's supposed to."

Raj laughed, then sobered. He leaned forward on the table. "It's further payment for the favor you did me," he said in a quiet voice. "Thanks again."

The favor. Oh, yes . . . another one of Raj's shadowy doings. *Find out what you can about Father Jermaine Harmody,* Raj had asked. *Nothing special. Just keep your ears open. And if it's any trouble, don't worry about it.* Those were indeed the magic words: "if it's any trouble, don't worry." Justice was not sure he wanted to be involved in any more of Raj's secretive doings . . . dangerous or not.

"I hope I was of some help."

"You were," Raj said. He glanced around: the tavern was not full, for the dinner hour had yet to come. "And I've got a piece of advice for you."

Justice lifted an eyebrow.

"Word's out on the canals that someone, or maybe more than one someone, is damned interested in deathangel."

"Oh?" A thousand thoughts clamored in Justice's mind—more mysterious goings on? Which was it this time? A poisoning war between two powerful houses? A blackleg setup, prelude for a crackdown on drug traffic? "Why?"

Raj shrugged. "Don't know. It might have something to do with hallucinating. You can get a great grandmother of a high off the stuff."

"And die from it, too, if I remember correctly."

"Right. Now that you've started to attend the affairs of the high and mighty—" Raj winked at Justice. "—you might run into some of it at the parties. I wouldn't have anything to do with it, if I were you."

"Don't worry." Justice sipped at his beer, trying to remember if he had seen anyone talking with God at the recent parties he had attended. "I have enough trouble mixing with hightowners as it is without doing it drugged."

"I don't exactly mean it that way," Raj said. "If someone's interested in deathangel, then someone's going to be willing to *pay* for it . . ."

"And that means dealing in the shadows," Justice added. "Could be dangerous."

"Could be. Most likely *will* be. If anyone asks you to make contacts—"

Justice grimaced. "Why me? I'm no canaler, to have access to deathangel."

"Ah, but you're a student and—"

"—students get hungry. Point well taken. Don't worry, Raj. I've seen enough weirdness lately to last me for a long time. I won't go hunting for more."

Raj looked embarrassed. "I don't want to get you involved in . . . in my troubles," he said. "That delivery you made for me to Petrescu . . . if it makes any difference, you're well thought of by my friends."

"From what little I know of your friends, I'd hate to be *disliked* by them."

A sheepish smile spread across Raj's face. "And another thing about you, Justice, you don't ask questions."

"What kind of a fool do you think I am? In cases like that, the less I know, the happier I am."

"Just watch out for deathangel. I've got the feeling things are going to get real strange around here before long."

Real strange? Justice shook his head. Coming from most people he knew, he would have shrugged the statement away. Coming from Raj, —well, it wouldn't be a bad idea to avoid traveling the canals after dark.

The more Rhajmurti thought about what Father Alexiev had told him about the cardinals' interest in deathangel, the more the notion bothered him. He had known for years that many people tried to attain enlightenment through use of drugs, but he had always frowned on the idea, preferring to conduct his spiritual quests unaided by pharmaceuticals. The idea of the cardinals becoming interested in the hallucinogenic properties of that deadly fish gave Rhajmurti cause for deep thought.

From his earliest days of priestly training, Rhajmurti

had been taught that seeking and finding spiritual enlightenment took years and years. But in the same breath, his teachers had told him that certain drugs—if used sparingly and in very moderate amounts—could facilitate such a search. They likened limited drug use to the mantras each priest had selected to repeat and ponder—aids to put the mind in the proper attitude for inner visions.

Deathangel, however, if not carefully dealt with, could send one on a spiritual quest without a return ticket.

He frowned as he neared Hilda's tavern. Not until recently had Justice been included in the hightown party circuit, and Rama knew all sorts of drugs were available there. In some ways, Justice was an innocent when it came to what went on behind the closed doors of Merovingen above. Now that he had become socially acceptable after the Governor's Winter Ball, perhaps it was time for a little priest-to-student talk about the evils that lurked behind high society glitter.

Hilda's was crowded with patrons eating their dinners, but Rhajmurti easily spotted Justice at his usual table, his nose buried in a book and Hilda's gold cat asleep in a chair by his side. The empty plate shoved to one side was evidence that Justice had already eaten. Rhajmurti left the doorway, nodded to Jason and Hilda, and crossed the room to Justice's table.

"Busy?" he asked, and smiled as Justice looked up. "Mind if I join you?"

"No, Father." Justice pushed a chair out and gestured. "Please sit down."

Rhajmurti placed his order with an attentive Jason, then turned back to Justice. "So. Exams aren't far away. How do you think you'll do?"

"All right, I suppose. All I can do is study and hope

for the best. Oh. I saw Raj today. He tells me he's been accepted into the College."

"He has?" Not for the first time did Rhajmurti wish he was higher placed in the College. He was still young—only thirty-eight—but his progress had not been as swift as he would have hoped. Hearing a piece of news like this, secondhand from one of his students, made it painfully clear how much he was missing out on by not cultivating the priests in power, or by refusing to flatter the cardinals. "It must have been recently. Who's sponsoring him?"

"House Kamat."

"Hmm." Rhajmurti could not resist. "How'd you hear about it?"

"I saw Raj just a little while ago. He told me."

"He must be happy."

"That's an understatement." Justice fell silent as Jason delivered Rhajmurti's dinner, swept up the offered coins in one hand, and went back toward the kitchen. "He's fit to burst."

Rhajmurti nodded, fully aware after all Justice's talking about Raj's talents how much this sponsorship would mean to a young man who otherwise would have never stood a chance to get a higher education.

"Raj also told me something I think you might like to know." Justice lowered his voice. "He says someone's really interested in getting their hands on deathangel."

"Damn!" Rhajmurti met and held Justice's eyes. "Where'd he hear that?"

"From the canalers, I suppose. He has a friend who runs a skip."

Rhajmurti frowned. First Father Alexiev proposed that the cardinals wanted all the deathangel powder priests found students carrying; now Justice said the word was out on the canals that deathangel would fetch a good price.

"That's odd," he murmured, taking a bite of his fish and following it with a sip of beer.

"What's odd?"

"I was just going to have a little talk with you about the . . . let us say, overindulgence in drugs that goes on at hightowner parties."

"Then I'm warned twice," Justice said. "Raj said the same thing."

Rhajmurti stared a moment. "Good for him. And I want you to promise me you won't start experimenting."

Justice shook his head. "Why does everyone think I'm such a thick-skull? I've got more sense than that."

"You do now." Rhajmurti leaned forward on crossed arms. "I'm sure you mean every word you say. But remember what you've said when you go to your next party. What if you're offered something by your new friends? What if everyone at the party decides to get high?"

It did Justice credit that he had no quick answer for those questions. "I could always say I have a delicate constitution and can't mess with the stuff," he said.

"What if Sonja decides to get high?"

"That won't happen." Justice's voice was full of certainty. "We've talked about it. She doesn't like doing drugs. Says it clouds her mind, and if she wanted a cloudy mind, she wouldn't be spending all this time going to school."

Rhajmurti's estimation of Sonja Keisel went up another few notches. He took another bite of fish. "You take care to remember what we've talked about. Sonja won't always be around."

"I know." Justice dropped his eyes, then lifted them again; when he spoke, his voice was very quiet. "Something else, Father. If deathangel's getting this popular, someone's going to be willing to pay for it . . . and pay well. I'm worried about Krishna."

"You? Worried about Krishna? After all the karma he's heaped on himself from bothering you?"

"I can't help it, Father. He's already sold drugs. If his father ever finds out. . . ." He shrugged. "If Krishna'd only grow up, I don't think he'd be all *that* bad."

"Huhn. Maybe so. But don't look for him to grow up any time soon. And I wouldn't spend my time worrying about him. Krishna can take care of himself."

"Dammit, Krishna, listen to me! Now's not the time to pass out."

Krishna opened one eye and then the other. Pavel Suhakai sat on the floor beside him, a curiously intent look on his face.

"Shit, Pavel, —d'you always haveta ruin a good buzz?" He lifted his glass, frowned when no liquid hit his tongue, and turned the glass upside down. Not a drop left. He belched, wiped his mouth with the back of his hand and, with studied care, set the glass back down on the floor. "Whadya want?"

"Money, Krishna! Listen to me. *Money!* Maybe *big* money. Am I getting through to you yet?"

"Money." Krishna's head was beginning to spin. He set his teeth, slid his back higher up on the wall, and tried to focus. His words came out very slow—his tongue was not cooperating at all. "Big money. All right, —you have my attention. Where? How?"

"You've heard what I've heard. Deathangel. If we can buy up as much deathangel as we can get our hands on, we'll drive the price up. Are you listening to me?"

"Huhn?" Krishna rubbed his eyes. He looked around Pavel's expensively furnished room and winced at the bright electric light overhead. "I'm listening. We buy up deathangel." His head ached and he slapped his hand on the floor. "But who wants it, Pavel? It's damned dangerous stuff."

"Hell, I don't know who wants it. Who cares? All I know is that someone's real interested. Ask around school. If the market's there, and we move quickly, we can fill it."

"Where'd you hear all this?"

"Same place you did. Esteban overheard two priests saying the cardinals wanted all the deathangel powder they found any student carrying." Pavel's brows drew together in a frown. "Would you sober up, Krishna!"

"I'm not *that* drunk! All right, smart-ass, —where are we going to get the money to buy it?"

"I thought about that. We could always sell some of our things and then claim they were stolen."

"Maybe. So Esteban heard two priests talking. How do we know the cardinals are interested? It could be a trap." Krishna belched again. If he did not eat something soon, he would be too drunk to make it back to Hilda's. Food. His stomach turned at the thought of it. "They could be setting us up, Pavel. Then, the moment we say we've got some of the damned fish, they'll make the buy, and slap us into the darkest, smallest room in—"

"It might not be the cardinals. They might be getting it for someone else."

Krishna shook his head. This was all getting too complex to follow. Why would the cardinals be buying deathangel from students, when they could easily hire some canaler to get the fish for them at a cheaper price?

Unless they were after the processed powder which they figured the students might already possess.

That put a new slant on things. If he and Pavel

bought up deathangel, the fish would have to be processed to obtain the powder. On the other hand, if they were clever and moved quickly, they might be able to buy the powder from their hightown friends *before* word of what the cardinals wanted leaked out. In either case . . .

"Talk to that friend of yours. Justus. He's friendly with canalers. It's our best bet to find someone to get us deathangel. If you approach him right, maybe he'd be willing to— "

"Mister Good? Ha!" Krishna snorted a laugh, bumped his head against the wall, and cringed. "He's so squeaky clean I've never seen him drunk."

"Maybe so, but he's poor. Offer him money, Krishna. Money talks. It may even speak Justus' language."

True to form, the following morning dawned dull and gray, though not as chill as Justice had feared. He sat alone at his table, lingering for a last few moments over his second cup of tea, trying to sort out exactly what had happened the night before.

Krishna had come in late, so drunk he was stumbling. Drink, however, seldom silenced the hightowner, and he had latched onto Justice like a barnacle. Justice had wanted to leave his table, to go off to his room and go to sleep, but Krishna was insistent. His words slow, obviously chosen with the care induced by overindulgence, Krishna had apologized for being an overbearing ass during the past few months, confessing that it was the pressures put on him by his father who so desperately wanted a youngest son to succeed. He had even gone so far as to pay Justice the last of the money he owed.

It was this repayment of a long-overdue debt that set alarm bells ringing.

And sure enough, as if right on cue, Krishna had

mentioned deathangel. *You know canalers, don't you?* Krishna had asked. *Do you think maybe you could talk someone into getting me some deathangel? Oh, don't worry . . . it's not for me. I wouldn't* touch *the stuff. Booze is good enough for me. . . . It's for a few of my friends. . . .*

And so on and so on. Justice had listened politely, trying his best to look attentive, all the while searching for some diversion to get away from Krishna. *I'll see if I can find someone,* Justice had promised, hoping like hell Krishna would forget everything the following day.

He had not seen Krishna yet this morning, but that was hardly a surprising event. Krishna was more than likely sleeping off his drunk, thereby missing another morning of classes. If there had not been a brain inside that uptown head, Krishna would have failed his courses long ago. As it was, he passed with marginal grades, his quickness and good memory (when liquor-free) keeping him from total disaster.

Justice frowned. Now what? He could always deny that he had promised to look for a canaler to get a hold of deathangel. Drunk as Krishna had been last night, Justice was fairly sure he could swear the entire conversation had been a leftover from an evening spent with a bottle.

Still . . . Justice sat up straighter in his chair. It might not be a bad idea to have another talk with Father Rhajmurti.

The day was still overcast enough that Rhajmurti found the lighted lamp on his office wall welcome. Justice sat opposite the desk, his face bearing two conflicting emotions: lack of sleep and worry.

Rhajmurti leaned back in his chair and crossed his hands on his chest. It would be Krishna again. There was something about that lad . . . something that led Rhajmurti to think Krishna must have done terrible things in his last life to be so confused in this one.

"You don't think he remembered what you said?" he asked Justice.

"No, Father. If he does, I'd be surprised. He's been drunk like this before and not remembered anything that went on."

"Let's hope you're right." He studied Justice a moment, verging on telling him about the secretive goings on in the College. He finally shelved the idea, not only to keep hidden maneuverings from a student, but to prevent Justice from becoming embroiled in a situation that might get out of hand.

"What's going on, Father?" Justice asked, looking away from a complex rendition of the wheel of life hanging on Rhajmurti's wall. "Why is deathangel all the rage now?"

"I'm not sure." Falsehood . . . lying to one's own son? *Bad* karma, that. "It might have to do with the state the drug can put people in." There, that was better . . . a small omission of truth. "Some people think you might be able to remember previous lives if your mind's put into the proper frame of consciousness."

Justice lifted one dark eyebrow. "Remember former lives? I thought only some yogis and other spiritually blessed could do that."

"You're correct. Usually, Sometimes, the uninitiated stumble across enlightenment, but it's not normal."

"I wouldn't think so. But none of this solves my problem. What do I do about Krishna? He's offered me a fair sum to make a contact with someone who can get him as many fish as possible. *He* says he's getting them for his *friends*. Ha! Likely story. He's probably heard something that makes him think someone will pay him a good price. I'll be willing to bet he wants to drive that price up and then sell what he has for a tidy profit."

"Do you know someone who would help you get your hands on deathangel?"

Justice shook his head. "I can't think of anybody. The only canaler I know on a first-name basis is that skip-runner I mentioned yesterday—Jones, Raj's friend. And I don't think she's the type to deal in drugs."

"Huhn." Rhajmurti rubbed his forehead. "Were you telling me the truth when you said you were worried about Krishna?"

"Yes." Justice grimaced slightly. "Though this morning I'm inclined to leave him to his problems and spend more time trying to deal with mine."

"I think . . . if we play this right . . . we might be able to scare Krishna off from drug dealing for a while—" He met Justice's eyes. "—before things start getting too dangerous for someone who doesn't know what he's doing. And Krishna will help us by being greedy as usual. But to make it work, you're going to have to look guilty, too. Are you interested?"

"You'll have to tell me what kind of punishment I'm to expect before I tell you," Justice said, the hint of a smile on his lips.

Rhajmurti leaned forward in his chair. "Nothing that you won't be able to handle. Are you going to be seeing Sonja this morning?"

From his perch on one of the benches in the College hallway, Justice could easily see the students pass him by. Sonja sat quietly beside him, her nose buried in a book, seeming to pay no attention to what was going on around her. Justice attempted to look equally disinterested, but when he saw Krishna approaching, he felt his stomach tighten.

"Hssst," he whispered to Sonja. "He's coming."

A brief smile crossed her face, then disappeared. "Good luck," she murmured.

"Justus." Krishna stopped by the bench. "M'sera Keisel," he said, bowing slightly to Sonja. He motioned to an alcove a few steps away. "I need to talk with you a moment, Justus, if you don't mind."

"Not at all." Justice set his book down at his side and stood. "I'll be back in a moment, Sonja," he said, and followed Krishna.

"Well?"

"Well, what?" Justice said.

"Have you got in contact with anyone yet?"

Damn! Krishna had remembered. The *one* time he should have been stewed enough to forget, and he remembered. Justice frowned slightly. As for professing to have been an ass, Krishna had probably forgotten *that* particular part of last night's conversation.

"Maybe." He looked up and down the hall. "Maybe I've got something better."

Krishna's eyes narrowed. "And what might that be?"

"There's a rumor going around that the priests are very interested in getting their hands on deathangel. Have you heard the same thing?"

There was just the slightest hesitation. "I have."

"Well, I overheard someone whispering in the hallway this morning that certain priests will pay good money for a student to get them some deathangel powder."

"Oh?" A flash of greed passed behind Krishna's eyes. "Who'd you overhear talking?"

"I didn't recognize the voice and when I came round the corner, whoever it was had gone."

"That's a mighty flimsy lead,' Krishna said. "It could be a setup."

"I suppose. But I thought I'd let you know . . . if you want deathangel for your—friends, you might be able to get enough money from the priests to buy some for everybody."

"Hmm." Krishna's forehead furrowed in thought. "Maybe. Did you hear how much the priests were willing to pay?"

"No. Just that the money was good."

"And how the hell are we to get in contact with the priests?"

Justice noted the use of the plural and winced. "Supposedly there's always one of them waiting behind the steps downstairs."

Krishna frowned. "If this is a false run, Justus . . ."

"I've told you all I heard. That's the only information I can give you on deathangel. Take it or leave it."

For a moment, Justice thought Krishna would stalk off, but the hightowner kept his temper in check. "All right. I'll tell you what . . . why don't you and I pay a little visit to the steps."

"Me?" Justice tried to look startled. "Why do you want *me* to go with you?"

"Simple." Krishna smiled nastily. "To make sure it's not a setup."

Justice shrugged. "I can only tell you what I overheard, Krishna. Nothing more. But if you want me to go with you, I'll come."

Sonja waited until she had seen Justus walk off with Krishna, then gathered up her books along with the one Justus had left behind. Counting until she reached thirty, she stood and casually walked off down the hall toward the stairs. As she nodded in passing to other students, she asked herself why she was doing this. Why was she getting herself involved in another of Rhajmurti's and Justus' plans? Was it simply to get back at Krishna for all those years when he had been after her to pay attention to him? Or, was it because she truly *liked* Justus . . . liked him more than many of her hightowner friends?

She could not answer that question to any satisfaction. Her parents were puzzled and concerned over her new choice of friends, though neither of them had said anything derogatory about Justus. It would not do for her to become overly fond of someone with no House, no money, no position. As it was, she had been affianced a year ago to enter into a contract marriage with Jorge Kuminski when she finished College.

A familiar anger welled up inside. Dammit! Was she not free to pick and choose as she wished? Had she no say in her own destiny? Not that Jorge was a bad sort; she was as fond of him as she was of many other hightown young men, but . . . She shook her head and walked on. Her parents had married for love. Why not her? All these contract marriages, these formings of alliances between Houses, bored her to tears. She could play politics with the best of them, but she had a fatal streak of outright honesty that could doom her in political maneuverings.

And what, by Krishna the Thrice Blessed, was wrong with her liking Justus? He was smart, talented and would go far in his chosen profession. An artist who catered to hightown could become as wealthy as some of his patrons. All the great Houses had to start somewhere.

She descended the stairs, refusing to follow her thoughts on to a conclusion. Justus was sometimes far too good a person, if the word good applied here. She supposed it was his own honesty that appealed to her . . . his earnestness, and his dedication.

And, by the gods, he wanted to make something of himself, to become more than he was at the moment. *That* kind of ambition she admired.

She smiled slightly. Getting back at Krishna would have to serve as her reason for going along with Rhajmurti's plan . . . for now.

Justice followed Krishna down the wide steps that led to the first floor of the College, all the while keeping his fingers crossed that Rhajmurti knew what he was doing. Krishna had reacted as expected, his greed being the one thing about him that never changed. Money given to him now, in partial payment for the future delivery of deathangel, was far more attractive than *spending* money to purchase the fish and getting paid back for his trouble later.

As for his own part in this plan, Justice hoped he could pull it off convincingly. The last thing he needed was Krishna mad at him again. Ever since the Governor's Winter Ball, Krishna had been careful not to step on Justice's toes too often. It was one thing to bait a student with no ties to Merovingen-above, and another to bother someone Sonja Keisel seemed to like.

"You sure this priest will be waiting there?" Krishna asked over his shoulder, his words nearly lost in the hum of conversation around him.

Justice shrugged. "All I know is what I heard. If he's not there, he's not there, and we're back at our starting point. But we won't have lost a thing."

"This better be on the up-and-up," Krishna growled when he reached the foot of the stairs. He turned to face Justice, trying to look grim. The effect was spoiled by his lack of height: it was hard to appear threatening when one had to look up at the person one threatened.

"Look, Krishna," Justice said, putting an edge of weariness in his words, "if you don't want to bother, just say so. You asked me to see if I could help you, and this is the only lead I've got."

"Huhn."

Krishna turned and stalked off, turning right at the edge of the stairs and heading back toward the rear of the great entry hall. Justice followed.

For a moment, he thought no one was waiting, but then he saw a cloaked and cowled figure standing in the shadows under the stairs. Krishna had evidently seen the same person, for the stocky hightowner stopped, turned toward Justice, and made a quick motion for silence.

"Do you think that's him?" Krishna murmured.

"How should I know? I suppose all we can do is ask."

Krishna's face darkened but he evidently could not come up with a flippant reply. He set his shoulders, glanced once about to see if anyone might be interested in what he was doing, gestured for Justice to accompany him, and slowly walked toward the stairs.

It was a priest . . . Justice could see that now: the saffron color of the cloak showed a bit more in the shadows the closer he and Krishna came.

"M'ser?" Krishna said in a soft voice. The priest looked up, but still Justice could see no face in the shadows thrown by the cowl. "I've heard that you're looking to buy something. Is that true?"

"That depends," the priest said. Justice tried to place the voice, but could not. "What do you have to sell?"

"Nothing yet," Krishna said, "but if you'd tell me what it is that you want, I might be able to help you."

Justice lifted an eyebrow. Such finesse . . . never really committing himself, Krishna was still letting the other man know he was available, and that he knew more than he was saying. An old hand at this game, and it showed.

"Could be." The priest shifted his weight in the

shadows. "I'm interested in obtaining a certain fish. . . ."

Krishna glanced sidelong at Justice, his eyes glittering in the dim light. "And what kind of fish would m'ser be interested in?"

The most beautiful . . . with long, trailing fins of deepest black, set on a silver and yellow body. Do you know the fish, young ser?"

Justice heard Krishna's quick intake of breath.

"Deathangel," Krishna said.

"It is called that," the priest acknowledged.

"Ummm . . . as I said, I don't have any now, but I could *find* some, if the price is right."

Lord and Ancestors! Justice groaned. *Greedy as ever, aren't you?*

The priest reached beneath his cloak and extended a gloved hand. Even in the shadows, Justice could see the flash of gold.

"Would this be appropriate as partial payment for . . . shall we say, twenty fish?"

Krishna took the coin. "A demi," he breathed, turning the gold piece over in his hand. He glanced up at the priest, then back at the money. "I—I think this would be more than appropriate, m'ser."

Justice stared at the gold glittering on Krishna's palm. Damn! That one coin could keep him going for weeks and weeks!

"Then I can trust you to fulfill your part of the bargain, m'ser Malenkov?" the priest asked.

Krishna's head jerked up at the mention of his last name. The priest knew him! He swallowed heavily.

"Yes, m'ser. A Malenkov doesn't break his word."

"That's good to know. I wouldn't want you to have to return the full amount if you fail. I'm sure you understand me, don't you, m'ser?"

"Oh, yes. I understand you."

"Then it's settled."

"Uh . . . where should I deliver the deathangel?" Krishna asked.

"What in Vishnu's hells is going on here?"

Justice had been so intent on the bargaining going on, he had failed to notice the arrival of another person to the shadows beneath the stairway. He spun around and came face to face with Father Rhajmurti.

And Sonja.

Three things happened so quickly Justice could barely follow them. The cloaked and cowled priest turned away and vanished around the stairs; Krishna started to break and run; and Rhajmurti reached out, grabbed Krishna by the arm, and spun him around.

"Selling drugs now, are you?" Rhajmurti asked in a voice like polished steel. "I'm ashamed of you, Krishna." He glared in Justice's direction. "And *you* . . . of all people, Justus, I wouldn't have expected to find you involved in this!"

"But—"

"Don't you say another thing, Krishna!" Rhajmurti snapped. "You've already heaped enough karma on your soul without lying! You know it's a rule of the College that we won't tolerate drug usage or drug selling!"

"But—" Krishna's face had gone white now, visible even in the shadows.

"The demi," Rhajmurti said, extending his hand, keeping the other firmly planted on Krishna's shoulder.

"But . . . the priest . . . his money . . ." Krishna dropped the gold piece into Rhajmurti's hand.

"How do you know that was a priest?" Rhajmurti asked. "Anyone can don a saffron cloak and stand in the shadows beneath the stairs."

"He *knew* me," Krishna said in a plaintive tone of voice.

"That doesn't surprise me. You're quite notorious in certain sections of town."

Krishna lowered his head.

"Think of the karma, Krishna," Rhajmurti said, lowering his hand. "And you, too, Justus. You've both brought a good deal of it down on you today. And you've broken a College rule. Punishment seems to be in order here."

Justice had been watching Sonja, who had remained silent through the whole thing.

"Were you going to sell drugs, Justus?" she asked.

"Uh . . . no."

"Oh?" Rhajmurti looked stern. "Then what were you doing here?"

Krishna swallowed again. "He was here because I made him come with me. He overheard someone saying that the priests were looking for deathangel. I was going to sell it to the priests, not him."

A look of genuine surprise crossed Rhajmurti's face. "That's one of the most responsible, adult things I've ever seen you do, Krishna," he said. "By being truthful, you've escaped a good lot of your karma."

Krishna looked hopeful.

"But I still have to punish you both. If word gets out that the two of you were caught negotiating the selling of drugs and then not punished . . ."

"Just don't tell my father," Krishna begged. "Please, Father Rhajmurti. You can do with me what you like, but don't tell Papa."

Rhajmurti seemed to think about that request for what Justice considered an overly long time. "All right. Since you've been honest, Krishna, I'll keep this from your father. But if I ever so much as hear a *whisper* that you're involved in drug dealing, he's the first one I'll go to."

The threat had a visible effect on Krishna. He licked

his lips nervously, nodded, and put his hands behind his back.

"You won't, Father."

Rhajmurti drew himself up. "All right. The two of you come to my office. I'll have to think of a suitable punishment." He turned to Sonja. "We'll continue our conversation later, m'sera, if you wish."

Sonja smiled her most charming smile. "Of course, Father. Any time." She extended Justice's book to him. "I'm glad you weren't selling drugs, Justus, or . . . or I wouldn't have wanted to be seen with you for a very long time."

Krishna stiffened at this pronouncement, and glanced forlornly at Rhajmurti. "I wasn't exactly *selling* drugs," he began.

"No, just thinking about it." Rhajmurti looked at Krishna and Justice, and gestured toward the stairs. "My office. Now."

He turned and walked off, expecting to be followed. Krishna nodded to Sonja as he passed her, but Justice merely smiled slightly at her, and exchanged a conspiratorial wink.

"Are you suffering suitably yet?" Sonja asked, turning away from the blackboard, chalk in hand.

Justice sighed. "Actually, yes. You've chosen some of the hardest math problems I've seen since the last test." He rubbed his eyes. "Are you *sure* you want me to do these?"

"That's what Father Rhajmurti served up as your punishment," she said, a smile tugging at her mouth.

" 'You, Justus, will have to spend ten nights at the College, doing what you hate the most . . . math,' " Justice repeated, mimicking Rhajmurti's tone of voice. He grinned. "He's right. I still don't like math, despite your love of it."

Sonja sat down at the table. "Who knows . . . you *might* become fonder of it as time goes by."

"Maybe." Justice cupped his chin in one hand and stared at the blackboard. "I wonder who Father Rhajmurti got to play the priest buying deathangel?"

"I suppose we'll never know."

Justice laughed. "I'm just glad I'm not Krishna right now."

"I bet you are. But I think he might have had some good sense scared into him."

"Let's hope so." Justice grinned at her. "You know what I'd like to be? A fly on the wall of Hilda's kitchen. Can you see it? Krishna Malenkov, son of The Malenkovs of Martushev of Rimmon Isle, washing Hilda's dirty dishes for ten days!" He took the chalk from Sonja's hand and stood. "I'll tell you something else . . . as much as I hate math, I'd far rather be doing this."

A HARMLESS EXCURSION

by Robert Lynn Asprin

Pietor Gregori did not like being the head of the House, but the death of his father had left him no choice in the matter. For the better part of a year he had done nothing, or as little as possible, while House Gregori languished from neglect. The minor details of maintaining a functioning Household went untended, while major decisions . . .

Had it not been for Terrosi stepping into the void as family doctor when winter's fever penetrated their holdings, House Gregori might have been wiped out completely. Pietor, for his part, had done nothing to take command or make even the smallest gesture of leadership during the crisis—while Demitri seemed bent on destroying himself with alcohol since the elder Gregori's death, —though in truth Pietor had never considered his brother and father to be that close. Still, he hesitated to dictate behavior, so Demitri's drinking continued unchecked.

Meanwhile the census was grinding toward its end, in the slow way of Merovingian affairs, and the family still argued the best course to follow: did they exaggerate their headcount to keep their mortal enemies the Hannons at bay, or report accurate or even reduced figures to keep their tax burden with the government in bounds? In lieu of agreement, someone would have to decide, yet few hoped that Pietor would rise to the occasion.

Sharrh-inspired fireworks terrified the city, and strange plants multiplied in the canals—unprecedented occurrence. Things changed in Merovingen, and there were stirrings of ambition in various Houses high and low, —but Pietor did nothing to advance House Gregori.

And worst of all, Pietor did absolutely nothing at all about the Feud. The entire city had braced itself for the bloody vengeance of House Gregori on House Hannon when their rivals succeeded in poisoning the head of the Gregori household (for no one really believed the old man's death to be natural)—yet fall passed to winter and winter wore on to spring without any sign of counterattack. In fact, the famous Feud not only failed to escalate, there were no signs that it was even being maintained at its earlier levels.

Now, while nearly all of Merovingen traditionally deplored the Gregori-Hannon feud as an obsessive waste of money and personnel, there were many in the city nonetheless disquieted by its absence—in somewhat the same way as a cat is upset by rearranged furniture. The Feud was a constant, a part of native Merovingen, and the prolonged lack of activity seemed to leave a void in the ordinary goings-on and gossip of the city—while certain people whispered dire rumors of extremist activity and speculated that fear had driven the Feud to subtler measures; and while the foreign Sword of God acted unchecked and impious Nev Hettek folk walked unmolested in broad daylight in Merovingen of the Thousand Bridges.

In short, there was *no* one who was pleased with Pietor's performance as head of House Gregori . . . including Pietor himself. He knew his hopes that family affairs would take care of themselves were in vain. Sooner or later he was going to have to take an active hand in running the House, which meant accepting the responsibilities of his actions as well, and that day was something he would avoid indefinitely, given a choice. Unfortunately, one might not always *have* a choice. . . .

"It's not that I expect you to *do* anything, Pietor . . . God knows you've done little enough since father died. Stephan insisted I should tell you, that's all. Everyone loves little Nikki so, though for the life of me I can't see why. He's a mediocre artist for all his claimed devotion, and no use at all in the Feud. . . ."

Pietor avoided meeting his sister's eyes as she prattled on. Sister Anna was one of his greatest personal decriers . . . certainly she was his loudest. Anna Gregori had had a caustic tongue for as long as Pietor could remember, and he had been secretly glad when she had married out of her House on a five-year contract, thinking they were free of her at last—or at least free until the contract expired—but instead of taking her from the House, her hew husband, Stephan, had simply moved himself into their holdings—since it turned out he seemed less fond of Anna as a partner than as a passport into the Gregori fortunes.

Needless to say, this discovery had done little to improve Anna's disposition, but strangely Pietor felt more sympathetic toward her since that unfortunate discovery. He had always envied Anna the inner fire which he had always seemed to lack, and now that that fire was sputtering with frustration he was willing to make the extra effort to make her five years of suffering minimal.

"Could you tell me about it again, from the beginning?" Pietor said, interrupting her in mid-grumble.

"Really, Pietor. I've already . . ."

"Yes, yes. But you yourself have commented on how slow I am. Please, Anna?"

She grimaced and rolled her eyes melodramatically, but she complied.

"Baby brother Nikki . . . you *do* remember Nikki, don't you? —Well, he's decided that he's tired of being sheltered from the slings and arrows of the real world . . . not to mention the swords and knives of the Hannons. Some drivel about how artists have to experience life, not watch it through a window. Anyway, he's decided to slip out for his appointment with the College this afternoon without a bodyguard or escort, says he's *tired* of bodyguards in his life, —says *other* folk go out unescorted, he's *tired* of living with guards."

Pietor pursed his lips.

". . . And you heard this scheme from one of the servants?"

"Old Michael," she nodded. "He claims to be afraid for the boy, but it's more likely he's afraid of what would happen to *him* if anything happened to Nikki and we found out he'd known about it all along."

"Well, for whatever reason he's alerted us. Now just what is it you want me to do about it?"

"Do? Why, I want you to stop him! Just because you haven't the stomach to kill Hannons doesn't mean they return the feeling! If Nikki goes out alone, in a place like the midtown, he's a sitting target for the first Hannon or Hannon retainer that sees him. He's got to be confronted and kept behind our defenses! I know I've said a thousand times I don't like the little twit, but still he's . . ."

"No," Pietor said, shaking his head. "I won't do it."

"But he's our own brother! think of our reputation! You can't just—"

". . . Because if I do, he'll just sneak out again some other time!"

They locked gazes in stony silence. Anna's dark eyes still held the wildness of her sudden anger, but her lack of argument told Pietor louder than words that this was one of his rare victories.

"Think about it, Anna," he urged her, "if brother Nikki has taken it into his mind to go outside on his own and we stop him, he'll simply try excursions like this again and again until he succeeds. This time we were warned because he confided in a servant. Next time, he might not be so open."

His sister turned and dropped heavily into a chair.

"So what do *you* propose?" Anna said sullenly. "If we let Nikki try his little venture, the Hannons will eat him alive."

"Maybe not," Pietor muttered, then added hastily, "still, it's a risk we can't take."

Secretly, he was rejoicing. This was the first time since their father's death that Anna had asked his opinion rather than immediately chiding him for being too foolish to follow her recommended path. He suddenly realized with no small surprise that preserving that small spark of respect in Anna meant as much to him as saving his brother, and for the first time Pietor Gregori actually started to *feel* like the head of the household.

"What we've got to do," he said in that heady moment, "is convince him that traveling alone is dangerous for him, and the best way to do that is to let him go on and try his little venture."

"But you said . . ."

"Oh, he won't *really* be alone. He'll just think he is. Hurry along now and pass the word to the rest of the family. We have a lot of planning to do before little Nikki makes his escape! What time's his appointment?"

Demitri Gregori was in a foul mood, or, to be

accurate, fouler mood than normal, which these days took some doing.

Ensconced at a sheltered table in the small open air cafe across from the Gregori apartments, he watched the kitchen delivery entrance via the walkways that led up from the water-stairs—Pietor's instructions—while vainly trying to offset the aftereffects of yesterday's drinking with a fresh onslaught of wine.

Pietor was obviously going daft from the weight of his new responsibilities. His little scheme to trick their little brother was far too elaborate to be practical. If nothing else, Demitri was aware of the peculiar dangers of being overly subtle in one's planning.

At which thought a sudden wave of guilt broke over Demitri Gregori, and he hurriedly fought it off by tossing down what was left in his goblet and refilling it, as he forced all thoughts of his father's death from his mind.

On the surface, Pietor's hastily improvised plan seemed simple enough: let Nikki wander a few isles along the walkways toward the College and his appointment, apparently unescorted but actually covered by available Gregoris and Gregori retainers from hiding, then scare him back to the House with the appearance of several hired "Hannons" in his path.

Simple in concept, perhaps, but execution was another thing entirely.

It wasn't until the Family had hastily tried to figure how to position people along the anticipated route that dear Pietor had begun to count just how many routes and shortcuts there were in the three tiers between the Gregori apartments and the College. In the end, by whatever calculations, it had proved impossible to cover them all, so Pietor had had to settle for trying to establish a "floating" circle of spotters around feckless Nikki that would advance before him and cover his back as he moved.

Of course, this also meant trying to devise a system of signals to let the others in the guard party know which way dear fool Nikki was heading, which of course increased the chances of Nikki spotting his shadows and thereby negating the point of the whole exercise. There was also a shortage of good hiding and lurking places along the most likely route, that lay along Archangel, forcing them to "cover both ends of the tunnel" in some stretches and ignore some stairways and passages as unlikely. All in all, Pietor's crackpot idea of trying to shadow the fool was proving more difficult than anticipated, and it was altogether so cumbersome as to introduce the possibility of the escorts tripping over each other in their own maneuverings.

Then again, there were the Hannons they had hired . . . or rather the bully boys they were paying to play the role of Hannons. Could they be trusted? What if they decided to increase their earnings by selling the information to the Hannons . . . or, even worse, if they took advantage of the situation to collect the Hannon-offered bounty on a Gregori themselves?

No. *Not* likely. The whole plan was far too complicated and too hastily conceived for comfort, but Pietor had insisted and the Family had gone along with him, if for no other reason than to encourage slack-handed Pietor to take an active hand in running the household: among themselves, they had admitted a fear that if they had refused to aid Pietor in this, his first effort at involvement, he might retreat back into the lethargy he had been showing to date—a laissez-faire Demitri privately reckoned more dangerous to House Gregori than Nikki's fecklessness.

Better to get him moving by cooperating today,

then, the consensus in the House was, and once Pietor had a bit of momentum and confidence behind him, they could try to guide their Househead's steps into wiser courses of action.

That was, of course, providing House Gregori survived the day.

Demitri grimaced wryly at the thought. He had disagreed with Pietor's plan from the start, and still remained skeptical even after younger House members had teamed up to vote him down. He felt that Anna had been right in the first place, that Pietor should have simply confronted Nikki and acquainted him with the facts of life. As head of the household, Pietor should have met the challenge of the established procedures squarely and dominated their younger brother with the sheer force of his personality and his anger. That was certainly what their father would have done. . . .

Demitri groped for the wine again, only to find the pitcher empty.

Damn! Why couldn't he keep his thoughts away from his father? He had made a conscious choice between the old man and his pregnant Hannon lover before arranging for the elder Gregori's assassination. Was his current guilt a matter of second thoughts, or was it merely anger that Teryl Hannon's death—and, unknown to either House, Demitri's own unborn child's—had made his father's demise both unnecessary and pointless?

If the latter were true . . .

A furtive movement at the delivery entrance caught his eye.

Nikki.

Demitri had to smile to himself as he leaned back into the shadows and averted his face. If he had not been forewarned and watching, he probably wouldn't have recognized his little brother in that getup. The youngest Gregori was decked out in the garb of a common laborer several sizes too large for him, creating the illusion of underfed poverty in scrounged clothes. With the added touches of a few artfully placed streaks of soot on his face and a slouch cap pulled low over his eyes, Nikki bore little resemblance to the dapper young artist who was prone to spending such considerable time in front of a mirror polishing his appearance and manner.

Demitri waited a few more moments to insure he would not be spotted, then rose casually to follow his brother. Fumbling for a few coins to leave as a tip, he glanced down the walkway . . . and froze. Nikki was nowhere in sight!

In a flash Demitri was up and well along the walkway, casting about in all directions for a glimpse of the disguised artist, but it was as if the walkways had dropped him abruptly elsewhere, into the nether tiers of the city. There were a few people strolling along the boards, but none bore the slightest resemblance to Nikki!

Demitri waffled for a few more precious moments between trying to find his little brother himself and alerting the waiting net of the watchers. Finally, he swallowed his pride and sprinted off to find Pietor—who would curse him for a careless drunk perhaps, not without justification—but Nikki might now be wandering Lord knew what tier of the walkways and bridges without anyone protecting him, and that took priority over any personal affront Pietor might deal him.

As he ran, Demitri prayed that one of the other watchers had spotted his little brother's course somewhere across the bridges and taken up guard duty. If not, if Nikki came to harm . . .

He forced the thought from his mind and plunged on.

"I don't like it. I should've thought it out more before takin' this job. No sir! I don't like this one bit."

Gordo nodded at his companion's growled complaint. He had been experiencing similar reservations himself.

"I know what ye mean," he said. "I was just thinking the same thing. It sounded easy enough at first, but what if one of the *real* Hannons comes along and finds us wearing their House colors? It's not going to endear us to them any, I tell ye that much."

He found himself nervously fingering the bits of gold and orange ribbon pinned to his sleeve, the traditional mark of the Hannon household and their retainers. They had been given these badges by the Gregoris when they were hired for what had seemed like a harmless masquerade. The more Gordo thought about it, however, the less comfortable he was with the arrangement.

"Ye got a point there, Gordo," the original speaker grunted, "but that weren't what I was thinkin'."

"Oh?"

"I was more worried about us bein' set up."

"Set up?" Victor, the third man in their group said, joining the discussion. "How d'ye figure that?"

"Well, it occurs to me that if I was the Gregoris and I planned to do some mischief, it wouldn't hurt none to have a couple Hannons around to pin the rap on . . . and here we are, standin' around when and where they done told us, wearin' ribbons to mark us as Hannons."

Gordo felt a quick lance of fear shoot through him, but he tried to laugh it off.

"Come now, Curt. You don't really believe they'd do *that* to us, do ye?"

"Well I, for one, don't," Victor stated emphatically. "I've worked for the Gregoris afore, and they've always dealt me fair."

"That was *old* Gregori," Curt shot back. "How about Pietor, this new head of the House? Either of ye dealt whatsoever with *him?* I haven't. What's more, I'm wonderin' how smart it is to be wearin' Hannon colors out on the walks on nothin' more than his say-so that it's all right. Not that I'm sayin' he'd *be* up to no good, mind you. Just that we should look sharp if we want to be sure to come outta this in one piece, is all."

They had been stationed at the foot of the last bridge on the direct route between the Gregori apartment and Kass Isle, a point young Nikki would be certain to pass on his self-engineered adventure. Though warned to keep their faces toward Kass so that he would only see their Hannon colors, the three men found themselves glancing around nervously as they continued their debate. What had seemed like easy money now looked increasingly hazardous, and their feeling of vulnerability was growing by the moment.

"It's a possibility," Gordo conceded. "Still, we can't walk off a job because a' some *possible* danger. We should've thought of all this 'fore we went and took their money. All we can do now is . . ."

"Hullo there!"

Three heads snapped around and fixed on the figure approaching them.

A figure wearing Hannon colors.

"*Now* what do we do? —Lord, if he recognizes us—"

"That's Lonnie Hannon. Don't worry, he's blind as a bat. So far he only sees our ribbons."

"He'll see well enough to tell we ain't Hannons if he joins us."

"Let him," Curt growled softly, slipping his belt dagger from his sheath.

"Lord, what are ye doing?"

"Can't ye see? This is our chance to be away and free from here. Ain't nobody expects us to hang around after we was jumped by one o' the Hannons, can they? And he ain't tellin' nothin' t' anybody."

Without waiting for a reply from the others, he turned and waved a welcome to the oncoming Hannon . . . hiding his dagger behind his leg as he did.

Helwein Hannon was surprised to find himself regretting, in such bewildering times as this, not having attended the funeral of old Gregori. It was true that old enemies could be as dear as old friends . . . especially when they were known quantities that were reliably consistent.

Of course, his presence would have been interpreted as gloating, though the Hannons had had no part in that notable's demise . . . a fact no one in Merovingen was inclined to believe, especially the Gregoris. With a sigh, Helwein returned his attention to the subject at hand.

"How many are there, again?"

Zahn, who had been haranguing the other family members assembled, broke off his oration to frown at his Househead.

"But, Uncle, . . . I already told you . . ."

"So tell me again!" Helwein snapped, then softened his tone."Have patience with an old man. My ears aren't as good as they were . . . or my mind as quick."

This, of course, fooled no one, as Helwein held his position by the strength and speed of his judgment and could wield a sword with an agility that denied his years, —but it did cause Zahn to swallow his impatience and repeat some of the highlights of his report.

"At least a dozen, maybe two," Zahn said. "It's hard to tell for sure, since they're scattered singly or in small groups on the walkways and bridges around the Pile and Kass and Borg. More important is . . ."

". . . But so far, they're mostly around their old holding?" Helwein interrupted. "They're not near *our* House?"

"Yes . . . but I think it's important that they aren't wearing House Gregori colors, any of them. If anything, they seem to be trying to avoid being seen, staying mostly in shops and in shadowed walks and cut-throughs on the middle tier. To me, that means they're up to something."

A low growl from the others assembled showed their assent, an opinion that was noted by the head by the head of the House as he tried to collect his thoughts.

"It's important, yes," he said. "But so is the fact they aren't making any direct moves on us or our holdings. It's also important to know how many of them there are . . . exactly . . . as well as where each is stationed. Once we have that information, we can decide . . ."

The door burst open before he could complete his thought.

"They're killing us! PAPA!"

Instantly, the room was filled with exclamations and babble.

"I knew it!"

"Who was it. . . ?"

"But what about. . . ?"

"We've got to . . ."

"Quiet! ALL of you!"

Helwein's voice, seldom raised, now roared, shocking the assemblage to silence.

"Now, you tell *me,*" he demanded, fixing the interloper with a steely gaze, "who's been killed."

"I . . . don't know, Papa," the youth faltered. "It was just reported downstairs by a deliveryman. He said that one of our House had just been killed . . . stabbed in broad daylight and dumped off a bridge by three men who ran. He didn't know . . ."

The head of the House was suddenly on his feet, towering in his anger.

"Who's outside right now?" Helwein Hannon asked, not waiting to hear the balance of the report.

"Five, I think," someone volunteered. "William . . . and Uncle Lonnie . . . and—"

"Six. Tellon went out early."

"Tellon can take care of himself. There isn't a Gregori who can match sword with him."

"One on one, maybe. But there are dozens of them on the walkways."

"Enough talk!" Helwein bellowed. "Zahn, assemble everyone in the House who can carry a weapon and follow as soon as you can. The rest of you, come with me, *now!*"

Despite his earlier impatience, Zahn was taken aback at the sudden flurry of action.

"But Uncle, shouldn't we wait . . ."

"There's no more time if the Gregoris have already started their move," was the snarled response. "We've a chance, though, if we can make our countermove in force while they're still scattered. Aye, catch them in their small groups before they can unite or scuttle back to their hole. All of you now . . . *with me!*"

The assemblage followed Helwein out of the room, caught up in his urgency and excitement, though more than a few were chilled by the bloodlust that shone in his eyes.

* * *

Damn Demitri . . . and damn Nikki!

Anger and worry warred within Pietor Gregori as he half walked, half ran toward Kass Middle Bridge.

If harm came to his youngest brother because Demitri had been too busy drinking to keep proper watch . . .

He prayed that Nikki was already at the College. If so, then he would fetch him home if he had to drag him kicking and screaming every step of the way. Safety was more important now than teaching a lesson.

He was nearly at the Pile West Bridge now, but his path was blocked by a shopper speaking with a walkway vendor. Beside himself with impatience, Pietor started to edge past just as the shopper turned . . . revealing a bright gold and yellow sweater beneath his cloak.

Tellon Hannon! Said to be the best swordsman in his House!

The two men stared at each other in shocked recognition.

"Tellon . . . Have you seen my brother Nikki?" Pietor blurted suddenly, voicing the first thing that came to his mind.

The Hannon blinked in surprise and bewilderment.

"The artist? No, I haven't . . . You're asking *me?*"

The absurdity of the situation began to creep into Pietor's mind. Here he was, seeking assistance from a Hannon, the very ones he feared were threatening Nikki. Still, he had blundered into a conversation with one of the Gregori's arch rivals, and he set himself to make the most of it.

"That's right. The young fool is out here somewhere. . . . Say, Tellon, while we're talking . . . I wanted to tell you how sorry I was about your sister's death."

"Teryl?" Tellon's bewilderment changed to a scowl.

"Why should you be sorry? I heard the Gregoris paid for her murder."

"My father did," Pietor admitted, "but even he didn't order it. I'm the head of the House now, and . . . Look, my father was killed by your family, but I'm still willing to talk. Can't we. . . ?"

"We had nothing to do with your father's death," Tellon said. "I won't try to tell you we wouldn't have killed him if we had the chance, but no one from my House is laying claim to that death."

"Really? See what I mean? No, . . . I'm saying this badly. Look, Tellon, can you tell Helwein that I'd like to meet with him? If we can't stop this feud, maybe we can at least modify . . ."

"*Pietor!* There's no sign of Nikki at the . . ."

Demitri Gregori halted his approach and his news in mid-step as he realized who his brother was speaking to. His hand flew to his sword hilt at Tellon drew back, mirroring the move with his own weapon.

"Stop it! Both of you!" Pietor ordered sharply, stepping between them. "Demitri. Take your hand off your sword! We were just talking. I was telling Tellon here how sorry I was about Teryl's death."

"Teryl?"

Demitri blanched at the name, his shoulders tightening as if expecting a physical blow.

"That's right," Pietor continued hurriedly, wondering what was ailing his brother. "You remember Teryl. She was . . ."

"Tellon! 'Ware!"

They all started, then turned toward the hail. No less than eight Hannons were hurrying toward them across the bridge.

" 'Ware the Gregoris! *It's an ambush!*"

"What?" Pietor gaped. "No! Wait!"

Tellon's sword leapt from its scabbard as he backed

away from the Gregoris, his head turning back and forth between the two groups in confusion.

Demitri stepped forward, shoving Pietor toward the upstairs of the Pile as he fumbled for his own weapon.

"Run for it, Pietor!" he hissed. "I'll try to hold them here!"

"Stop, Demitri!" Pietor cried desperately, seizing his brother's arm in an attempt to keep him from drawing his weapon. "We've got to . . ."

"Let go, dammit! I can't . . ."

That was how they died when the Hannons swept over them . . . Demitri trying to do something right, even if it meant sacrificing his life to save his brother, —and Pietor struggling to keep a Gregori sword in its scabbard.

"It were terrible," Old Michael returned to the House to report—

Which report stopped cold midway, at the sight of Nikki Gregori on the stairs, paint-smeared and smelling of turpentine.

Everyone stopped . . . of those servants who were there to hear. And Anna Gregori, who came from the parlor to hear the account.

Nearly a dozen had been killed, mostly Gregoris . . . though a few Hannons as well as innocent bystanders had been cut down in the fighting that had ebbed and swirled through the walkways near the College for nearly an hour.

Pietor lost, his brother Demitri—both killed. The servants, realizing the status of things—gave new deference to Anna, who cast a look of amazement and outrage in Nikki's direction.

"Where did *you* come from?" Anna asked; and Nikki, puzzled, answered his new Househead:

"Upstairs. . . ."

—It being that he had left the House only briefly, to turn back when he realized the afternoon light was perfect, falling on the face of the upper tiers opposite his studio window—and his study arrangements with Rhajmurti in the College had been informal at best.

Damn you, Anna might have said. But Anna said nothing at all. Anna only stared at him.

And Nikki Gregori, who had a houseful of such stares to face, instead went upstairs and methodically put away his paints, folded down his easel, and threw his latest work down from the topmost tier into the dark of the canals.

He took his disused sword from the armoire then—his middle brother had given him the blade—and sat down on the bed, taking up a discarded canvas-knife to scratch a name patiently and deep into the shining metal.

Tellon Hannon, it said.

MYSTERY

by Chris and Janet Morris

Early spring in Merovingen was cold and wet—that was normal enough, nothing to ruffle hightown feathers or put canalers on their guard; not even enough on its own to trouble Tom Mondragon, who never slept soundly in his exile's bed, whether that bed was, on any given night, in luxurious Boregy House, or filthy cold Moghi's, or stilt-leaning Petrescu.

But there was plenty this spring to trouble Mondragon besides the damp, which bit to his very bones and made his white skin whiter among the dark folk of Merovingen.

After the winter of the sharrh's overflight, of Sword of God attacks on the noble houses—attacks that had culminated in the assassination of a daughter of Nikolaev House—Adventist nerves were frayed and Revenantist thoughts were turning to Retribution in all its guises. And Retribution troubled Mondragon, as a concept and as a reality: he was a fugitive, a hunted man, an ex-Sword agent caught up in Merovingen politics; he was as guilty as you could be in Merovingen. When Retribution came, it would have his name on it.

He knew it in his soul as he knew his time was short and his leash here shortening. He had too many masters with too many conflicting agendas, and no one to count on but himself and a canal-rat named Jones . . . sometimes. He knew it as he knew the way to Petrescu, and the way to the safe-house used by Jones' canalers when things were too desperate to risk any of their usual haunts.

On his way to the safe-house, he didn't have to think about the direction in which his feet were taking him, or the shabby clothes appropriate to the lower tiers, or the hunched posture of the hopeless that must accompany such clothes: all these were second nature to him now.

This winter in Merovingen had nearly killed him; he'd taken sick and in that miasma of illness, he'd made enough mistakes to kill any but a very lucky man. A part of the spirit that had always sustained him might well have died. His luck surely had died in the cold, exhausted and pushed beyond human forbearance—as was the rest of the tall, pale man who floated between the worlds of Merovingen like a wraith.

He was so tired that he couldn't summon even the strength to be angry at the boy who'd used codes reserved for real emergencies to call Mondragon, a once-noble son of Nev Hettek, into the slums for this meeting.

God in all his manifold attributes and his myriad guises was testing Merovingen, so the faithful said and looked forward to being reborn into a better life. Mondragon knew that God had tested Merovingen long ago, found it wanting and gone away—gone somewhere pleasant where people were civilized and the air didn't stink; where buildings weren't built on teetering pilings and tied to each other with rotting, spindly bridges; where people weren't so desperate or so selfish or so sure of their afterlives that they failed to tend to their present lives.

Sometimes Mondragon thought that the concept of

reincarnation was the chain binding Merovingians in their hopeless servitude, which kept them spinning on the wheel of misery that they called the hope of rebirth. Without the promise of a better life next time, perhaps these folk would do something about the lives of misery they currently led.

Mondragon shook his pale head, shouldering by a fish stall where fries could be purchased with coin he didn't have. The smell tortured him momentarily. Then it was gone, replaced by the stench of the canals that, this year, was somehow different in the thaw: sweeter, less reminiscent of a garbage dump.

The sharrh, aliens of unparalleled power, had come from beyond the sky and blasted the planet of Merovin back to the early industrial age. It was afraid to recover, afraid that technology would act as a beacon to the sharrh. In their fear, Merovingians had found religions to comfort them in a night they wouldn't hold back with electricity or knowledge.

Reincarnation was the Revenantist creed, and the people packed like fish in the multitiered stilt city dreamed technodreams of being reborn where there were fields of waving wheat, bright lights, fragrant springs, and a chance once more to fly among the stars.

Until that time of change and rebirth, the citizens of Merovin had only themselves to blame for their sad estate. They fought among themselves over everything: over religion, over politics, over a scrap of tech or a crust of bread or, in Merovingen, over a home on the highest of the tiers.

Change was what they wanted, they thought. The Sword of God, a revolutionary front, had changed Nev Hettek and wanted to change Merovingen, destroy entrenched and repressive power structures—to entrench new ones.

Mondragon didn't blame the Merovingians for resisting the change that the Sword offered. Mondragon had resisted the Sword, and now Mondragon was nearly run to ground, his back against the wall that was Merovingen, facing Sword vengeance as sure as death.

If Mondragon had been a Revenantist, maybe he wouldn't have been so worried. Or so tired. Maybe he'd have been looking forward to rebirth in a better place. But he didn't believe in Revenantism, or in Adventism, or in Janism, or in any other *-ism.* Once he had believed in the Sword of God, when he and Karl Fon had tried to liberate Nev Hettek and succeeded in liberating only their own greed. So revolution was not the answer, Mondragon was certain—and that certainty was one that had made him a marked man in the eyes of Sword agents in Merovingen.

Whether or not reincarnation *was* the answer, the way that the Revenantists said it was, life in Merovingen was changing; on this everyone was agreed. And no one Mondragon knew, in Merovingen-above or Merovingen-below, liked the coming changes any more than he did.

First had come the lights in the sky, wakening long-dormant fears—as the Sword of God had intended when it faked the lights that the superstitious mistook for the returning sharrh.

These lights in the sky, which some called the return of the sharrh from heaven, might have been enough by themselves to galvanize the superstitious into fundamentalist fervor, but other things had happened—troubling things, ominous things, things no one could quite forget or quite ignore.

Things that Thomas Mondragon knew, from careful investigation, were not the work of the Sword of God: the Janes had dumped *something* into the canals, before winter's grip grew tight, and now that something was beginning to sprout.

Whether the plants would flower, no one knew; whether their roots would choke the canals, none could say. But the plants were already changing the smell of Merovingen and the look of Merovingen. And the saltwater-loving deathangel, a rare fish prized for its flesh and the drugs extracted from that flesh and its spines, had been spotted darting among the proliferating roots where deathangel fish had never ventured before.

"Get me deathangel, Denny," an acolyte of the Revenantist College had commanded the young drug-running juvenile delinquent, and Denny had had no choice but to obey.

"Get me deathangel," Vega Boregy had demanded of Thomas Mondragon, and Mondragon had had no choice but to obey.

"Get me deathangel," Mondragon had demanded of Altair Jones, and Jones had said, "Hey, get it yourself. I dunno nothin' about the College's druggie games and don't wanta."

This was another change come to Merovingen: the College was growing bold, and its sudden hunger for a fish whose spines produced a lethal poison was only one inscrutable indication of the changes going on among the hightowners out on the Rock, in the Justiciary and across the bridge in the College itself.

The Revenantist College had gone into the business of dispensing portents, it was whispered—dispensing them to the ruling mercantilists, to the Boregys and the Nikolaevs and the Kamats . . . and to the family of Governor Iosef Kalugin himself.

Down at canalside, all the changes going on in Merovingen-above were a matter of rumor and innuendo, of resultant pressure and unintended distress.

Here the changes were impenetrable in their motive, if not their effect. First had come the census, to mark everyone and give each soul a number; then had come the canal-rats hunting the sharrh for a bounty posted by the College. Then (or was it simultaneously?) had come the Janes doing their dirty work of "salvation" that had changed the pollution of the canals to something else.

Some said this was a different sort of pollution, nothing more. Some said that the disturbances that trickled down from Merovingen-above were nothing shocking, just signs that the Kalugin dynasty was coming to an end.

But all of those folk discounted the hand of the Sword of God in Merovingen affairs, as Mondragon was too wise to do.

And none of those folk had looked closely at Altair Jones' private war against the slavers of Megary, as Mondragon made it his business to do.

Nor had any of them noticed Mondragon's late-night scurryings, hither and thither on his masters' errands like a rat in a Boregy-constructed maze. And none but Mondragon, it seemed, had remarked on the way that the Kamat family was quietly strengthening its defense force, or that the Boregys were doing the same.

And not a single soul among those who protested that this spring would be like any other, that the rising tide of fundamental Revenantism and Jane-spawned revolutionary fervor and Adventist buttressing of defenses already more than sufficient—none of those folk were privy to the information gathered by Thomas Mondragon. Or by the Sword of God.

Sword agents swarmed Merovingen, gathering news like ants collecting crumbs. And every crumb they gathered went back to the Sword's Chance Magruder, on-site tactical officer, who sat in his embassy's office, a few hundred yards of Nev Hettek property smack in the middle of Merovingen, like a queen in a hive, and wrote reports that went, by diplomatic pouch on Chamoun Shipping vessels, straight to Governor Karl Fon in Nev Hettek.

One such report had it that Cassiopeia Boregy, wife of Michael Chamoun, one of the Sword's agents in Merovingen, was subject to mantic fits of prophecy under the direction of Cardinal Ito Boregy, high official of the Revenantist College. Mondragon knew this because Magruder had asked him to confirm or deny the truth of it, though he'd done neither.

Another dispatch had it that Cassie Boregy was pregnant by her husband, and that the child's survival—and the strength of the merger between Boregy House and the Chamoun family of Nev Hettek—was imperiled by the drugs the cardinals were giving her to bring on the visions of her prophecies. This intelligence was no more than what every privy party in hightown was whispering.

Yet another report, scrawled hastily in Ambassador Magruder's own hand, suggested that Thomas Mondragon, once Sword agent in good standing and now Boregy confidant and Sword pawn by virtue of blackmail and maneuver, was "out of money, out of luck, and out of time. Vega Boregy, Cassie's father, is using Mondragon to smuggle deathangel spine poison into the house—a clear sign that the Boregys consider him expendable at the moment, since Ito Boregy's College faction has a stranglehold on the deathangel catch in town. If Ito finds out that his brother-in-law Vega is using Mondragon to smuggle deathangel meant for the College into Boregy House, Mondragon is dead in the water. Although the flesh of the fish isn't illegal, possession of poison extracted from the spines is a Judiciary offense. My recommendation to Karl Fon is that we use Mondragon now, to secure more than reports—use him against the College and whatever it thinks to do with Cassiopeia Boregy—before we lose him to Collegiate justice."

This was what Thomas Mondragon had come all the way down here to read? *This* was the reason for the urgent summons? For the danger of exposure he'd sustained, just by coming here in broad daylight? For the possible unmasking of the safe-house?

For a moment Mondragon thought he was rightly and solely angry. Then his denial crumpled and fear took hold.

He'd been winded from climbing the stairs. This objective fact bothered him suddenly—bothered him so much he couldn't concentrate on the import of the document he held. He wasn't in good shape. He wasn't in good shape at all. He was too weak, still, to run again—if he could think of any place to run. Which he couldn't.

He had to make his stand in Merovingen. He had to. He had to be up to the task, up to the exertion, up to a duel of wits with Magruder, who was far from unarmed.

His hands were shaking. He stared at them until they steadied, then tried to use a similar discipline to clear his head. He should be accustomed to stairs by now, but the fever he'd had this winter had scarred his lungs, or his fear was binding his chest so that he couldn't take decently deep breaths. He focused on a point on the horizon, far distant, and took three painfully deep breaths, each of which he held for a count of ten before exhaling slowly.

He'd come quickly, quietly, and carefully. He had made no mistakes so far. Upon arrival, without a word he'd taken the document from the hand holding it, reserving judgment. This, too, was action free from error.

But that was before he'd read what was on this piece of paper. Even steeled to confront the indictment he held, his heart skipped a beat when he reread it.

Now Mondragon nearly crumpled the report in his hand as he leaned on the safe-house balcony overlooking Fishmarket, trying to think clearly—trying to think at all. The report was damning; coming here to read it was twice so. Better admit that much, and go on from here.

He could stop this report from going to Nev Hettek, but that wouldn't stop Chance Magruder, Nev Hettek's Ambassador to Merovingen, the Trade and Tariffs man who was covertly the Sword of God's tactical officer. The only thing that would stop Magruder's hounding of Mondragon was death—Mondragon's, or Magruder's.

At last, Mondragon rounded on the person he'd come here to meet. He tossed the piece of paper in that direction. The sheet sailed crazily.

The teenager who stood shivering in the shadows lunged for it, caught it, and smoothed it against his ragged breast.

"Ha' come ye do that, hey?" the boy named Denny wanted to know. "We gotta help each other, Thomas. We gotta."

"How'd you come by that piece of paper, Denny? And how come, if you're so smart, you didn't make a copy—you can read and write—instead of doubling everyone's risk by stealing the original? Now you've got to get it back to wherever—"

"To the *Det Queen*, one of the Chamoun ships." Denny's lower lip was thrust out, his eyes sparkling with hurt. "C'mon, Thomas. I did good, didn't I? Bringin' this t' ye? My mother was Sword o'—"

"Sword of God. Yes, I know. What I don't know is why you're so damned proud of it. Why you think you have to be part of all this, when what it leads to is misery, years in hiding, losing everyone you ever loved and having no one you can ever trust."

The teenager, who was risking life and limb to aid Mondragon, stared at him without a word. The round eyes told Mondragon that the boy knew that Thomas was talking about Thomas' own experience with the Sword of God, but didn't want to believe it. The Sword was romance, adventure, all Denny had left of his dead mother. If the Sword was bad, Mother had been bad. . . .

When the boy's stare didn't waver, Mondragon continued remorselessly: "You didn't answer me. How'd you get this? Why'd you bring it to me? If you're a good Sword trainee, or want to be, you should be helping Magruder, not double-crossing him."

"You're the Sword—the *real* Sword; we all know that. You're the Sword like Mama thought she was, not like those hightown leeches, not like Chamoun and his fancy embassy connect—"

"Denny, you fool, the Sword's a bunch of terrorists and murderers, revolutionaries bent on bringing their own form of oppression to Merovingen—"

"An' that's worse than Kalugin's oppression?" The boy's defiant interruption was loud, exploding out of his mouth so that Mondragon glanced reflexively over his shoulder and the balcony, in case someone outside should have overheard.

"Denny, how deep are you in this?"

"I've been . . . gettin' deathangel for the College, best I can. There's not that much around, an' this priest tol' me to." Denny's voice rose with a plaintive edge that was nearly a whine. "You knew 'bout that, Tom. You know 'bout everythin'; we all make sure you knows what you needs . . ."

"That doesn't explain robbing dispatches out of dip pouches."

"Well, there ain't much deathangel, so I been usin' what I got fer resources, like you tol' me."

"I never told you any such thing."

"Like you showed me, then—I watched you, Thomas, doin' what it takes. I'm Sword, by my mother's word and all. So when I couldn't get no more deathangel from Fishmarket, an' when the price gets so high 'cause the College's buyin' so much and then Rita's friends all want it 'cause Cassie's chewin it like candy—"

"*Rita's* friends?"

"Rita Nikolaev, *you* know. The highs and mightys, they's just kids too, even if they're College kids. So Rita's little sister wants some deathangel, and I says, no, I can't git it but fer the priests, but I takes 'em fishin' fer it . . ."

"That doesn't answer my question, Denny."

"Well y'see, since I'm Sword, I went to Mike Chamoun when I couldn't git none, cause the swamp's fished out an' the canals is full o' that weird weed and the baby deathangel's too small t' bother with—poison's not strong enough or sompin' . . . Rita's little sister said Mike Chamoun, he'd listen, cause them's so friendly, Rita and Mike, what with the business they're doin' an' all."

"I bet. And you told Chamoun what?"

"That iffen any o' his big boats could troll fer a little deathangel, or happened on any, it'd make everybody's life easier—his wife's, 'specially."

"Denny, you didn't tell him you were Sword, did you?" Mondragon's eyes narrowed as if against a blinding light as he waited for an answer he didn't want to hear.

"Well I had t' tell 'im somethin', Thomas. T' git his attention. Then he says, sure, anything his boats git, I c'n have to give to the College. So I'm on every Chamoun boat, sometimes when they come t' port, sometimes just before they leave, 'cause I take the deathangel they got. And sometimes I take a message over to the boat, from Mike, when I'm goin'. Sword business." Denny's chin jutted. He folded the paper back on its original creases and put it carefully away. "He pays me when I do. I need the money, Thomas. So do you, so don't tell me I'm wrong to take—"

"Get out of my sight, Denny. You're going to drag down everyone else with you. Don't bring me any more messages from Magruder, not ever—not if one of them's my death warrant. Don't tell me what Mike Chamoun thinks. Don't tell me how their money spends like any other. And most especially, don't come around me canalside, not at Moghi's, not anywhere. You want to be Sword of God, you're my enemy—now and forever. Is that clear?"

Mondragon didn't wait for an answer. Denny was just a kid and Mondragon's emotions were the emotions of a duelist confronted with a deadly enemy. He had to get out of there before he hurt the boy.

Hurting innocents, even dangerous innocents, wasn't something Mondragon could stomach. Not yet. He still had that much self-respect. He was mucking around with the Kamats for money, but that was harmless, he told himself—at least not more venal than was necessary for survival.

And Denny was right. Mondragon could hear the boy's outraged honesty chasing him down the stairs: unanswered questions, uncomprehending hurt at being so bluntly upbraided. Denny was smuggling diplomatic dispatches off a Chamoun vessel, dispatches that were demonstrably key to destabilizing the Kalugin government. And he was smuggling documents back *on* to those same Chamoun vessels. Smuggling deathangel spine poison wasn't half as bad as being privy to plots against the Kalugin government. But then, the punishment for smuggling controlled substances wasn't a long, slow, and interrogatory death.

Everybody in Merovingen was smuggling something this season: Moghi was smuggling fancy foods and nonhallucinogenic contraband; Chamoun and Magruder were smuggling information; Denny, and even Jones, because Mondragon had asked her, were smuggling deathangel; the Janes were smuggling their religious husbandry and hydrocultures . . .

And Thomas Mondragon was smuggling himself—in and out of dark and narrow places and some of the wrong beds, this season.

At the foot of the stairs he stopped, meaning to head for Fishmarket. He had his own quota of deathangel to acquire and deliver. And he didn't want to see Jones, not now. Not with this whole mess of Denny's hanging fire: Jones would hear about it, as she always heard about Mondragon's doings from that damn clutch of adulatory kids she fed as if they were kittens.

Either those kids of hers or Jones herself would be the death of him, he'd long known that. But he couldn't shake Jones, and she couldn't shake those kids . . .

Some other canaler would have left it at kittens. Could have left it at kittens. But now, when everybody was winter-poor and the unknowable was going on in the College and Boregy House, Jones had to be involved up to her neck with someone like Denny, who simply wasn't smart enough to survive this mess he'd made.

Well, kittens rolled out of the rag basket onto the

cold floor and then they died there, when the mother cat was out hunting for rats to feed them. And the canaler who took in the cats got over it.

Jones would have to get over Denny, who'd marched up to Michael Chamoun and announced that he, Denny, was Sword of God, too. Magruder ate kids like that for breakfast. All Chamoun or Magruder or anyone aboard a Chamoun ship had to do was even wonder if Denny had been breaking into the dip pouches, and there wouldn't be enough left of Denny to give a canaler's burial.

"Damn," said Mondragon out loud, and made for Fishmarket with a determined set to his shoulders. But that wasn't where he wanted to go. He wanted to go to Vega Boregy and ask (impolitely) what Vega was letting the College do to his daughter.

But Mondragon couldn't. He was strung between too many posts to risk losing even one—partial—supporter. And they'd all find out, those with hightown access, what the College was doing with Cassie Boregy, soon enough.

Mondragon had been invited to a College "tea and seminar" that was "fancy dress" and "an evening of utmost important and revelatory significance," according to the engraved invitation Vega's people had sent him.

And the R.S.V.P. had been either Ito, at the College, or Vega, at Boregy House.

By party evening, Mondragon better have scratched up enough cash to buy himself a new suit, or he was going to go in there looking like what he was: a pawn on the run, a bedraggled, exhausted ex-Sword agent hounded to ground by Magruder's agents; the dregs of the man he'd once been, a petty criminal who couldn't even make a living committing crimes.

Smuggling wasn't the best way to make a living, or

the surest. The surest, for Mondragon, was always women. Right now, that meant Marina Kamat or Altair Jones. And he couldn't risk Jones, not with Magruder's dogs so close on his heels that Denny—*Denny*—was an unwitting agent of Magruder's provocations.

He didn't know how honest he could be with Marina, or with her brother Richard, but he knew he needed to get some money—and fast. If the party that Vega and old Uncle Ito were throwing was really full of "revelatory significance," Mondragon wanted to have enough money in his pocket to get out of Merovingen—get out clean—before things got so bad here that you could stand in fear of Judicary action not only for the secrets of your current lives, but for the sins of your past ones.

For Mondragon knew that much about what Cassie Boregy—and the College—were using the deathangel for: to facilitate regressions into purported past lives. And in Cassie's case, if rumor could be trusted, to read the future as well.

"Almost ready, Cassie?" came her father's voice through her bedroom's closed door. "We can't afford to be late. Ito needs to walk you through the hall, he says, before you . . . go into your meditation."

"It's all right, Daddy. You can say 'before you eat the deathangel.' That's the truth of it, isn't it? Before I bare my soul and all of ours to the College and its assembled guests?"

Her voice sounded nervous to her own ears, though she'd meant it to sound defiant, controlled, the voice of an intrepid voyager who laughed at danger and sacrificed without hesitation for the good of Boregy House, Revenantism, and Merovingen.

"Cassie," came her father's voice again, followed by

a rattling sound as he tried her locked door. He didn't demand that she unlock it and let him in, though. He sighed audibly and said in a cajoling tone, "Please hurry, daughter. We're all waiting for you. If there's anything I can do to help . . ."

The unfinished sentence dangled, hopeful and restrained, the only proof that there was anyone else in the world beyond her locked door and her blue and gold bedroom and the mirror before which she stood, fussing with her hair.

"Nothing, thanks. Unless you can find Michael and send him up here, I might be a little late." She kept her voice steady, but the demand in it was clear. Her husband was upsetting her and she wanted her father to see to it.

There'd been a time when, if she'd behaved this way, Vega would have called houseboys to break in the door and swatted her backside personally, to make sure she understood the demands of being a daughter to Boregy House.

No one dared demand anything of her anymore.

"I'll send someone over to the Nev Hettek Embassy and to the docks to see if we can turn him up, dear. But you hurry if you can. I promise you we'll have your husband at the College waiting for you, if we can't locate him sooner. But you mustn't be too tardy for your . . . debut."

Everyone, including her dear father, Vega, was polite to her now.

At first she didn't answer. Let him wait. She'd waited plenty in her life. She heard him shift from foot to foot, then clear his throat.

Finally she said, "Daddy, go downstairs. I can't get ready with you standing out there distracting me. And I'm not coming down until I'm ready. If Michael returns, send him up."

She heard her father mutter something unintelligible, then his footsteps descending the stairs.

She was no longer simply Vega Boregy's daughter and the collateral for a political merger with Nev Hettek. She was a power in her own right.

And powers in their own right led very lonely lives, she was finding out. Now that her father was gone, she thought she'd wanted him to stay—to tell her to come to her senses, to break down the door, to shake her and yell at her and treat her like the child she still was.

Or had been, until she'd been blessed or cursed with knowledge of Merovin's past and of its future. She wasn't sure she cared to have such knowledge and such power, right now as the moment drew near when she'd display her talent to all of those who counted in Merovingen: the Kalugins, the Nikolaevs, the Kamats, the others from the great Houses.

She wasn't sure she wanted to know their future. She wasn't sure she wanted to know even as much as she knew now, without the help of deathangel or Uncle Ito's clever guidance.

Right now, all Cassie really wanted to know was what the baby she was carrying had been in its last incarnation. The baby was hiding its previous lives from her.

She cupped the nearly imperceptible bulge at her belly, then smoothed her thickened waist. In the mirror, as she squinted at her reflection, she fancied she could see the baby in her womb, a white and tiny form about the size of a man's thumb, attached to her by a glowing cord. . . .

But there was no such sight in the mirror. In the mirror was only the pregnant darling of Boregy House, dressed in a smock of pale blue velvet trimmed with gold: Cassiopeia Boregy Chamoun, the woman on whose slender shoulders the merger with Chamoun Shipping had been built.

The woman on whose slender shoulders all Daddy's hopes rested, she amended and made a face at her image, which mocked her in return. She'd taken to thinking of Vega as Daddy, as she'd taken to thinking of Ito as Uncle Ito, now that she was a mother to be.

Now that she was more than that: now that she was a power in her own right, a woman endowed with the gift of prophecy and the wisdom of previous lives—the precious gift of Boregy House to the Revenantist College and the future of all Merovingen, as Ito continually reminded her when the drug haze grew too thick to see through and the way back to her body grew hazy as well.

Now that she was all she'd ever dreamed, she wished she wasn't. Before the regressions, before Uncle Ito and Daddy had believed in Cassie's powers and Cassie's wisdom and the import of Cassie's previous lives, she'd been freer. Now, whatever she thought and whatever she said was imbued with symbolism that only the College could decipher. Whatever warnings she gave of the future were studied by Working Groups and declared part of the Mystery of the College.

When she had a bad dream or an attack of indigestion, the cardinals scurried over the bridge to Boregy House to closet in Daddy's office and worry, to stand around her bed with their hands in their sleeves while scribes took notes.

She had no privacy. She had no peace. But she had power, and when she hadn't, it had seemed worth any price.

The price right now was increasingly high, so it appeared. Her marriage, her husband . . . everything but her baby seemed to depend on her performance tonight.

Performance: that was what it was, though nobody but Cassie would admit to that. She would take the deathangel and pontificate for the gathered masses of hightown power: read their futures, tell them of their pasts.

It was what Ito wanted, what Daddy needed. But it wasn't what Michael wanted. Her husband was being driven from her by the College as if they'd planned it. Michael looked at her askance and shook his head. He talked to her of propriety and of honesty and of her power being a great responsibility.

And Michael had made it clear that he thought she shouldn't let the College use her for their own ends.

When she'd said, this evening, "So you can use me to yours?", he'd stalked out without a word, slamming the door behind him so viciously that a piece of ormolu fell to the carpet in his wake.

She'd been frightened by that: by the slam of the door that had dislodged a piece of inanimate decoration. She'd gone over and picked it up. It had been one of the cupids that held the ormolu bunting.

The fall of the naked cupid, with his fat belly and his little wings, had shaken her. It was an omen, she was certain. She must find a way to make it a good omen, not a bad one.

She'd placed it on the dressing table and examined it. One wing was cracked, where it had fallen. The trumpet it had held to its lips was shattered: the trumpet's bell was still on the door; the stump was sharp and ragged.

Of all the decorations in her bedroom, Cassie had loved the cupids best. Since childhood, they'd been her favorites. She rummaged in her jewel box, found a gold chain, and tied the chain around the cupid's neck, then put the chain around her own.

The cupid dangled between her breasts, broken and divested of the bell of its horn.

This suited the mood she was in, and the image that her father and the College were making of her. And it would speak clearly to Michael of things she couldn't bring herself to say.

When he came back, he would see that their love was like the cupid: shaken, damaged, misplaced, and yet something she'd go to any lengths to salvage. Michael Chamoun was her perfect mate. Michael had guided her to her previous lives by virtue of his own.

In a previous life, Michael had been a great warrior against the sharrh. No lesser man could be considered as her companion, not when she was the long-prophesied seeress of Merovingen's salvation, whose life was dedicated to preparing Merovin for the day when the sharrh would come again.

Before that, of course, the horrible truths of her visions would be made real in Merovingen: there would be flame and revolution. The riffraff from the canals would rise up against their betters.

By then, the great Houses must be ready. This was her message to them tonight, the message that Ito and her father had so carefully orchestrated.

Before she left here, she must make peace with Michael, though. She couldn't let her mind float off on the wings of deathangel while she was worried about her husband.

Decided, she strode to her bedside and pulled on the needlepoint bellpull there. Twice she pulled on the strap, three times, four: she would tell Daddy she wasn't leaving until Michael was by her side. That meeting her husband at the College wasn't going to be good enough.

Downstairs, people were already scurrying. Before Cassie had discovered that within her was another woman, a noblewoman who'd been murdered by the colonials when the sharrh scourged Merovin and mobs looked for technocrats to blame—in those days, Boregy House didn't jump to obey her every whim.

She knew she mustn't abuse her privilege, understood that these were gifts from on high, and nothing she'd earned—or at least she remembered Ito's warnings.

But Ito didn't realize what courage it had taken to become a voyager on the astral plane. Ito was a small man who craved temporal power with a giant appetite. He'd never remembered how he'd lived and died and lived again. And died again, in the formless dark. And gone beyond life and death and differentiations of male and female, past and future, to a place where space and time were simultaneous and all futures were equally real, all realities equally desirable.

Ito had never risked anything. Not his unborn child. Not a lover, a mate. Not his sanity or his body.

Cassie risked her body with every deathangel-facilitated excursion out of it.

Someday, she might lose track entirely and become trapped among the planes, never to find her way back to her body again. When she told Ito how this worried her, he said only, "Don't bother your father with such talk. You're tired, Cassie. You're new to this. And the responsibilities are weighing on you, as they weigh on us all. That's why I'm here, to guide you through. To help you sort out what wisdom should be given to the people, and what truths are too frightening for any but the cardinals to hear."

She knew what Ito was doing. He was trying to make her a creature of the College. Michael was right about that. Daddy was right about insisting that she tell her father everything.

Vega Boregy was due her first loyalties, and she

knew it. He didn't have to keep telling her. She never kept back anything from Daddy, except what she and Michael talked about when they were alone.

Daddy had a right to know all that the cardinals knew. Although Vega was more difficult to talk to: whatever she told the cardinals, they merely nodded. Of course, she told Ito everything, first, and Ito helped her decide what the rest of the College should know.

But when she told her father that Merovingen must steel for a revolution—when she spoke of her visions of fire and wild mobs and conflict and destruction, then Vega would pace and browbeat her, hoping to force her to renege, to prophesy what was safe, and what was prudent, and what was helpful.

A parent was a parent, and Vega deserved respect and honesty. But not even her father's demands could make her take back the truths she saw, or unmake the visions that drove her. If Daddy wanted her to tell him that Boregy House would last forever, increasing in glory and power, then Daddy would have to do what Cassie told him, when they were truly alone.

Daddy would have to accrue more wealth, more power, more men at arms. Daddy would have to stop being content with maneuvering behind the scenes, and prepare to supplant the Kalugins.

Vega didn't like to hear such talk. Vega was a good adherent of Anastasi Kalugin's. The fortunes of the House of Boregy were tied to Anastasi's, Vega Boregy had insisted numerous times.

And she could only reply implacably with what her visions prompted: "Boregy House can save Merovingen, but only if I am free to speak my mind, and all of Merovingen listens. Under my guidance, and ruled with a steadier hand than the Kalugins', we may escape the worst. When my child is of age, he must be master of all Mero—"

"Stop it, Cassie. That's treason!" her father would say then.

But he'd heard her. He knew the truth of it. He must feel it in his bones, as she did in hers. The canalers were their enemies; the filthy rabble must be controlled, before the uprising in her visions came to be.

This she would tell the College and its invited guests, tonight. What else she would tell them was a matter to be left up to her mantic power, and to their perspicacity.

She could never be sure what the deathangel would being her, what she would see or what she would say. But she was sure of what the College would see and what the cardinals would say.

Ito was not totally devoid of visions, himself. Ito was envisioning the day when the Revenantist College, interpreters of the wisdom of Cassiopeia Boregy, mantic prophetess of the Wheel of Life, would be the sole authority controlling Merovingen—every House, every company worth mentioning, every heart and soul.

This, the high Houses would see tonight, when Cassie's powers were formally introduced to them. And formally offered to them, in a consultative structure allowing each House to consult Cassie, through Ito, as to what were their best courses of action, to ensure the future all in hightown wanted, and prevent the horrid one of anarchy and destruction that Cassie had foreseen.

If Cassie had to do all that, to put up with the manipulation of the College and the cast that politics and her father's best interests put on her pure revelations, then the least that the College and her father could do was make sure she had her husband by her side.

So she waited, combing and then brushing her hair until it flew about her head, for Michael to return.

And when he did, her husband was very angry.

She could hear him arguing with someone as they came up the stairs. Then she realized that the someone was her father, and that Vega's voice was hushed and trembling with anger, and that someone else's voice was also part of the argument.

She listened harder, but couldn't make out their words. But in the back of her mind, she thought she could hear them with a different ear, an inner ear, as if she were right beside them on the stairs.

The vision was so complete, so complex, so full of sight and sound and smell, that she started visibly.

Her heart began to pound. She hadn't taken the deathangel yet. She wasn't supposed to be able to do this without deathangel. She wasn't supposed to be able to do it in the present—she'd never heard of anyone who could.

Yet it was as if she floated, disembodied, so near to Michael Chamoun she could count the close-shaven whiskers on his chin, even see one he'd missed, just where his lower lip curled.

And she could see Chance Magruder, the Nev Hettek Ambassador, with Michael and her father on the stairs. And see her father's white skin go whiter as Magruder put a hand on Vega's cyan velvet jacket and said, in a low voice, "Get hold of yourself, man. It's just a circus for the gullible, after all."

"It's my daughter's sanity at stake here. And I expect you, Magruder, to be respectful—keep your cynicism to yourself—and you, Chamoun, to use your influence to control your wife, since you're the only one she seems to listen to, any more."

"Not true, if I may say so, Respected Ser," said Magruder in Cassie's mind. "She listens to Ito, and to the cardinals. And she listens to the deathangel's—"

"Chance," and this was Michael's voice, louder so

that she was sure she heard what her husband said as the three men reached the landing and her door: "Let me handle this."

"I've been waiting for you to do just that, Mike. So has your father-in-law, here, by the sound of it."

"Both of you," said Michael, "go downstairs. We'll be with you shortly."

Her father and the Ambassador left meekly, without a word of remonstrance, as if Michael were the lord of Boregy House already.

Already?

Had she thought that? Her eyes filled with sudden tears and she started to shake. She grasped the edge of her dressing table and held on with both hands as tightly as she could while vertigo overswept her.

The dressing table was the only thing that was real. Her father's death was far in the future, not near at hand. All portents were only that. Every disaster was avoidable.

She was suddenly so frightened that she doubled over, still holding the edge of the dressing table as if she were a tiny child and she was trying to pull herself up by it.

The whole table came over on top of her with a crash.

Michael came through the door, shoulder first, with another, louder crash.

She was only vaguely aware that she was lying in a mess of pomades and spilled powders, of costly crystal perfume bottles, shattered and emptied, of hand mirrors and combs and jewelry.

Nevertheless she was aware of her husband's arms, of Chamoun's worried eyes and beautiful face.

She reached up to touch his lips. He kissed her fingers.

He was saying things to her. She couldn't really hear him, and yet she could hear him in her mind.

Everything 'll be all right, you crazy hophead. Chance and I've got just the thing for you. And it'll save the baby, at least. And you, my love . . .

Michael's lips hadn't moved. Yet she had no doubt that she'd really heard those words of his, not imagined words for him to say. Because she never would have imagined him talking to her that way. And he never would have risked it.

But in his mind, or in hers, he'd called her his love.

And that was one piece of truth in a world where there was precious little truth but her own.

Then she realized that he was still talking to her:

"Cassie, you've got to stop this. You're eating too much of this stuff. You weren't supposed to have any until we got over to the College . . ."

She didn't let him finish. There mustn't be misunderstanding between them. There mustn't.

"I didn't eat any, Michael. It just . . . came over me, the feeling—this feeling. It's as if I had eaten some, but I haven't had any today, honestly."

He was smoothing her hair back from her forehead. She caught his wrist. "You've got to believe me," she added.

He was helping her up, out of the wreckage of her dressing table. "That's worse—if you haven't had any, and you're flashing anyhow. What about the baby, if you don't care about yourself or me? What if you stop taking this stuff, and it doesn't stop: the effects, I mean. Do you want to live like this, going off into trances without any warning, without preparation?"

He didn't usually speak that way to her. His diction wasn't usually that formal. But there was no mistaking the care with which he chose his words or the intensity behind them.

He seemed angry with her. Yet he had her on her feet. His arm was supporting her. He was smoothing her tunic down, over her baby-belly, and brushing her off as if he were a batman.

She turned in his arms and leaned against him bonelessly. His embrace was strong and firm and real. She considered telling him that she'd heard what he was thinking, and asking him if what she thought she'd overheard of his conversation with Magruder and her father on the stairs was accurate.

But something stopped her and that something was fear of his reaction. He didn't want her taking the deathangel as it was. If she told him she thought she'd . . . read his mind . . . or at least heard the words he was thinking, what then?

It could be the end of their marriage. But so could towering dishonesty. Yet, though she struggled, she couldn't get out the words. She merely let him hold her as she shivered.

He was saying, ". . . bring a doctor down from Nev Hettek, with your father's permission—someone who's got all the technical knowledge of modern medicine at his command. Just in case something goes wrong. You've got to agree to it, Cassie, or your father and Ito will never allow it."

"A Nev Hetteker doctor? Why? I'm fine, really." She straightened up to prove it, stepping back against his embrace.

He let her go. His fingers laced in his belt. "An obstetrician," he said. "A professional, best we've got. Please, Cassie—if you won't stop taking this stuff, then at least help me make sure you don't lose our baby."

"Yes, all right." What did she care? "If it makes you happy, that's fine. I'll tell Daddy I want an—an

. . . obsetician, if it means we won't fight about the deathangel anymore. Or my talent."

"Promise," Michael said brusquely. "No problem. You can whack yourself silly three times a day, as long as you don't risk your health or the baby's." He sounded exhausted, but his smile was bright and wide as he came forward and offered her his arm:

"Now, can we get this show moving, Cassie? Everybody who's anybody's waiting for you over at the College."

"And your friend Chance? He's here, isn't he? I didn't imagine it?"

"Ah . . . yeah, downstairs with your father. We're all going over together, one big happy family, showing the strength of the merger and how well Nev Hettekers and Boregy House get along. Okay? Take my arm and let's go?"

She went with her husband, down the stairs although they seemed miles long and she bit her lip rather than admit to him that each stair seemed to be wiggling and humping itself like a staircase of restless cats.

She held tight to his arm, as if by doing so she could hold onto the reality she was supposed to be living in, instead of the one that kept creeping around the edges of her perceptions, the one that deathangel brought her.

Why was this happening? She hadn't eaten any deathangel for three days. She kept blinking to restore her normal sight, but everything was too bright and too particulated, and the walls seemed to undulate as she reached the bottom of the stairs and greeted her father and Michael's mentor, Chance Magruder.

When she took Magruder's hand, a shock went through her that made her slump against Michael in front of everyone.

They were all fussing over her now. Was she all right? Could she continue? Did she want water? Tea? A physician?

She told them no, over and over. She called for her coat.

And she couldn't take her eyes off Ambassador Magruder, whose hand had been so hard and sharp like a sword, and whose whole mind had collided with hers for an instant that left her breathless and afraid.

Michael's friend and mentor was her enemy, this the touch of his hand had shown her clearly. In his mind was destruction and treachery, murder and deceit. And Tatiana Kalugin.

Cassie had seen the other woman, during that brief instant of contact, so clearly that she might have been in the same room when Chance Magruder undressed the Madame Secretary, very slowly, very passionately, and climbed on top of her to scheme about changes to come.

"That wife of yours is really getting to be a problem," Magruder told Chamoun after Cassie had been handed over to the College cardinals and the two foreigners had been shooed out front to wait with the rest of the theater's audience for Cassie's performance.

There was tea in Magruder's hand but precious little sympathy in his eyes.

"She's okayed the obstetrician, though she can't even pronounce the word. That ought to count for something."

"Stop helping her get the deathangel, Michael," said Chamoun's controller unequivocally.

"It's not that easy, Chance. She'll get it anyway."

"Maybe. Maybe not. Don't facilitate it. Don't accept it. Don't look the other way."

"That'll destroy my marriage just as surely as . . ."

Chamoun paused while two of the gathered luminaries wandered too close.

They were standing by a buffet that would have fed the whole population of Ventani Isle for a week. There were canapes and whole smoked fish, ice sculptures keeping unseasonal fruit cool and delectable, expensive wines and cheeses, meat pies and pastry rolls. And the rich and powerful loaded their plates from that buffet as if they hadn't eaten in months, though fat rolled over their waistbands and flopped under the women's bare arms.

This place needed the Sword of God, that was certain. But the Sword was a hard taskmaster, and Magruder was the Sword in Merovingen. ". . . just as surely as the deathangel," Mike Chamoun finished when the couple moved away. "She's having flashbacks, anyhow. What good's stopping the drug when she's got so much in her system?"

"I'm not a specialist. If it gets too difficult, she'll have an overdose." Magruder shrugged as if he'd just made a comment on the weather, rather than warned Chamoun that Cassie might have to be assassinated.

"What about the child?"

"What about the reason we're here?" Magruder reminded him, looking off into the crowd. Chance Magruder's profile was sharp and hard; his graying, pale hair had grown long this winter but now he'd cut it short and the shape of his skull was clearly visible. Around his mouth, the punctuation marks of shadow were deep tonight. Yet when he turned back to Chamoun and smiled with paternal affection, he was positively handsome. "Let's not take our eyes off the target, Mike. This is a mess, let's be clear on that. How bad, we don't know yet. Maybe you can control her."

"Everybody and his brother's trying that. She knows and she's resentful."

"Everybody and his brother, if you mean Vega and Ito, aren't her husband. Trust me, I know a little about women. It's your kid in the oven; your words will carry a little weight."

"Like about the doctor, yeah. Okay, what else?"

"Let's get her off the deathangel. Maybe she'll still be able to do whatever it is she does without it. Be better if we got her faking it altogether, the way we'd like. Think you can do that?"

"You bet. Right after I turn myself into the Angel of Retribution, wings and all, and clean out this nest of cardinals."

"Try. For me. At least don't lose whatever influence you've got. The medic we send down will have a pharmacy of his own to work from. We'll get her tractable for you. What's that ritual you kids were using? The 'listen only to my voice' part might be a good place to start."

"Chance, you're underestimating her . . ."

"A male failing. We'll huddle on it. Meanwhile, I've got my own female problem to deal with, coming up behind you." Again, the quick and energizing smile.

Chamoun looked over his shoulder and stepped reflexively from the path of the Governor and his entire family, bearing down on them.

Iosef Kalugin, white-haired and charismatic, with ribbons on his chest and striped hose to match, had one arm around his idiot son, Mikhail. Mikhail was dressed like an imitation of his father, which was what Iosef was trying to make of his dimwitted but good-hearted son.

And behind them swept the sharks of the family: Anastasi, with a colorguard of blacklegs trailing him, his quick dark eyes darting over a hawk's nose, checking out everybody and everything in sight, including the rafters of the College hall above their heads.

To his left was m'sera Secretary, Her Excellency, Tatiana, arguably the most beautiful woman in Merovingen, if you liked them arch and harsh, with shadows under flaring cheekbones and a mouth born for giving orders. Her nose was thin and its nostrils dilated suddenly.

Then she smiled and stepped out of the family procession, instead of passing by them. "Chance, I was hoping to see you here."

"I thought I was here by your command," said Magruder with a distinct bow of his head that didn't humble the sudden sparkle in his eye.

"No doubt you are," Tatiana said, "m'ser Ambassador. We've a question or two for you regarding the paperwork on our desk for the departure of the *Det Queen,* and we wouldn't want the ship held up, would we? Perhaps after this is over we could . . ."

"I'll leave you two . . ." Chamoun started to back away.

"Oh, no. Young Chamoun, isn't it? Stay and tell us what your wife is going to say tonight, so we won't be surprised. We hate surprises."

The fact that Chamoun knew Tatiana and Magruder to be an item obviously wasn't lost on Iosef Kalugin's daughter, who was locked in a power struggle with her brother Anastasi for Iosef's legacy.

Chamoun stumbled back into the conversation: "I don't know what she's going to say, m'sera Secretary. Wish I did. My wife's doing this under the guidance of the College cardinals. . . ." He shrugged, not knowing if he should complain to Tatiana overtly, or let Magruder take over from here. Or even if he'd already said too much.

Chance's expression gave him no hint. Over Magruder's

shoulder, Michael glimpsed Iosef and Mikhail, the reed-thin son who'd have been an engineer or an inventor if only he'd been born a Nev Hetteker. They were taking seats on the low dais reserved for the governor's family, while blacklegs descended on the buffet like skits with Anastasi, to bring the best of the delicacies to the family where it sat.

And then Tatiana responded to Chamoun's comment and he lost interest in the other Kalugins: "We're concerned about the College's involvement. We'd like to take your comment to mean that you are, too, m'ser Chamoun. As Cassiopeia's husband, we'd like to feel free to call on you from time to time for an assessment of her health and welfare—given the delicacy of the situation, of course."

Oh shit. "Of course, m'sera Secretary. Whenever and as often as you please." *Chance, it wasn't my fault. Please, man, don't blame me.* But he'd walked right into Tatiana's clutches.

He looked to Magruder openly, pleadingly, and Chance's face didn't give him a hint of how bad the damage was. "Don't you have to remind Vega about Cassie wanting you right by the stage, Mike?"

"Yessir, I mean, you bet. I'm on my way." Blindly, Chamoun backed out of proximity to the Kalugin woman, whose face was equally as unreadable as Magruder's.

They didn't look angry. They looked like a couple of cats who'd found and emptied a milk pail. But you never could tell . . .

Find Vega, fool, Chamoun told himself, afraid now that if he said or did anything out of the ordinary, Tatiana's eagle eye would see and he'd wake up in a Justiciary holding cell where Chance kept worrying they'd both land. . . .

Mondragon was the last person Chamoun had expected to bump into, and he would have pushed by the outlaw agent.

But Mondragon put out a restraining hand. "How's the deathangel business, Chamoun?"

"I ought to ask you the same, traitor," Michael said, voice low enough and temper high enough to risk it. If there was someone in this room vulnerable and more despicable than himself, it was Tom Mondragon. "And while I'm at it, how's your canal slut? Still blaming Megary for something that was all your fault?"

"You know, kid, if anything happened to Chance, all this brave talk of yours could stick in your craw and kill you."

"It'd take a man to do that," said Chamoun, his pulse pounding in his ears. This was no place for a fight with an ex-agent who was still, Chance thought, a passable duelist. "Out of my way, crud; go slime over somebody who thinks you're worth the trouble."

Chamoun turned and muscled his way through the crowd, past the Kamats in their magnificent finery, and found Vega in the shadows where cardinals came and went.

"Vega, is she handling this well enough?" said Chamoun to his father-in-law without preamble.

"We were just about to send someone for you, now that you're through mingling." Vega's tone said that Chamoun ought not to be talking to the sorts he'd been talking to—but he knew that.

"I'd be happier backstage with Cassie," he offered.

"She wants you where she can see you," said Vega Boregy heavily. His dark hair was startling against his pale skin tonight. Above their heads were chandeliers, and on either side of the curtained stage were oil lamps on tripods as tall as Chamoun.

For the first time he really looked at the stage, at the gold-leaf carvings and the red velvet curtains heavy with braid—at the scenes from Revenantist theology bracketing the stage.

What was he doing here? Michael Chamoun was a poor kid from Nev Hettek who happened to have parents who got mixed up in the revolution, and who happened to look like someone Chance Magruder could use for an operation so risky no professional would volunteer for it.

He didn't belong here; his whole life here was a lie. There wasn't any Chamoun Shipping line, at least there hadn't been until Karl Fon and Chance Magruder generated enough paper to create one. There wasn't any Michael Chamoun, really—not the Chamoun that the Merovingians knew.

But there was a baby, he reminded himself. And there was his wife.

At that moment, he wanted to cut and run because his wife was a drug addict controlled by the Revenantist College and soon enough Magruder would see that. And when Magruder saw that, Michael Chamoun was going to become expendable, having failed resoundingly despite all the time and money put into his cover and his mission. . . .

"Hey, Captain," said a soft voice by his ear.

"*Rita!* What are you doing—?" With yet another stupid question half out of his mouth, Michael Chamoun closed it with a snap. Rita Nikolaev smiled and took his arm, snuggling it against her breast because she was that kind and these Revenantist women were loose as women came.

He hadn't understood that at first, or he'd have saved himself endless misery. Now that he did, Rita was less desirable. But she was very accomplished, and that stirred him.

His body remembered the tryst in the boat with her, though his mind told him he ought to let things lie.

But her warm, soft breast was telling his arm things that telegraphed down the length of his trunk and precipitated a reaction that his Merovingen short tunic and leggings weren't meant to hide.

He disengaged from her. "I'm worried about Cassie," he said severely, trying to get another message across.

She took his arm a second time and squeezed it. "So am I, dear; so am I. But I told you I'd help you. It's really only the two of us who know the extent of the danger—who were there at the beginning, so to speak."

Was she threatening him? She did know way too much, and he hadn't been completely honest with Magruder about the night he and Rita had found Cassie doped into a stupor and thrown her in a cold shower, then walked her, then . . . Well, that was what he hadn't told Magruder.

He kept envisioning Rita's lips parted in passion and then he shut his eyes so he could concentrate on what she was saying.

"So, Michael, any help you need from Nikolaev House, just ask. As long as we're all still friends, and Cassie remembers that, I'm sure whatever she's into with the College can only benefit those friends. Aren't you?"

"Aren't I what?"

"Sure," she said. Her body went out of contact with his. "Tell me you're sure, Michael. No one wants to perceive this turn of events as a threat to business as usual."

"Or as a threat to Cassie's welfare," he added carefully. On his own level, he could play this game. Chance hadn't schooled him personally for nothing. "I'm most concerned about our baby. We're bringing in an obstetrician from Nev Hettek for her."

"Really? Well, should I be relieved?"

"Depends on what your concerns are. Want to talk about this later?" he offered as the lights started to dim, because that was what Chance would want him to do. And because, given that his wife was going to be high as a kite for the next several hours, he didn't mind. He had to make sure that relations stayed friendly. It was a sacrifice for the Cause he was glad to make.

"Later, then," she said and drifted away.

Then Ito was coming out on stage, between the claret curtains, and Michael's heart nearly stopped beating entirely.

The cardinal said, "Friends and colleagues, we have promised you a revelatory evening, and we are as good as our word." Ito had on one of his most ornate robes, and it glimmered in the light with an ethereal brilliance as he raised his hands to chest level and held them out to the crowd. "A wondrous event has befallen us, as the Ancestors predicted. Lo and behold, from our midst a prophetess has been given unto us, and that mantic seeress long foretold is none other than our own Cassiopeia Boregy."

Ito paused for the crowd to make its noises. Some clapped, some murmured, some merely shifted uncomfortably, unsure of what to do now that rumor had been confirmed.

"Boregy House and the College together have decided that this gift is one that should be shared among us all. The wisdom coming through this humble girl of Merovingen is too crucial to our futures for it not to be accessible to all. So, without further ado, and with the single advisement that private counseling by Cassiopeia Boregy may be arranged through your cardinals, I give you the jewel of the College, our special gift from God, Cassiopeia Boregy."

Michael's neck was hot. He was glad no one could

see him blush. How must Cassie feel? *What a bunch of tripe.*

He wished he could see Magruder's face, but he dared not turn around.

Ito was holding back the curtains for Cassie.

And even Michael was astonished at what he saw.

Cassie was in a white gown, riding on a litter of gold and glittering stones, held high on the shoulders of red-robed cardinals—not acolytes, but actual cardinals—in full regalia, including ceremonial headgear that made them seem as if their heads came to points.

Not a one of these old charlatans wanted to be upstaged, or to have it thought that he had less access to Cassie's "wisdom" than any other, Michael realized.

And there was his wife, herself, slumped upon the litter, eyes half closed, head lolling sideways.

Chamoun felt his nails digging into his palms. How much had they given her? She couldn't have stood unsupported if her life depended on it.

But she didn't have to stand. The cardinals lowered the litter in a practiced minuet and stepped back on either side of her. He saw the lips of the closest cardinal move, and realized it was some sort of prompt, though he couldn't hear the words.

As Cassie started to speak, Michael got a glimpse of Ito, hands in his robes, beaming as if she were his daughter, not the child of Vega, who stood beside him, in the wings.

Cassie said, "People of Merovingen, beware! Beware the canalers, who will rise up in flames. Beware the children of the Det, who come with their treachery and blandishments."

Great. Terrific. Michael was going to wring her neck, if Chance didn't wring his first.

"Beware your own selfishness," Cassie continued in a voice that seemed too large for so small a girl. "Beware the demons within. And the sharrh who are hiding beyond the clouds. The sharrh will come and we must make ourselves ready! The sharrh are full of guile, and we must be more canny!"

That threw Michael into a quandary: what was she saying?

"And we must learn our pasts, in order to shape our futures," said the woman in the trance, who was his wife but didn't sound anything like her now. "We must find our previous lives, and our future lives, and our current lives as well. We must take control of our destinies. We must gird our loins. We must root out the venal and the criminal among us! And we must put the canalers in their places or drive them from the city! Beware the poorest and the meanest of us, for they have torches that will light Merovingen like a beacon to the sharrh! When those flames rise, our doom is nigh! So heed me and join together with me, or all is lost. I have seen it! It is your future! It need not be your present! But listen to my voice, listen only to my voice. Listen. Listen. Listen. . . ." Her head fell forward.

One of the cardinals, and then another, began to clap. Uncertainly the crowd took up the ovation, as cardinals closed around Cassie, shielding her from public view.

Michael had heard most of this before. He was surprised only at the reaction of the crowd around him—surprised that anyone could take this ranting seriously.

Then he realized that the people in this room, the powers of the city, wanted to believe Cassie's warnings and Cassie's demands for harsher controls and disciplinary measures: they'd been looking for an excuse to tighten their rule here in any case.

He eased back, away from Rita, who was buzzing

excitedly to one of her own family about private militias, and heard others taking up the cry for more personal security, for less leniency in dealing with the lower tiers, for all the paranoid measures that Cassie, as a Boregy, would naturally dream up when stoned out of her conscious mind.

They were afraid, he realized—everyone in this room but him and Magruder. And they were afraid *of* him and Magruder, though they didn't have the names and faces right. They were afraid of the Sword's revolution, that was all.

That was what Cassie was talking about!

Suddenly, Chamoun needed to see Magruder, just touch base, get a look at Chance's face.

Rita forgotten, he headed off through the electrified crowd to find Chance, thinking as he eavesdropped his way that wisdom wasn't what got people excited. What got people excited was hearing what they wanted to hear, was having license to do what they'd wanted to do all along: was, in short, more absolute power, more control over everyone not in this room.

More of what they already had was what they could gain from tonight, and gain it with the College's sanction, as a religious mandate.

Michael Chamoun wanted to be sick. This was all his fault. If he hadn't undertaken that first, damnable regression that got Cassie started, none of this would have happened. He wouldn't blame Chance if Magruder took him down to the docks and cut his heart out.

But when he finally caught sight of Chance Magruder, who was leaving with Tatiana, already holding her cloak for her, Magruder waved and contrived, during the wave, to give Chamoun the high sign. Chance's mood wasn't show, then: Magruder was *pleased*.

Michael was nearly reeling with relief and confusion. He seemed to be in a world of his own where all these people around him were insubstantial ghosts. None of them could touch him, feel him, hear him, and they were all immaterial to him.

Until Rita found him, he felt that way. Her magic touch burst his bubble, and the offer she made him was real and opportune, tactically as well as personally. He needed to know what she thought of Cassie's performance; Chance would want to know.

But first, Rita wanted to see Cassie. "Oh, Michael, please can't we go backstage and talk to her? They'll let *you* back there, surely."

It was a matter of prerogatives, he realized. Rita wanted to be seen as a close confidant of *the* Cassiopeia Boregy, the emergent power of the moment in Merovingen.

"Sure, I guess. If it's okay with Vega and Ito . . ."

He led her up into the wings as if he had every right in the world, which he did: Cassie was his wife. When they found her backstage, where they were led by a maddeningly proprietary acolyte who had to "check with cardinals, m'ser and m'sera, of course you'll understand," someone was in Cassie's dressing room before them.

The door was open. Rita and Michael weren't eavesdropping. In fact, the man within beckoned them from where he sat on the dressing table. The mirror behind it reflected Cassie, slumped and staring distractedly at her hand, and the man who had that hand in both of his own and was talking fervently to her, his face aglow.

"Wasn't she, as I said, just wonderful?" said the man. "So wonderful, Cassiopeia, that I feel as if my whole life has changed. You've made a new man of me, a man with clear and resounding purpose. You must grant me a private interview, and guide me through my own past lives. Please. Please say you will."

Rita's hand closed on Michael's arm even as he came up behind his wife as if he could somehow, at this late date, protect her. He touched Cassie's shoulder. It was clammy through her robe.

He looked at the man who was begging for an audience and said, "Mikhail, Kalugin or not, you'll have to let her rest until tomorrow. When she's ready to give private readings, I'm sure you can be the first."

"And who are you?" Iosef Kalugin's designated successor asked archly.

"I'm her husband, m'ser. Her husband."

Rita was tugging on his arm. And from behind him he could hear Vega, calling his name.

Chamoun knew he either had to leave or face the consequences of cold-cocking Governor Kalugin's son. The idiot was going to make a terrific first adherent to Ito's little politico-religious coven.

Wait until Chance heard about *this*.

But Chance wasn't going to hear about it right away. Rita was insistent that he keep his word and come with her and her cronies to Nikolaev House, "where we'll get a few minutes alone, I promise."

Ito and Vega wanted him out of the way as well. "Be a good son-in-law," Vega told him in a tired and flat voice. "Let me take care of the delicate matters here. You go deal with your peer group and let Ito and me handle ours."

So he was ousted from his wife's presence, and he wasn't even sure she'd known he was there.

She'd looked so frail and tiny there, so exhausted, so pathetic with her dilated pupils and her loose lips.

He couldn't banish the memory of Cassie sitting there letting Mikhail Kalugin pump her limp hand. She had his child in her belly. What did they think they were doing?

But it didn't matter what he thought, or what he

felt. And eventually, Rita Nikolaev managed to get his attention and banish his distress, at least temporarily. But it all came back again when they rejoined the others and he saw the deathangel carefully apportioned on Nikolaev china for everyone to try.

He couldn't even storm out. He had to play his part. He'd tell Chance to send him back to Nev Hettek, if he thought Chance would. But Chance wouldn't. This was just the kind of mess that Magruder was here to make.

And it was just the kind of mess that Mike Chamoun was here to make. So, if he was succeeding, why did he feel so damned bad about it?

Maybe, he told himself, it was because Rita and her friends—*Rita,* one of the shrewdest of the new generation of Merovingian mercantilists—had swallowed Cassie's performance hook, line, and barbed sinker.

Not a one of the young lions of Merovingen commerce at that table, chewing their deathangel with giggles and sighs and chattering wide-eyed to one another about the "importance" of everything Cassie had said—not a single one of the elite and the elitist realized that Cassiopeia Boregy was prophesying the revolution that the Sword of God had come here to make!

After all, she was a home-grown seeress, a magical creature in their midst. Michael methodically chewed his own deathangel tail, because he couldn't risk *not* doing it, not in this company, not when his wife was the rising star of Merovingen's new fortune.

As he chewed, he listened and he grunted in the appropriate places, and the part of him that wasn't Sword of God felt increasingly sorry for these spoiled magnates-to-be. They followed fashion with such a passion that none had a single qualm about the effect of repression on the lower tiers, of paranoia among the ruling class, of beefed-up security and personal militias—or of deathangel on their own psyches.

Michael had risked deathangel before, for a lesser prize than being intimate with the Nikolaevs and their powerful playmates. He'd risk it again, if he had to.

But he didn't like his wife risking it, and risking their child in the bargain. He didn't like it one bit. And he was so absorbed with that concern that the deathangel magnified his worries. The tiny amount of drug in the deathangel flesh turned into an amplifier of those fears, and soon enough Mike Chamoun had all he could do not to run out of there, yelling at the top of his lungs that Cassie must stop this before it was too late.

It was too late already. His sweaty face and his glazed eyes and his shaking limbs were a testament to that. And all over Merovingen that night, in the homes of the rich and the powerful, wherever money and connections were strong enough to secure deathangel, young men and women looked into each other's eyes and asked: "Who was I, in a previous life?" and "What does my future hold in store?"

And everywhere the answer coming back from drug-assailed psyches and imaginations titillated by Cassiopeia Boregy's performance was the same: "I was rich and powerful, a traveler among the stars." "I will be there again, in Cassie's army of the newly aware and the carefully prepared, immune to the onslaught to come."

Tatiana Kalugin leaned back on her taupe velvet couch and stretched her naked arms high above her head. Her hair was loose and she ran her fingers through it, eyes on Magruder, who was still undressing.

"And then Anastasi grabbed me," she told her dangerous lover, "—nearly shook me, actually, but you saw that—and said that if it turned out I had anything to do with this, he was going to . . ." She forced a grin that she hoped was insouciant. ". . . ah, do away with me, would be the most polite way to say it. But Anastasi wasn't polite. And when my brother loses his calm, you can be sure there's something very wrong."

Magruder didn't comment. She loved to watch him undress. First he'd take off his velvet jacket, then his shirt, revealing all that well-used muscle on a broad-shouldered frame that was built for action, and for speed. Some would call Magruder stringy, aging, rangy or lanky; to Tatiana he was like the pistol belted against his spine or the knife on his hip: hard, designed for a purpose, and exciting beyond anything built for less.

He always took his pants off last, and she was sure it was because his weapons were around his waist. Tonight, barefoot and bare-chested, he padded toward her with his belt still cinched and sat on the edge of her couch, stern concern in his eyes. He put a hand on her naked flank, slid it up, past her waist, along her ribcage, down her naked arm until he could take her hand. He guided that hand to his belt.

She said, because the silence between them yawned dangerously and something real might fall out of her mouth into it: "What did Vega say to you about Cassie's performance? Anything? Do you think they can control her, Vega and Ito?"

"I'm more worried about Anastasi threatening you. Just what did he say, exactly?"

She wasn't going to tell him, then she did: "That he'd 'tear me a new asshole,' should it turn out that I had anything to do with Cassie's debut—or the things she said. I know I didn't." She took a quavering breath, while her hands undid Magruder's belt and the weight of his weapons made it fall away from his hips. "Did you? Or your boy, Chamoun?"

If her question shocked him, or frightened him, there should have been some sign.

Magruder didn't push her hand away from him; he didn't shrink from her; his desire didn't abate. He leaned forward and down, kissing her breast. Then she felt the sharpness of his teeth.

Her free hand ruffled his short hair. Her attention strayed from the question she'd asked to the answers her body was giving his, and the promises his was making.

When he lifted his head and stood to allow her to slip his pants down, he said in a thicker voice than usual: "Michael said he'd talk to you about Cassie whenever you wished. Don't bring that business to bed with us, Tatiana. Not tonight."

Out of contact with him as he kicked his legs free of his pants and made sure his weaponsbelt was in easy reach, she had enough presence of mind to say, "Chance, you're underestimating the danger here. Anastasi's feeling threatened by your protege's wife."

"Anastasi's in bed with Vega," said Magruder as he put one knee on the couch and then swung the other over, straddling her. "And I'm in bed with you. Looks like parity to me."

Then he lowered himself onto her and there was the remarkable pleasure of the length of him against her. There was something about the feel of Magruder's skin against her own that was unparalleled in her experience. It was more than simply his heat and the slide of his lean muscle, the brush of his body hair, or the strength in his limbs: the very contact with his skin took her breath away.

And it took her senses away, as well. The man who might well be the most potent weapon in Merovingen split her legs with a practiced hand and, when he took that hand away to delve her most intimately, she was devoid of questions as to his loyalty . . .

Almost. The uncertainty of his motives was part of the attraction, she knew. The very threat he represented, the risk of being intimate with a man as ruthless and as motivated as Magruder, made the stakes so high her body leaped to meet his.

She locked her arms around his neck and willed him to say that he loved her. It was the only protection she could possibly secure from Chance Magruder. But he didn't say it. He murmured that he loved her breasts, that he loved the feel of her, that he loved the taste of her. But none of that brought any safety to this union of wholehearted lust.

Magruder liked control games. He watched her as he made love to her, holding back, teasing, intent on making her respond and react, rather than initiate and act. And her body arched under him, saying in its own language how it longed for the climax he could give her.

She was just raising her lips to his ear to whisper, "Now, Chance . . ." when a bright light intruded.

The door behind them had opened. Someone stood there.

She froze, her arms and legs locked around her lover, and craned her neck in horror. She *had* locked the door! She knew she had.

Therefore, whoever stood in that doorway either had a key, or was an enemy capable of picking locks soundlessly . . .

She squinted at the figure silhouetted there and it moved toward her, flipping on the electrics.

"Father!" The agonized groan burst out of her as Magruder's weight left her. There was a scramble: Magruder's feet hitting the floor, Chance snatching up his belt—not for his pants, but for his weapons.

She realized what Chance was doing and lunged for him, naked before her father. Bare-assed, caught with a lover Iosef would never have approved. . . .

"No, Chance!" Her arms went around Magruder's, to stop him from pointing knife or gun at her father.

"Get dressed, daughter," came her father's voice. "I'll be waiting."

And Iosef Kalugin stomped out through the door, slamming it behind him.

Alone in the bright light, they looked at each other. Magruder's chest was heaving; the hair on it sparkled with perspiration; his desire had wilted. "What now?" he asked.

"Do as he said." She shrugged into her wrap. "I'll talk to him. Stay if you—"

"I don't think so. I'm not sure we can—"

She couldn't let him say that—not that they couldn't see each other again. "Don't be ridiculous, Chance. I'm a grown woman with my own sphere of influence."

"You're still the governor's daughter." Magruder's voice came from deep within his chest. He was buckling his belt, stooping over for his tunic. He looked up at her. "You do what's best for you, Tatiana. I'm not expecting anything more. I'll go out the back way. We knew this wasn't the most politic of unions. . . ."

"But it is, Chance. Trust me. At least," she hurried as, shod and buttoned up, he headed for the back door, "tell me where you'll be if you won't wait and I'll come to you, when I've talked to Iosef."

"I don't know. The embassy, I guess—"

Then the door opened again, and her father said, "Don't leave, Ambassador Magruder. I need to talk to you, as well."

Tatiana Kalugin squeezed her eyes shut as if, when she opened them, her father wouldn't be standing in the doorway ordering her lover to bear witness while he lectured his daughter.

She wasn't a child. Why did she feel as if she'd been caught necking in a fancyboat? She wished with all her heart that it had never happened. Never in her life had she dreamed of anything as awful as her father coming upon her with her legs wrapped around a man's buttocks. . . . Not only her pride, but her dignity as well, was wounded.

Iosef cared for none of that. He stalked right up to the couch where she sat, her wrap pulled around her, and glared down at her. He was still her father. Standing there, he towered over her as he had when she was young. She nearly wept.

Then her father said, "Tatiana, Ambassador Magruder, what do you think you're doing, frolicking here like this? It's bad enough my daughter is consorting with the enemy, but *now?*"

She tried to retort, "Chance isn't the—"

Iosef cut her off brutally: "Are you both blind? Or did you plan all this? Confess you did, and things will go easier for you both."

"Plan 'this' what, Governor?" Magruder said in a tone that snapped like a whip, with no hint of guilt or embarrassment in it.

"Mikhail and Cassie Boregy. Don't play the fool with me, Ambassador. I know your boy Chamoun's up to his ears in this plot."

"What plot, father?" This time, Tatiana wouldn't be silenced. She stood up on shaking legs, holding her wrap closed, and took a step toward her father. "If there's a plot here, it's come from Vega Boregy and Ito, possibly with Anastasi's collusion."

"It's not Anastasi, Ito, and Vega I find missing and unaccounted for when I need to discuss matters this evening—and then find in carnal—"

"All right, Governor," Magruder said, coming to Tatiana's side and putting an arm around her shoulder—a protective arm that at any other time she'd have shaken off, to then slap the impertinent fool across the face.

But Magruder's support was curiously welcome. Magruder's touch, in this moment, wasn't a sign that he thought her to be weak. It was display for her father's benefit, and one she appreciated.

And Magruder continued: "Your daughter and I are lovers, have been for some time. We think this is our business, and not only that. We're forging a better understanding, a basis for cooperation. We're not ashamed, only prudent. People will talk. Assumptions will be made. But I assure you, ser, my intentions are honorable and Tatiana's never displayed anything but a wholehearted support of your best interests."

"Nice speech, Nev Hetteker." Iosef's mouth was dry, Tatiana noticed. She could see the way his tongue couldn't wet his lips; they parted with an audible smack when he talked. "But not the speech I need to hear. Both of you, look me in the eye and tell me you had nothing to do with Cassiopeia Boregy's little performance."

"Chamoun's against it, ser," Magruder said very softly, as if he were reluctant to discuss the matter at all—which he was. "His wife's pregnant. He's afraid the drugs that the College is giving her will hurt the fetus."

Tatiana looked at Chance, shocked. There was so much he'd held back. She edged away from him. His arm tightened about her shoulder, saying *don't misconstrue; don't jump to conclusions.*

"Father, Chance is right. It's Ito, and Vega—probably under Anastasi's direction. Look at what's before you: who wants unrest in Merovingen if not Anastasi? Who's enamored of military might? If this ploy works, Anastasi will have all the men he needs to make his war upon Nev Hettek—he'll only have to commandeer the private militias that the houses will commission. He doesn't even have to go against your quotas . . ."

Now Magruder squeezed her, nearly imperceptibly. But she was just fabricating, guessing, casting straws to the wind.

Her father frowned. Then he positively glowered. "Did you see Mikhail's reaction? Did you listen to him? He's sure Cassie Boregy is the Angel of Retribution, never mind that she's a woman. He's got religion, and she's it. If you two aren't part of the problem, then you'd better prove it to me by becoming part of the solution."

"Of course, father," Tatiana said through her own dry mouth, aware of the danger, and the opportunity, at hand.

"Whatever you say, Governor. Anything I can do," Magruder offered, and she could only hope that Chance realized where this might lead.

"Magruder, I want you to tell the Chamoun boy we want to see him."

"I did that already, father. He's agreed to come discuss his wife's . . . ability . . . with me tomorrow."

"I want control over this woman—over what she says and whom she says it to. Or I want her silenced. One way or the other, is that clear?"

Tatiana nodded, struck dumb, and watched Magruder out of the corner of her eye.

Chance said, "If it's Anastasi's gambit, there's not much I can do but ascertain that for you, Governor—to the extent that Chamoun knows anything. We can't get into the College and find out what kind of rubbish they're feeding Cassie . . . what kind of preparation goes along with the drugs they're giving her."

"You'll do what I tell you. If she can't be controlled, she must be stopped."

"Stopped?" Tatiana knew what her father meant, but needed to be sure: "Do you mean formally, or informally? Accused of treason, along with Ito and Vega, and possibly Anastasi—of fomenting this or that? Or do you mean . . . disappearing?"

Iosef looked hard at his daughter, then at her lover, then back to Tatiana again. "I mean, stopped. Or controlled. Let's try the controlling, first. Tatiana, you see Chamoun. Magruder, whatever your influence is, use it. The next time Cassie Boregy speaks, she's to speak to the advantage of the status quo as I've determined it. I want a copy, before the fact, of whatever she's going to say in her next public appearance. I also want assurances, from you, Magruder, and yours—Chamoun and by association, his wife,—that when Cassie Boregy gives my son Mikhail his 'private audience' tomorrow, nothing will be said in that audience of which I would not approve. Nothing that will turn Mikhail's head. Nothing that will involve him in something I can't sanction—nothing that will limit his future. *Is that clear?*"

Her father's roar echoed around the room so that Magruder reflexively let go of her and she, in her turn, stepped back a pace. So that was what Iosef was really angry about: not her and Magruder, not whatever Ito and his allies might have fabricated in the person of Cassie Boregy—but Mikhail. Nothing must happen to make Mikhail any less likely a successor. Nothing could be allowed to affect precious Mikhail's chances of acceding to Iosef's power in Merovingen.

Suddenly she wanted to strike her father, leap upon him and scratch his eyes out: Mikhail, Mikhail, Mikhail. All her life, no matter how well she'd performed or how hard she strove, that idiot brother of hers was always in her way.

Dozens of times, she foiled Anastasi's clumsy plans and maneuvers to build his own strength at Iosef's expense, and never had her father so much as admitted that she'd done well, or done anything. No matter what she did, she could never prove herself more worthy than Mikhail, who was guileless, stupid, worthless . . . but a man, and Iosef's choice of successor.

She gritted her teeth and endured the rest of the interview. She was no longer sorry that her father had found her with Chance. Perhaps she'd acquire some of Chance's power by association. For Iosef was treading carefully with Magruder, though the Nev Hetteker might not have an inkling that this was the case.

Maybe now Iosef would notice her—at least as something more than his daughter who squabbled with Anastasi and whose machinations must be held in check. Perhaps, at last, Iosef would give credit where credit was due.

He'd asked her to handle Chamoun, that was something. And he was using her association with Magruder to involve the foreigner in House business, which was even more: she and Magruder could go public now, if they chose.

There was, finally, a percentage in showing, rather than hiding, the strength she'd gained from forging an alliance with Nev Hettek's ambassador.

Otherwise, Iosef would have forbidden them ever to see each other again. She'd half expected it. Iosef had destroyed other relationships of hers, on grounds that this or that man wasn't suitable.

It seemed ironic that the one man her father hadn't dismissed like a house servant was one she herself didn't trust.

But respect is a different thing than trust, and when

Iosef left as abruptly as he'd come, in his wake everything was different.

She and Magruder were now under direct orders to collude to the benefit of Iosef Kalugin. Their relationship—or at least one facet of it—had official sanction.

Magruder sat down heavily on her couch and she noticed, distractedly, that they'd stained it somehow before father had showed up.

He said rubbing his jaw, "Damn, now what?" and looked up at her.

She was shivering with cold. She felt as though she was encased in ice. She looked down at him and shook her head slowly. "Now," she said, "you and I do exactly what we were told. Or we'll be the ones who disappear." She hated that euphemism, but it was the way imprisonment and/or assassination was broached in the Kalugin household. "I've never felt I could trust you, Chance— " She held up her hand to forestall any protest. "Now I have to. If you're half the man I think, you've had the same reservations about me. Whether it's Ito and Vega implementing a plan to supplant the Kalugin house with their own, or the Boregys in collusion with Anastasi to secure him the governorship, or merely an unrelated piece of bad luck, you've heard what my father expects from us."

"I don't have that kind of control over Mike. And if I did, he doesn't have that kind of control over his wife."

"Then we'd better secure that kind of control—before tomorrow, when Cassie meets with Mikhail."

"Tatiana," said Magruder carefully, "there are angles to this you aren't seeing. We just got caught with our pants down, literally. No way we're thinking clearly. Come sit with me." He patted the couch beside him.

"I'm not a pet," she exploded, crossed her arms, and stalked across the room to her closet. Suddenly she wanted to be completely dressed, even to high boots. Dressed in layers and layers of clothing, beneath which nothing could touch her. If she got enough layers over her body, perhaps she could banish the cold that seemed to have invaded her person.

He didn't respond, nor did he get up to leave. When she was totally dressed, she turned around, stiff-necked, and said, "I'm sorry, Chance. I didn't mean to snap."

"Come to the embassy with me," he said calmly. "We'll send somebody to find Chamoun. And we'll find ourselves again. . . ."

She couldn't imagine letting him touch her. The thought of it brought back the crack of light, her father's form in the doorway, the mortification of it all. But she didn't tell him that.

In time she might feel differently. In time, the cold might leave her bones. In time, they might be able to weather this crisis and go on to better days. Now, there was only the threat that Cassiopeia Boregy represented.

It wasn't until much later that Chance Magruder softly wondered if the threat might be turned to their personal advantage—if Anastasi might "take a fall over this, and Mikhail as well, leaving you as the only Kalugin your father can trust."

It was this supposition, so carefully voiced by Magruder, that melted the cold in Tatiana's bones and allowed her to begin to live again, to think again, to feel again and to scheme again.

And to enjoy her foray into Magruder's embassy, forbidden territory, and (as they waited for Magruder's men to find Chamoun and bring him to them) the warmth and privacy of Magruder's bed.

The next morning, Michael Chamoun paced back and forth in Cassie's bedroom, his face pale, making impossible demands as she sat there, fingering the cupid hung about her neck on a golden chain.

"Cassie, you've got to stop eating the deathangel. You insist you don't know what you're saying when you're entranced—fine. Then that's even more reason to stop doing this. You don't know what kind of prompting Ito's giving you, either. You're mucking with heavy politics, here, stuff you don't understand."

"That's not true. Daddy wouldn't let me do anything that wasn't. . . ." She trailed off, choking back a sob, and started again. "Please don't be angry with me, Michael. This is what I'm supposed to do, what my life's purpose is, I know it. I just know it. Everybody but you's so happy for me . . . happy about the prophecies. . . ."

"*Who's* happy? Think, woman: Ito's happy; he's a snake, you used to tell me that. Your father's happy? I don't think so, not when his daughter's hyped out of her mind at the College's orders. Anastasi's happy, I bet—this whole thing is giving Governor Kalugin conniption fits."

"You can't know that. How can you know—"

"*Chance* chewed my butt to ribbons last night, because old Iosef's told *him* how *un*happy the Governor is! That's how I know. And what about us? What about what I want? How about what our baby would want, if it's ever going to get a chance to be born? Cassie, you've got to stop this."

"I *can't,* Michael! How can I?" She was whimpering now, and hating herself for it. She should be angry at him, not blinking back tears. She *was* angry at him, but she was more frightened that she'd lose him over this. "Please, Michael, what can I do to make you understand that I can't stop the prophecies. . . ? It comes without the deathangel, now—"

"Because you've had too much! Retribution's hangnails, woman, can't you see you're risking our lives, and the life of our child?"

She sniffled out loud. She hunched down. Her shoulders began to shake. In a tiny voice like a child's whimper she managed to say, "But Mikhail Kalugin's coming for his private interview in just a few minutes. I can't not do it, Michael. He's the governor's son. And if his father's mad at me, then maybe he'll tell Daddy so, because Uncle Ito will be so disappoint—"

"Don't talk to me about 'Uncle' Ito! Uncle Ito's to blame for most of this. Don't forget, Uncle Ito doped me, too. And almost really messed my mind around. That's his specialty, isn't? Messing with people's heads? Keep doing what Uncle Ito tells you, Cassie, and you'll either end up a vegetable or floating in a canal somewhere because these prophecies are scaring the hell out of the *current* Kalugin government, which is what we have to worry about, not some future in which Ito and Vega want to cut themselves a bigger piece of the pie using you to do it."

"What do you want me to do, Michael?" she moaned.

"I want you to stop doing deathangel. Tell Ito the circus is over."

"I can't, I told you I can't."

"I won't accept that. Maybe you can't stop—yet. Not today, not before Mikhail's blind date with destiny. Okay, then control what you say. Don't let Mikhail go back to the governor with anything you said that seems the least bit threatening to the stability of the Kalugin government. You *can* do that, can't you—control your tongue?"

"I don't know; I don't know; I don't know."

"Damn, don't cry like that."

Michael came over, knelt before her where she was doubled up, and took both her hands in his. "The doctor's coming—the obstetrician from Nev Hettek I sent for. You just hold on until he gets here. And you don't say anything that will scare the Kalugin dynasty into thinking you're its enemy. And don't you dare lose that baby of ours. Or let Mikhail get some dim-witted crush on you so I end up disappearing and you end up marrying into the governor's family. Hear?"

"Michael! Is all this because you're jealous of *Mikhail?*" The thought was so ludicrous it dried her tears. Strength came back to her. She pulled her hands from his and palmed her eyes. She sniffled and straightened up. "I've got to do something about the way I look. Mikhail will be here soon. And don't you worry, I won't run away with the governor's son."

Her husband grabbed her and shook her, hard, lifting her off her feet. "Cassie, this isn't a game. This is serious. I don't care who you sleep with. I don't want you dead, and I don't want our baby dead." He let go and she fell back on the bed.

"Michael . . ."

"I'll be down at the dock, on the *Detfish,* if you want me. If I stay around here, I'm going to tell your father what I think of him. If you're not doped out of your head by lunch, why don't you come down there? Bring some things. We're not sleeping here—at least I'm not—until this whole thing is settled. And don't bring any drugs with you if you come."

He stomped out, slamming the door behind him, leaving her crushed and terrified and confused.

She called after him, "Michael, don't leave me," but he was already gone.

She sat hugging her stomach and crying as quietly as she could. She was going to lose the baby, Michael thought. She didn't see why she had to lose the baby. She felt fine. No, that wasn't true. She felt horrid. She was going to lose her husband over this, because of the prophecies, because of Ito, because of Daddy, because of her . . . gift.

How could he do this to her? How could he leave her when she needed him so? She sat there until someone knocked on the door and said that Mikhail was downstairs, waiting for her.

Then she panicked. She had to do something right. She was spoiling everything. She looked a mess, nothing like the cool and composed prophetess of all their futures.

She struggled in vain before the mirror. Then she had a blinding flash of insight: she'd wear a veil to mask her puffy eyes and lips, her runny nose.

She found one in her closet and put it on, right after she opened her drawer and got out all the deathangel spine powder she had left and sniffed it with a little silver spoon that Ito had given her.

She couldn't prophesy without it, not in the state she was in. And if Michael was deserting her, or was lost to her because of her revelations, then all she had left was her talent—and Daddy.

Daddy said she was doing fine.

As the drug began to take hold, she hurried down the stairs. She needed to get into the room and sit down before the full force of deathangel poison hit her, or she might fall. The staircase was already beginning to undulate like a staircase of restless, if familiar, cats.

Mondragon caught Jones at Moghi's and grabbed her when she tried to slip away, out the back. In the kitchen, she spat in his face.

"How couldya? Denny's nobody to catch up in yer hightown games! What'd ye think, we wouldn't hear 'bout it? Ye ain't welcome here, Mondragon. Go back where ye—"

"Jones, this is serious."

"So hey, what's new? With you, everythin's serious—serious trouble, serious danger. And none of us to blame fer any of it." Her eyes flashed like signal fires.

"Jones, listen for a moment. One moment. Cassie Boregy's Ito's pawn. It's clear to a blind man that the Boregys have thrown in with the College. They're beefing up defenses. . . ." He trailed off. From her face, she wasn't listening: It was stony and uncomprehending. She was watching his fingers where they held her, enduring him, waiting for him to speak his piece and let her go.

Into his silence, she said again, "Denny. How could ye? Ye want yer deathangel fish fer yer hightown games, from now on, fetch it yerself." And she shook her arm as if to shake him off.

He let her go. You couldn't explain to her how these things were going to affect Merovingen-below. She wouldn't listen.

Once freed, she headed off through the stewpots and the kegs. He called after her: "Jones, you've got to warn the canalers not to get deathangel for hightown. And to curtail all smuggling, all arms caching, everything illegal. Purges are going to start. People are going to be arrested. Everything's going to be watched much more closely down here. They're looking for scapegoats, those hightowners. Signs of revolution. Signs of—"

But Jones was gone, and there was no use in any of this. He had enough troubles of his own to deal with. If Jones hadn't just about destroyed Megary with her private war, he could have used that second channel now, to get word to Karl Fon how Magruder was bungling things.

This was going to be one rough springtime. By summer, the folk of Merovingen-below, who thought they had it tough now, were going to learn how to spell "oppression" and what downtrodden could really mean.

Because hightown was nervous. So nervous that, if there'd been enough armed and trained men to go around, by this morning there would have been a blackleg in every hovel and on every corner.

But there weren't enough blacklegs in Anastasi's militia and the private security forces of hightown combined—not for that.

Not yet.

But if Cassie Boregy was allowed to continue prophesying unchecked, there would be. And only the Revenantist College was going to be happy about it.

"Get a doctor," Cassie had heard her father say, sometime after Mikhail had gone.

She didn't know how long after Mikhail had gone. She didn't remember being carried to her room. But here she was.

She remembered the pain, and that was still here. She remembered the awful pain in her belly, the cramps.

And she remembered screaming.

She remembered the doctor, vaguely—and Vega asking someone if she'd lost the baby.

And the doctor, or someone else, had said, "No, but it was close. She needs bed rest. And peace and quiet."

And then she remembered nothing until she heard Uncle Ito's voice. She didn't want Uncle Ito. She wanted Michael. She kept calling for Michael, but it was Uncle Ito who answered, every time.

Uncle Ito would tell her that Michael couldn't be found, and she should put her trust in God.

But she'd seen God, and he was angry. He looked just like Michael, and he was mad at her.

She'd been bad. She hadn't told Mikhail Kalugin the truth. She'd tried to lie and, behind her veil, she'd managed it—because her husband had wanted her to lie.

She said to Uncle Ito, "I lied to Mikhail. I lied and I told him everything was going to be just like he wanted it to be, because I was afraid to tell him the truth. So God punished me. I've got to tell him the truth."

"Ssh, Cassie, ssh. Mikhail was pleased with his session. You did fine. But you mustn't lie. You must let me help you."

"Make Michael love me. Make him come back." She tried to open her eyes, tried to sit up. She couldn't do either. "Make Michael come back to me, Uncle Ito."

"I promise, Cassie. You must rest."

Then she thought about Michael and she reached out blindly to Ito, who took her hand. "Don't tell him about the baby. Don't tell him I lost the baby."

"You didn't, Cassie. You and your baby are going to be just fine."

"But I will. I saw it in my vision, Uncle Ito. If I keep prophesying, I'll lose the baby. And Michael. But I can't stop prophesying or God will be angry and the flames will consume us all."

Now fear gave her the strength to sit up and she did. She opened her eyes and the whole room spun, her beautiful blue and gold room with its ormolu cherubs. She grasped the cherub around her neck and pulled with all her might. The chain broke, and she held the cherub out to Ito: "See, I'm going to lose the baby! Help me, Ito! Help me!"

"Lie back down, Cassie, lie back down."

She did, and Ito stayed with her. She wanted to die. But she knew it was too soon for that. First she had to tell Mikhail the truth, what she'd hidden from him in her vision. Then she'd lose the baby. *Then* she'd die. Then she could die, and God wouldn't be angry with her.

But now she had to live, even if she'd already lost Michael. Now she had to live and guide Merovingen through the flames and out again, into the new world Ito kept telling her they would make.

Listening to Uncle Ito droning on about her visions and what they meant, and what truths she would see when next she was entranced, Cassiopeia Boregy fell into a sick and troubled sleep.

And in that sleep was Michael, dressed like the angel he resembled, the one guarding the harbor, the one on Hanging Bridge. And Michael drew his sword and ran her through, killing her there and then, before he threw her body into the canal and she was eaten by all the fish so that little bits of her spread all over Merovingen. She was a part of all Merovingen forever, now.

Michael was the Angel of Retribution with the Sword in hand, and she was the sacrifice that God demanded in exchange for salvation—for saving Merovingen from the scalding wrath of the sharrh.

When her husband was finally found and brought to her, Cassiopeia Boregy looked up, smiled from her pillows, held out her hand to him, and said, "See, Michael, I didn't lose the baby."

There was no use in worrying Michael. He would leave her, she had seen it. She would lose the baby, she had seen that, too. In the end, he would kill her. But that was all in the future.

Right now, she had to regain her strength, see her father, and go to Uncle Ito for guidance. Not to escape her fate, which was fixed, but to save Merovingen.

When she'd touched Magruder's hand in the College theater, she'd known that Michael's mentor was her enemy. But not until she'd nearly lost the baby had she realized the rest of the awful truth: her husband was her enemy as well.

Michael Chamoun was Sword of God. That was why he'd told her to lie to Mikhail Kalugin. That was why he was so concerned with Ito and her father and politics. That was why, when she'd done as he asked and lied to Mikhail, it had nearly killed her—and the baby. She shouldn't be having a baby by her enemy. At that moment, she hated her husband and the baby inside her.

Michael *was* Sword of God. That was what the vision of Michael as the Angel with the Sword was trying to tell her: her husband, the man she loved, father of her child, was going to bring the flames of Retribution to Merovingen and skewer her through her child-belly with his sword in the process.

And there was nothing she could do to stop it, because she'd seen it in her vision, and what she saw always came true.

SMUGGLER'S GOLD

by C.J. Cherryh

"No, no, and *no,* you damned fool!" Steel on steel. Stamp and thump of advance and retreat. "*Dammit!*"

The boy lunged, Mondragon diverted the attack with a minuscule motion of his own and as the boy attempted the second, left-handed stab—

"*Damn* you!" He made the hit, dead-middle of the boy's unprotected gut and when the boy doubled and backed, followed step and step and step, beating the foil-guard left and right of the boy's undefended face, hit the boy in the side, kneed him in the groin and smashed him hard with the guard before he felt the ebb of his temper and saw the boy hit the wall—saw the shock in Raj Takahashi's bleeding face and stopped himself—stopped with a clutch of panic and a sudden weakness in his knees and his gut as the boy tried to keep his feet and get his guard up.

"Damned *fool!*" he snarled, and beat the blade down. "Damned *fool,* who was in line? *Who was in line?*"

The boy gasped for breath and shook his head, sweat flying from his hair as Mondragon hit him again, the guard of his blade against the boy's shoulder, not hard: but it staggered him. The boy's face was white, his eyes staring in panic.

Mondragon stopped himself, then, turned his back on a boy with practice-weapons in hand, felt that hazard in his gut and didn't walk away, just stood there. *Come on, boy,* do *it,* try *it—*

With a lump in his throat, too many dark memories tumbling one past the other.

For God's sake, do it. . . .

But the weapon-points were wrapped, the boy was bewildered as much as hurt, the boy *loved* him, dammit, too damned many people loved him, no matter that he killed them. It was a punishment from God that people went on loving him, it was the hell he lived in; it was part of that hell that sometimes he thought he could turn it all around and be content in it.

"Tom?" the boy asked, a faint, shaky voice. "Tom, I'm *sorry—*"

Not a blow in the back. One in the gut.

"Tom?"

He couldn't talk. He couldn't move for a moment. But the boy was in pain, and of course the boy thought the wrong was on his own side, of course Raj would, it was only Jones who ever accused Mondragon of his sins, sometimes yelled at him and sometimes, deservedly, hit out at him and called him a fool.

It was Jones who had kept him sane; and it was thinking about Jones that made him crazy now, because she had taken on his enemies, mistaking them for hers, that they had touched *her* and threatened *her* and that he had no way to stop her and no way to protect her—

It was Jones who *understood* where he got the rent money, in bed with Marina Kamat; it was Jones who was out there on the canals—running what she called the dark ways—running God knew what cargo, to get the gold she had brought him—two coins on the kitchen table this morning, just left there—when only Jones could have done it.

A year's living for a canal-rat. A year's living, in the terms she knew. . . .

Because for Jones' sake, for this damned *boy* she had dragged in out of the canals, —he had spent everything he had, and he had gone much further than that—he had spent money he did *not* have, had spent the gold Vega Boregy had given him, gold that ultimately had come from Anastasi Kalugin himself—

—because he had not been able to fail the only truly deep, outrageous favor Jones had ever really asked of him.

—because he was a damned fool who couldn't tell her no, even for her own good, because Jones' damnable sense of honor wouldn't let *her* stop looking for a young fool, and she would never understand a man who had no sense of honor left at all—

—because he had discovered then that he had one thing left to lose: he had her; and having her know him the way he was, and walk away from him in disgust, was more than he could bear. Jones only knew how to win, only understood Today, and Now; and in Jones' thinking, Tomorrow got along as best it could. She could snag him into thinking that way too, for a day or two, while the fever was on her, and while things were desperate—

But the bills came due. Finally the bills came due.

"M'ser Tom?" the boy asked, closer to his back.

But the boy went away then, slow footsteps that paused and paused again; and finally ended up at the side of the room where they had left their coats and their other gear. He heard the boy gathering up his belongings. He felt the pain in the air. There was no need for it. There was no justice in it.

"I'm trying to save your *life,*" he said without looking to see how Raj took it. "Dammit, you think it's smart to redouble an attack without a parry, smart damn rule-breaking duelist kind of trick! You don't give a damn about timing because you're too damn smart, aren't you?"

"No, m'ser. . . ."

"There's always somebody faster. There's always somebody with a move you haven't seen. You take care of your opponent's blade *first,* boy, you don't ignore it, you don't ignore *anything* that's not dealt with, not his *blade,* not his *knee,* not the chance that he could have a gun in his pocket or a partner coming up on your back, you hear me, boy?"

"Yes, m'ser."

"Think about that."

A long silence. A meek: "Yes, m'ser."

Eventually he heard the door open and close. He worried about the boy. They got night-rent of the salle, Raj's arrangement, Raj's money—another Kamat largesse, that only wanted a soul. . . .

Raj had to go out on the canals. Raj had to walk out of here alone, when there were people enough who had reason to know Raj was his, when there were far too many people who would find Raj Takahashi a much easier target.

He had to stop it, that was what it came down to. He had to stop it happening—to the boy—and to Jones.

Touchy going now—here near Hafiz's place, which was too close to damn-'em Megarys . . . a body had to let be on one Obligation for a while and take care of another, and it was damn bad business that one Obligation put her so close to the other—Hafiz's brewery lying as it did uncomfortably inside hostile territory.

So Altair Jones poled her skip with an eye to the

bridges and the overhangs and kept herself to the shadows where she could. She never ran a tight schedule on her special pick-ups—"I ain't no poleboatman," had been her word to The Hafiz, long since, "an' I ain't makin' any damn schedule. You want your special barrels to get where they're goin' and I want me to get where I'm goin' an' neither one's goin' t' do that if you got any damn notion of gettin' 'round what I'm telling ye, hirin' some other skip, either."

All of which old Hafiz had seen the sense in—Hafiz's businessman instincts being one thing and his under-the-counter business giving him better sense than to do what she warned him against—sending his goods out on any regular basis, with her or any combination of hire-ons.

So she made her runs in some trust of the old bastard—even when she had dropped the word on him lately that she was running more than the usual trade that passed between himself and Moghi.

And some of the things old Hafiz was into were things Moghi had too much sense to touch; and some of the things old Hafiz ran in his uptown barrels were things she suspected she didn't want to know about.

Damn fool, was what her Mama told her, in Mama's way—Mama having been dead a number of years now, and her knowing Mama a lot better than she had ever done when she had been alive. Retribution Jones had known a lot about the dark ways of Merovingen, Retribution had done a lot of things she had advised her daughter against doing—

Retribution Jones had had plenty to do just to keep an unplanned-for kid alive; and people in the Trade had criticized her when she had made her runs with that kid tucked into the ship's little hidey, gone places where shots flew and the blacklegs were hot after her, them and certain rivals in the Trade. . . .

But Retribution had never been one to shirk a responsibility either, and no matter to Mama that little Altair was a rapist's kid; that man had turned up floating one morning soon after, sure enough, that had been Obligation Number One, and Retribution never let that kind of debt go unpaid; but Altair had been Obligation Number Two, of a different kind, and Retribution, who had had ways to rid herself of her second problem, that had surely made itself known in a few-odd weeks . . . had undoubtedly sat on this same skip's deck and counted her coins and thought about the midwives and the drug-shops that could take care of that Number Two Obligation, cheap and fast.

Dunno why you didn't, Altair thought to her Mama sometimes, when things got bad, or when she got thoughtful. What'd you owe *me?*

And all her Mama's ghost would say (settling in her favorite position at the skip's bow, the same battered cap on her head, and shining-like, sometimes, like the Angel Himself) was: I dunno either, t' tell the truth.

So They could say what They liked about things Mama had done, taking a kid the dark ways, hiding a kid under the half-deck while she risked both their necks, but that was the second best thing Mama had ever done for her besides let her be born, —that Mama had known what it took to run alone, and Mama had taught her—taught her when she didn't even know she was teaching her, taught her in the way the skip moved and the water rocked her, taught her when the moment was to hide and when to run, and taught her, while she hid below, how you talked to old Hafiz and how you handled trouble when you got in narrow waters . . .

So here you are, Mama said to her, from the bow—Mama sat where nobody could, just showing off, because Mama didn't weigh anything and Mama wouldn't make the bow drop. *Didn't I tell you? Got yourself a man, and here you are, right in it, ain't you? Wasn't content with just some damn canaler that'd go short a few pennies, ney, ney, ye got yourself a hightowner, didn't ye?*

Shut up, Mama.

Mmmn, now ye get touchy.

I ain't.

Where's his help with the Megarys? Huh?

Jones took in her breath, shoved hard with the pole, knew with a little cold chill at her gut that she had missed a beat or two, watching around her—and she damn near scraped a piling, sorting herself out, missing the push of the current, she was so rattled. Mama had stopped being friendly. It wasn't Mama anymore, it was Retribution, it was Retribution the way she had never known her, so she was halfway afraid when Mama settled in and started talking to her—

Kill 'em, Mama said.

And she didn't want to see her Mama's face right then, didn't want to look where she was going, because Mama was so much like her that old canalers sometimes forgot which was which, Mama's pose there at the bow was so much like her it was like looking at a reflection, except when her Mama talked like that she could never see the face, just the hat and the hair: the rest was shadow, no matter where shadow really ought to be, and she was afraid to be in the dark with her, and afraid to go under the bridge-shadow with her sitting there—

Like Mama could trade places with her and take her over and *be* her from then on, Mama could get the Megarys that way, Mama could lie there in Mondragon's bed and look out of her at him and put her arms around him and Mondragon wouldn't know what was wrong—

(But he would know something was. Nobody could come up on him unawares—)

(Except he wouldn't know what to do then. He liked her too much. He did too much for her. He wasn't like the men her Mama had warned her about, her Mama had never met anybody like Tom Mondragon, that was why she kept having this feeling her Mama wanted to *be* her—her Mama wanted the life she had given her—wanted it *back,* wanted to run things, because her daughter wasn't smart enough—)

—But it's my life, Mama! It ain't yours, *get off my skip!*

Just as she went under Hafiz Bridge, and the dark was all around her, and her Mama's hands touched her, cold as Det-water, and her Mama said:

Ye're a damn ingrate, Altair. . . . See if I help ye after this. See if I help ye. . . .

She came out of shadow. Her Mama wasn't there anymore, just the water with the sheen of Hafiz Brewery's light on it, and the damned weed that piled up like scum on the canals in the still spots of the Tidewater canals, water that broke out in rings that laced and spread, fish feeding there.

Life. And deathangels.

She had helped those seeds. *Purify the canals*, Rif had sworn to her, word of honor. From a Jane.

Make the water clean.

Stop the fevers, the kind that had killed Mama. That was how the Janes had bought her help.

Do-goods are trouble, Mama used to say. They're the worst trouble. Revenantists got that one right. Maybe there ain't no karma, but there's sure as hell consequences.

So there were hers—the lantern-light shining on the weed, and on the steps that led up out of the water, at Hafiz's half-drowned door.

She pulled up there and found the ring that held the rope under the water, she tugged it free, and tied it to her skip's stern-ties. Then she rang the bell at the garde-porte, waited there, with the skip's sides all fouled in weed and the small, soft pop of fish feeding around her—till steps inside and a little rattle of the garde-porte meant she was seen.

Hafiz opened up then, chain running back, the watergate swinging back to let a skip into the low, black arch where a body had to duck fast and shove hard.

Not the regular door, but the Old Gate, that only opened to certain boats, at certain times.

On old man Hafiz's very special business.

There were boats to have hired—but anyone on the water might have carried word to Jones. Tonight Mondragon had no wish to have Jones know where he was going. There were the upper-level bridges where a m'ser of the class that belonged there might walk unremarked—except at this hour, night-guards were at their posts and gates along the balconies were shut and guarded, the occupants of the top-tier residencies, particularly in the midtown, defending peace and quiet by night.

So Mondragon took the low tiers, the canalside, as far as Fishmarket, where honest canalers at night-tie clustered along the banks, then climbed the dark and sinister web of steps to the middle tier, where a handful of walkers eyed one another with suspicion or predatory estimation. It was the hour for thieves and assignations, for banditry and burglary, and, on the water, for the honest night-traffic of huge barges and canaler-craft which could not pass in day-traffic . . . those and smaller boats like Jones' skip, running night deliveries—

So she told him, *—night deliveries.*

Deliveries for more than Moghi's Tavern, that was certain.

On trade that could win a canal-rat pay in gold, when copper was the coin of trade on the water, and Jones had, when he had met her, owned no more than her skip-freighter and one change of secondhand clothes.

Damn her.

He walked quickly along the boards, off Fishmarket's second tier and onto the walkways, wrapped in the cloak that spring chill still made ordinary enough on a rain-threatening night, with his ears and eyes alert not only for attack but for followers—

And that way led across the bridge from Ventani to Calliste and up to Golden Bridge by Archangel, where the Grand, if he had gone that way, followed its serpentine course up among the great Houses, past the front of Boregy.

But he had no need to go there, where gate-guards might have known him—and where Boregy would be only too glad to see him. There was a seagoing ship moored in Archangel, as it was from time to time, and from time to time docked down at Rimmon Isle—a black, tall-sided yacht which came and went where its owner chose, sometimes even to sea (but no one knew where its owner went at such times, or whether he ever truly absented himself from Merovingen.)

There was always a watch at night, on that yacht's deck, and beside her moorings on the wide Archangel walkway, a blackleg watch—the owner being, among other things, the advocate militiar, and this particular blackleg being no part of the civil department.

This particular blackleg knew him; and piped a signal to the deck. A head appeared over the rim, shadow against a cloud-shadowed sky, and the blackleg said to his partner: "Mondragon."

By the back ways of the Old Grand, which had been the Grand's course through the city before the Great Quake—but which now was a shallow, sluggish channel along dilapidated fronts of fading isles—and finally back to the open waters of the modern Grand, which led down to the present Harbor—or up again, past Hanging Bridge and past huge, three-tiered Fishmarket—

Nothing unusual for Altair Jones, except not turning cross-channel at Fishmarket, and not tying up at Moghi's, whose light at this hour was only a single watch-lantern, whose windows were shuttered and whose door was shut—in those few hours when, inside, Moghi's boys would be sweeping and scouring and getting ready for the breakfast trade.

Moghi would skin her, sure, that was what Jones was thinking: she passed that point with a little flinch, the same as if Moghi could dream she was going past, far across the width of the Grand—not that Moghi had ever outright said no independent cargo-carrying for Hafiz; not that Moghi had any right to say a thing like that except he paid her—but Moghi had a Policy about problems, and Moghi's problems went slip! splash! into Harborbottom, and Moghi paid her damned well (but not well enough for the kind of trouble Mondragon got himself into) and expected loyalty.

So she skinned past as fast as her pole could carry her, skirting the sterns of boats at night-tie, slipping along under bridge-shadow and cursing when the low whump-whump of a barge-engine announced the passage of a barge near as wide as the channel and as high as Fishmarket's bottom-tier. She eyed it coming, a shadow in shadow, under the flickering skies, a kind of on-coming wall that could ride a skip down and grind it to splinters.

She hove over against the side then, racked the pole and grabbed the boat-hook, hauling herself in by the pilings, holding there with the friction of bare feet on board while the wash from the monster made the skip buck and pitch.

There was the engine to use, the damn plants had brought that much to Merovingen, you could still the stuff to alcohol if you had room for the rig in your hidey or on your deck if you were a fool, which she didn't, and wasn't, and everybody was nervous about it anyway, not knowing how the priests were going to come down on the question whether it was Tech or not to let plants rot, and whether you could get hauled in for it and hung (the real question being, a practical Adventist knew, whether the importers of boat-fuel were influential enough, and that was Eber, and damned sure they had pull with the College)—

But fuel was cheaper and there was nothing too unusual about a skip using its engine nowadays, at least on the Grand where there was always chop and where the bottom was tricky; and especially at night, where a body could be more anonymous and no priest and no blackleg could say, Who's that? Got to have a source, don't she?

She was real tempted, standing there alternately fending off and holding to the bank against the heave of the water, she was real tempted to cut loose and run under the engines tonight, because it was also hell and away faster, and she had a terrible nervous feeling tonight—maybe it was just skinning past Moghi's, maybe it was the rain that was going to cut loose and make a nasty night, maybe it was thinking about Mondragon, and thinking about him waiting for her, and waiting and brooding, as he tended to do too much of lately.

Damn, he was going to be mad about that coin, she knew he was; and she hadn't wanted to be there today, and she was scared to be there tonight, but she was scared not to be, too—one image hanging in her mind, him sitting on the edge of the bed and saying once, arms on knees and head hanging, "Jones, I'm tired, I'm just damn tired—"

Not body-tired. Soul-tired. She knew the way he said it. It made her cold inside, because it was not like Mondragon to say a thing like that, or to look like that.

She was tired, Lord, she was tired, and he couldn't the hell quit on her. Not when it was her who had brought the damn kids to him and her who had let him get in moral debt to them, and damn-'im *Mondragon* had never told her he was spending to the bottom of his funds, Mondragon was rich, he always told her he had money, he was always throwing it around like there was no tomorrow, and she hadn't known there was an end to it—

Hadn't known Mondragon was such a damnfool as to spend Boregys' money.

Because *she* had put a debt on him.

And somebody had grabbed her and held *her* for some kind of cause, and she knew damn well it was Megarys, but she had her notions it was somebody else behind it, and Boregy was the likeliest—Boregy trying to put the scare in Mondragon and trying to get their money back, or another piece of his soul in trade for it—

That was what had jumped into her mind when he had said that, his voice so shaky and so near breaking down—that he was out of things to spend, and it was tired of living that he meant, and that the nights were the worst times to leave him, the dark times when things looked worst to him and nothing had its right shape. . . .

And somehow, against the wall with the wake of the barge battering at her she had a sudden bad feeling about being out here tonight, about the weather, about the trouble they were in and all, and how if something happened to her in this damn mess of Hafiz's it was going to happen to Mondragon, and how every minute Mondragon was out of her sight his enemies could come at him or his own despair could.

So she racked the hook as soon as the chop had died back and she let the paint scrape on the bow, same as if it was herself being rubbed raw, while she skipped back on the halfdeck and threw open the engine cover and started cranking her over.

Chug. Chug.

"Jones!" somebody hissed, and she turned around with her hand on her knife and that knife in her hand in a hurry.

Kid on the bank. *Raj* on the bank.

"What in hell d'you want?" she asked, and the boy skipped down into her well. "Get off!" He was right down where barrels were that she had no intention of anybody messing with.

But he paid no attention to that. He scrambled nimble as a skit along her well and up onto the half-deck and said, "Jones, Mondragon's slipped us, gone on Kalugin's ship—"

"Ye damned fool!" she hissed, grabbing for a shoulder, but Raj writhed out of her way and she only got sweater.

"I swear, I swear," Raj was babbling, out of breath, "I was with 'im, like you said, only he got mad and sent me off and I was following him, only—only he went straight uptown—straight to that ship—I'm sorry! I'm sorry! What c'd I do?"

She thought about Raj Takahashi's guts on a hook, that was what she thought of; she thought about Mondragon uptown, gone to Kalugin, and she felt sick at her stomach.

"—only," Raj was saying, "I come over Fishmarket and I saw you—" A gasp for air, a feeble attempt to disengage her hand from his sweater. "It hasn't been ten minutes—"

A second weight hit her well, a smaller kid clambered his way aft, rocking the skip: but that was guessable.

Both of 'em.

"Where'd you come from?" she asked Denny.

"I seen my brother," Denny said anxiously and came closer, put out his hand. "I dunno what he done, but you let 'im go, let 'im go, hear?"

Scared as she had ever heard Denny Takahashi.

And she realized she had a knife in one fist and Raj Takahashi's sweater in the other. So she let go, scared herself, and said: "Go to hell. Both of ye." And shoved her knife back in the sheath and felt the scrape of wood and stone. "Damn, get off my skip!"

"Where're you going?" Raj asked. "Jones, where're you going?"

"Where ye *think* I'm goin'?" She put the engine cover down, shoved Raj out of her way and grabbed up the boat-pole from the rack, half of a mind to shove both passengers in the canal. "Goin' t' get 'im *back's* where I'm goin', before he does some other damn fool thing. . . ."

She had a lump in her throat, she had another one in her chest, where her heart kept doing doubletime, and Raj said, damned obvious, "You can't get him out of there, nobody can get him out of there."

"I c'n be there," she said. No engine. Too damn noisy.

And Hafiz's damn cargo, that was worth her life if she didn't come through uptown, to Hafiz's anxious hightowner clients.

Damn, damn!

"Ye can *pole*," she snarled at Raj, who lingered with Denny trying to pull on him. "Dammit, ye can pole, an' if you foul me I'll drown ye both. *Move!*"

It was without the sword, without the cloak, without the small knife he kept in his boot, and in the company of two strong men—that Mondragon came down the steps and down the electric-lighted companionway and, ducking his head, into Anastasi Kalugin's private quarters.

"Well," Anastasi said, in his soft, slow way, and Mondragon took him in, smallish, thirtyish man in a dressing-gown, but you forgot whether he was tall or short, you forgot everything when you looked Anastasi in the face: pale skin, black hair, black, close-clipped beard, so, so immaculate no matter what the hour; and looking him in the eyes made you think of a killer, because he was; and he was the governor's youngest son, and he was Boregy's ally; and he was the one who held the highest call on Mondragon's often-mortgaged soul.

"You failed me," Mondragon said for openers, which was a foolish thing, maybe, but it was also true, and it was the only attack he had, when Boregy had a kill-order out on him and very likely it had come from here, from Anastasi himself. He could hear Boregy saying: *Mondragon's become a liability. . . .*

And Anastasi saying: *Take care of him.*

"Failed you?" Anastasi's dark brow arched, and Mondragon felt the presence of the guards behind him, knowing there was a weapon back there, sure that there was; and knowing that he could deal with it, if there were a percentage in it, which there wasn't. Nothing had a percentage any longer, except Anastasi's continued patronage.

"I told you," Mondragon said, "my price is Jones' safety. She hasn't been safe. The Sword got past you. And I spent your money."

The pole found no bottom, and Jones whirled and grabbed the back of Raj's sweater a second time, grabbed him and sat him down hard on the half-deck. He kept the pole, had it in both hands, give the fool that much.

"I—" was all he said, about two or three times, because when old Det went shy of bottom, you could go right in.

"Damned if I got time to fish you out," she muttered, and, seeing the skip across the broad part of the Grand, ran the pole in again and shoved. "Hin, dammit."

"I got it," Denny said, but Raj elbowed him out of the way of grabbing the boat-hook and Raj got up and kept going, breathing like a beached fish.

"Ware, ware," she said, "sit down." Denny sat, crouched in the well behind the barrels.

"What I do," she said, between breaths of her own, "is I let both you two off at Porfirio and you go on up to Borg and skit right on up close as you can to that thing. And I'm goin' on up the Spur Loop to Dundee, and back by way of Archangel to Borg, right past that ship to tie-up at Borg East and wait, so you'll see me if I pass—and if either of ye even thinks the name of Dundee after tonight I'll skin you alive, hear?"

"I hear you," Raj said.

"Denny?" That being the one to watch.

"Yey."

"You watch for 'im, you watch that boat close, and

you leech on and you don't let 'im go if you see 'im. But if there's trouble—you know where I am, you know how to find me, one of you—and I'm stayin' just long enough to drop my load."

"We got it," Raj said, panting.

"Rack 'er," she said, and the boy not understanding plain instructions: "Rack 'er, dammit! Get ready!"

She grabbed the hook out of his hands, shoved it at Denny one-handed and kicked at Raj to clear him out of her cross-deck path.

"Git!" she hissed. Raj skipped for the well and ducked the sweep of her pole; she grounded it and cursed, missing a skip at tie-up by a scant pole-length as she came in and skimmed along Porfirio East. "Git!"

They left, Denny first and Raj second, with a force that rocked the skip.

She shoved with the pole, leaned for all she was worth and cleared an oncoming piling and a couple of night-bound skips by less than that pole-length, skimmed right past the stern close enough to touch it, heart pounding, sweat pouring down her sides as she poled back along Porfirio's side.

She had to get the job done with, *had* to, that was all: no safety for her or for Mondragon if she failed it, but, oh, Lord, leaving him to Kalugin, leaving him to two fool boys who'd let him go off there in the first place—

She glided under the shadow of Porfirio Low Bridge, poling for all she was worth till she was clear of the boys. Then she drifted a bit at Cantry South, flung up the engine cover, pumped up the tank and got her going.

Damned noisy. If Hafiz knew she was running that engine on this job, he'd more than skin her, that was the truth, or Hafiz's boys would, more to the point, rough as Moghi's and twice as mean.

Not saying what Dundee would—the hightown folk who'd paid for this load by some means maybe gold and maybe just favors. Lord and Hafiz and the Dundee knew—and a canal-rat didn't ask.

No asking what was in the barrels, either. *Not* the usual stuff. Whiskey was what the bill said, she knew that. And it wasn't.

Beyond that you just took your precautions.

Brandy swirled into the glass at Mondragon's elbow, and the servant withdrew. Mondragon picked up the glass and drank, careless of poison—careless of the silk scarf with which the servant on his left was binding his wrist to the heavy chair arm—"Mild precaution," Anastasi called it, and Mondragon had consented quietly, acknowledged the hospitality of the drink with a lift of his brandy glass.

"So what happened?" was Anastasi's quietly patient question—but Anastasi was always quiet, and Mondragon sipped the brandy, steadied his nerves and said, once the servants and the guards had retreated from the cabin and left them in privacy:

"Magruder grabbed Jones, put it to me that it'd happen again if I didn't double on you. So I'm here."

"On whose behalf?"

"Mine. Hers. You told me she'd be safe. What happened?"

He succeeded at least in making Anastasi think a moment; but not in making Anastasi give a damn—nothing could do that, except what bore on Anastasi's own immediate wants, and Anastasi's own longrange plans, and he was no longer sure if they remotely included an ex-Sword agent.

"Obviously we slipped," Anastasi said. "But then —we can't be everywhere. Perhaps you'd care to have us bring this Jones in. *Then* we could guarantee her safety. Or perhaps you'd care to be more active against your own enemies. We've never forbidden you."

A chill touched him, the thought of assassinating Magruder—killing Karl Fon's Trade Deputy—*that* would make Anastasi's life easier; and Anastasi could ask that, and equally well have them arrested, then, and handed over to the Justiciary, the solely culpable party, with every motive in the world.

Anastasi might ask that. Anastasi might simply *do* that, and lay the bloody knife at his doorstep.

Or implicate Jones along with him—as might well happen in any case of his arrest. There was nothing Anastasi might not do—if it served Anastasi's ambition, or cleaned up loose ends.

"I did something else," Mondragon said. "I agreed. That's why I'm here."

"We know about Magruder. We know about Chamoun. There's very little you can tell us—except what you did with the money."

"Used it," Mondragon said.

"Searching for a boy." Anastasi turned the glass between his hands. "Not your usual taste, is it?"

"A Kamat client," Mondragon said, as composedly as he could. "Have you found *that* thread?"

Anastasi's brow lifted, a question.

"I won't suppose," Mondragon said, "you've missed the fact that m'sera Kamat pays my rent."

"And that you've hired out to her brother. Yes. Of course. A *financial* arrangement. An *informational* arrangement. You've betrayed Magruder and Chamoun to Boregy, Kamat to Boregy—do I guess, Boregy and Magruder to Kamat?"

"To certain extents. Boregy knows how much I betray him."

"Boregy wants to kill you. Do you know?"

"I'm not surprised," he said, quite, quite steadily.

"I'm not sure that's in your interest. But that's why I pursued the Kamat business, that's why I'm willing to double for the Sword, and that's why I'm willing to double again: that's why I came here."

Again the lift of the brow. "With what coin?"

"A warning about Boregy."

Anastasi smiled a predator's smile. "Asking what?"

"Absolution."

"Without warning Vega Boregy? How shall I do that?"

That *was* the sticky part.

"No answer?" Anastasi asked.

"I've no doubt," Mondragon said, "Vega suspects your suspicion. He's in too much, too deeply, he knows your contacts—I don't think there's any likelihood he suspects you might know, or will know, and he's preparing against that—through his other contacts. Magruder. Chamoun. —Ito. —Kamat hates him.

One hook after the other—all his pieces.

"Does this lead to the boy? And the money?"

"The boy went missing. I had the funds—I used—certain contacts, certain expensive contacts. It was possible, quite possible, it was Boregy or it was the Sword, and the boy—the boy involved my access to Kamat. Which was essential."

"*Was* it Boregy's action?"

Mondragon felt a trickle of sweat start, a little tickling, and heard the boom of thunder outside, the creak of the yacht against its buffers. "Even the boy doesn't know." A lie. But a good lie was almost all truth—except in the uncheckable points. "He was being stalked. He ran. We found him—Jones and I—found him in the swamp. Likeliest—likeliest, given it was the swamp, it was the Sword. Boregy's agents aren't that adept. Whatever it was—it was my invitation to Kamat. I've become trusted there—which is what I intended."

"What you intended. Where did *you* take the initiative?"

"When I knew my life was in danger. When I knew I knew too much in Boregy. When I knew I had to jump elsewhere, and I wasn't sure I could make it worth your while. Now I can. Now I know names, faces, dates, details: Kamat's—and Boregy's. Now you have your excuse to keep me alive."

"And what would that be?"

"That I've credit inside Kamat. That I've become too valuable. That you'd take it very hard—if an accident befell me—or mine."

Anastasi stared at him long and hard, with never a change in expression. "You're quite clever," Anastasi said. "Quite clever. But maybe there's nothing Kamat can offer me."

"You've lost Boregy," Mondragon said, conscious, too conscious, of the silk band that would hamper him entirely too much, and of Jones as much hostage as she had been in Magruder's hands—more, because Anastasi was her protection, the *only* side that offered that, when the others offered only threats. "If Boregy, then be careful of Nikolaev. And that's very major. But Kamat's organization has countering possibilities; and Kamat's interests are Kamat, and trade, and surviving—in Boregy's displeasure."

Anastasi leaned back in his chair. Smiled at him, not pleasantly. "How do you prove that? And how *many* times have you doubled, now, dear Thomas? And how do you prove *that*?"

"I can't," Mondragon said. "But I don't need to."

"And how is that?"

"Because you have the resources. Because the Sword *won't* guarantee Jones' safety. Boregy won't, certainly, and Kamat can't. And nothing else matters. *Nothing* else."

"Maybe that makes you dangerous."

"No. It makes me ultimately reliable. As long as you know where she is—you'll know whether I'm lying. It's just that simple."

"And will I know whether you've sold me out?"

"You already know."

"This kind of hostage is best kept under key."

Mondragon shook his head. The ship groaned against the buffers, rocked to the assault of wind. "No," he said quietly, rationally, "because she won't live that way. Because that's her condition. And mine."

"You think you're that valuable."

"Everyone who deals with me thinks I'm for sale. I am. And you can be sure you've got the high bid. That's more than you can say about your personal staff. *Isn't* it?"

The Lord was plainly against such undertakings and proved it, with a torrent from the skies and a torrent from bad guttering on the watergate side of high and mighty Dundee, that had poured down into her well, so she was ankle-deep in water, sweating and swearing and heaving barrels up by hand, because fancy Dundee didn't have a loading ramp, the servants just carried everything up the stone water-stairs.

And there was just one of him, and he went up the stairs and he disappeared and he came back down the stairs after another barrel, and he checked the numbers off against the bill.

He was damned mad when he came down and found her stacking barrels off on the steps.

"Don't you be getting in a hurry. This gate doesn't open till I have a count."

"I ain't hidin' any in my pockets!" Jones hissed at him, and thumped another one down on top of the load. "I'm dumpin' them, on your step or in the slip, I ain't got no preference, and you sign this damn sheet an' open that damn gate, or *I'll* go up them stairs myself an' ask the Dundee herself."

"It's fourth watch, you damned fool, keep your voice down!"

"Sign it! You got your damn count!"

"I want the numbers."

"Dammit to hell, here, *here*, I'll lift 'em, you check off the damn numbers."

"I'm not sure you'll be satisfactory."

"I ain't sure you ain't trying to hold me up. And Hafiz don't like that, either. And you better be damn sure it'll get back, if that paper don't get signed right now, and that gate don't come open damn fast."

Silence then. Sullen silence. Her teeth wanted to chatter. She had a notion a fool canal-rat could drop right out of sight in Dundee.

"He give me two hours," she said, "and then I got to have this list back, man, or he starts movin' on the thing, and you don't want to see that, do ye? I know sure and away your m'sera don't want any to-do on this order."

He snatched the paper. And signed it. Fast.

Rain came down in buckets, and if it did one thing, it made two boys harder to see, just a couple of lumps, Raj figured, among the lumps of debris along canalside, up against the massive side of Borg Isle, where Kalugin's yacht rode groaning at her moorings.

"Guard's gone t' cover," Denny said cheerfully, a warm knot of elbows and knees hard against him.

Raj sneezed and smothered it.

"Ties ain't guarded," Denny said.

"No!"

"Wind'd sweep 'er clear about," Denny said.

"Tom's all right," Raj said fiercely, and tried not to shiver. It hurt. A lot of things did, some physical.

"He could run for it."

"He went on there!" Raj said. "He did it himself, he'll take care of it."

"Then what're we doing here?"

Good question.

"Waiting," Raj said.

"F' what?"

"For whatever Tom needs," Raj snapped, and clenched his arms and shut his jaw tight, soaked through and feeling all the aches when the muscles went tight.

"How we goin' to—?"

"Shut up!" Raj said. So Denny shut up.

Fact was, Raj was scanning the dockside himself, and thinking that if worst came to worst it might be time to slip the moorings, —but that big yacht turned askew could take out a bridge or crush half a dozen skips and skiffs moored down at Borg East, and sleeping people could die down there, kids and babies and all.

And that set him to shivering for good and all.

"He might not *come* out," Denny said. "Kalugin could send 'im right to the Justiciary over there."

—Behind the Signeury, where the Kalugins' enemies went, and they chopped off your head in the basement if you were hightowner like Tom, they didn't hang you like some thief, just chopped you with an axe and threw the pieces in the Harbor. . . .

That was what you got when you got in with hightowners, and you didn't even need to be guilty of anything, you didn't even get a trial, except down in the Signeury basement, and they wrote what they wanted about it and that was that.

All you had to do was get afoul of the Kalugins or

the Kalugins' friends, and Boregy was enough—them with their money and their influence.

Money could buy lives in Merovingen. Money bought a doctor—or an assassin; or a judge; and Raj Takahashi sat there thinking about Granther, and about mama and about how if he was with Granther in Nev Hettek Granther could buy his way, (except the Takahashi honor said that wasn't the way, except Granther didn't send him the money Tom needed, Granther sent him the daggers—silk and steel. Silk and steel.)

Think Tom wouldn't have pounced on it faster, if it was gold.

Didn't do a thing for him. Didn't help.

Money would.

"S'pose that we could get onto the deck?" Denny asked.

"No," Raj said.

"Well, what're we goin' t' do?"

"We're not doing anything!" Raj hissed, overwhelmed with frustration. "There's nothing we *can* do, but wait."

Marina.

Marina with her money. That could.

He still winced, thinking of the bedroom at Petrescu, thinking about Marina—

And knowing, dammit, that Tom didn't love her, knowing that Tom didn't even want her—Tom did it to get money from her, Tom didn't want him to know that, but he had ears and Lord knew Denny had. He hadn't told that part to Granther in his letter. He was ashamed about that, he was mad about that—

But if it was dishonest money—

If it was, it had still bought a Takahashi neck, and Tom for honor's sake had risked *his* neck, and spent everything for a fool in trouble—

And Raj Takahashi had been that fool, that Tom bought out of his mess, by means that Raj didn't even want to think about; and Tom was in that ship because he was in trouble with Kalugin, in ways that he didn't know how to think about, and when he had written to Granther, Granther had sent him a reminder of honor.

He wasn't sure right now it was enough; or maybe a Takahashi, being a fool, had gotten himself in a mess there wasn't an honorable way out of, and you had to hire somebody like Tom, or you had to *be* somebody like Tom—

(There's always somebody faster. There's always somebody with a move you haven't seen.)

(Think about that.)

(*Think* about that—)

"We c'd divert th' guard," Denny said. "I c'd pertend t' fall in—"

Raj bashed Denny with his fist.

"What'd ye do *that* for? I—"

And grabbed his shoulder and jerked him hard, toward a movement on the ladder.

Somebody coming down.

Tom.

Denny sneezed and smothered it, while Tom descended the stairs, one guard above, the one on the dock coming out of the doorway he was sheltering in. They talked, a few words, Tom flipped his cloak over his shoulder and walked off the other way. Toward Borg East, and the Grand.

"Damn," Denny said in dismay, "man's in a hurry."

"*I'll* tag 'im,' Raj said; but Denny grabbed onto him.

"There's a guard we got to get by! Ain't your kind of stuff! Go fer Jones!"

Raj gulped rain and air, thought for the length of that breath about older brothers and precedence and how he *wanted* to be on Tom's case, wanted a chance to do right, pay things back—

But doing right meant letting kid brother risk his neck on the rooftops, risk losing sight of Tom doing it if they didn't hurry.

Doing right meant him slipping off down Borg to the bridge and hoping to the Lord and all the Ancestors that he didn't miss sight of Jones in the dark and the storm, or that she didn't pass too far from the bank to see him.

"Get!" he said, Jones' unintentional echo, and they split, himself down the walk and Denny with him for a brief way that left Tom completely unwatched.

Fools, he kept thinking, fools the way they had set it up, of *course* Tom was going out Borg East, they should have split from the start, should have posted themselves separately, but he had been so damned afraid of Denny doing some damn fool thing, and they had *had* to be in reach of Jones, this side of the guard and the ship—

He made the bridge, pounded across the rain-slick wood and ran, squishing and splashing through the gusts, his sweater twice its length and slopping around him with every step.

A quick drop, Jones had said. It was *long* past that.

"Back 'er up!" Jones cried, while m'sera fancy Dundee's nightman and a couple of the kitchen help fussed and fidgeted with the watergate wheel.

Stuck.

Fuss and fidget, two fools consulting with the chief fool.

"You got the damn gear fouled," she yelled, waking echoes in the barrel vault of the slip. "*F' Lord's sake, back 'er up a little, your damn wheel's off-center!"*

"Quiet!" the nightman said. "You'll wake the house!"

"I'll give you 'wake the house!' " It was too much. Jones flung her pole down in the well, flung up the lid on the number two drop-bin and grabbed her hammer. She jumped for the narrow ledge where the three servants were trying to tear the slotted wheel to flinders, grabbed the handle of the wheel right past one servant's arm and said, "Here! Back 'er up, fool, let me put 'er in line."

While rain was raising the level of the water in the slip and they were ankle-deep where they were standing.

"Get back!" the nightman said, shoving her hand off.

She brought the hammer up. "You back off, man, or I'll whack somethin' else into line. You got me stalled here, you give me trouble—"

"You don't come into this house and make threats!"

"I'll be givin' *my* report too, fancyboy, and I'll be givin' it to places you won't like if you don't back that damn chain. *Pull* it!"

"Pull it where?"

"Pull on the damn chain!"

"It's stuck!"

"With your pretty pink *hands*, ye damn fool! Haul 'er! Yoss! Ye got it!"

The wheel backed, she wobbled the wooden slot wheel with her hand, wobbled the metal cog-wheel, found the play in the metal wheel and whacked it, *clang!-clang!-clang!* while the nightman yelled about the noise.

"Noise, hell!" *Clang-clang!* "There she goes! *Pull*, now!"

The wheel turned, the chain rattled, the watergate began to move.

She splashed along the stone rim to the front of the slip and to the other side, and jumped for the stern, bare feet skidding and finding traction. She grabbed up her pole and started shoving before the watergate was wide. Water sheeted down outside, bad guttering.

Hell with the drenching. The nightman was still shouting at her when she cleared the slip and scraped out into the dark beside the Rock, out on Archangel again and clear.

She moved, no engine yet, didn't dare start it, Dundee would be on Hafiz about the whole mess as it was, and Hafiz would skin her—

But damn! oh, damn! she was way behind.

Going home, was Denny's conclusion. Mondragon came out of Kalugin's yacht, Mondragon headed down Borg East, headed the canalside way, first tier, by Porfirio, and Denny was mortally glad to pick him up, skinning not over the roof of Borg, which was a tall 'un with copper sheeting and hard to keep your footing on when it was raining this hard—instead he had cut all the way around Borg-canalside, around by Porfirio, fast as his legs could take him, which was considerable, Denny reckoned.

And Denny was ever so glad to come around that corner and see Mondragon cross Porfirio Low, a shadowy, rain-obscured man in a cloak.

He was so glad he stopped running and just followed, then, at a distance.

Till he got to Borg corner and Porfirio himself, and looked down the way past Porfirio, and realized there was more than one man in a rain-cloak ahead of him.

And the one ahead not seeing the one behind: the one ahead not, in the rush of wind and rain and water and full gutter-spouts dumping their loads into the Det, so much as able to *hear* the one behind him—

Jones sweated, cursing with every shove of the pole—old Det was helping, for once, she was going with the Greve Fork current and Det, full of rain, was helping shove the empty skip along nearly as fast as her engine could have done, but she was carrying a couple of barrel-weights of water in her well that she wished she could be rid of, and no time for the hand-pump, no time for anything but to shove and strain—opposite the Spur, now, where the militia had its headquarters, where there were blacklegs swarming thick (Anastasi's men, not Tatiana's) and where a skip moving under its engines just made too much unwelcome attention for her liking—

But she was coming up on the Justiciary ahead, was just passing under Gunnery Bridge, that linked the Spur to the Rock, when she heard *Jones!* from somewhere above the sound of the water and the rain—went into quiet just a moment in Gunnery's shadow and shelter, thinking *Raj!* and wondering if it was her ears doing tricks or whether she ought to ground the pole hard and try to come about, fast—

About which time she had her bow coming out the other side of Gunnery and this gawky dangle of limbs dropped down off the arch of the bridge, hanging there yelling *Jones!* at the top of his lungs.

She stepped hard aft, bottomed the pole with all her might and leaned, tipped the skip bow clear up and over, not enough to get him—the fool kid dropped, splash! straight as a rock, and went under.

"Dammit!" she yelled, minded to leave him, minded to be on down Archangel like a bullet, except the fool knew where Mondragon was, except the fool was going to drown in the dark—Archangel was fast, pushing her on around.

So like a fool she let the pole off the bottom and jabbed it right for the splash-spot and near took the kid's head off as he came up flailing and fighting and grabbing for anything in his reach.

Which was the pole, so she got him, she bent over, leaned her butt into it and hauled, holding on for very life during the series of shocks as the kid climbed the pole and while the kid acted like a sea-anchor and slung the skip broadside to the current.

Lot of room in Archangel, thank the Lord and the Ancestors.

But the boy was fighting hard for that transfer of hand from pole to skip-rim, and about to lose it. She hauled, hard, gave him the lift he needed, and an elbow aboard, both elbows came aboard, while the skip swung on about in the current and she hunkered down on the halfdeck and got a fistful of sweater and the back of an arm, the back of a pair of trousers, and anything else that writhed over her boat-rim on its way to the well.

Drowned skit looked better.

"He's gone Borg East," Raj gasped, still half over her rim, "walking. Like home. Denny's on 'im, but he—"

She headed for the engine, then, flung up the cover and got her started, right under the Justiciary wall, while the skip spun and turned in the current and Raj Takahashi fought to get his legs aboard.

He made it, about the time the engine took, slithered into her well limp as fish guts and just lay there trying to throw up.

Damn-'im Kalugin's ship was at Borg-side, no matter. Kalugin was awake, no question, and if he connected the skip making racket up the canal to the one that had gone past Cantry earlier, that was something for him to wonder about.

But they were moving now, current and engine and all, so fast it curled a white vee of wake side to side of Archangel, and sloshed the bank and the walkways far and wide, right up against the dark stone of the Justiciary and the College and all.

* * *

Calliste Old Bridge was ahead, and Mondragon thought of going up, there, to second-tier, the way he had thought about it back on Borg, and then decided, out of the morose condition of his soul, to keep to the shadows and the nether tier—where at least were simpler rules and simpler motives and where the banks were lined with skips and poleboats at rest, canalerfolk, Jones' folk—whose problems were enviously immediate and direct. He remembered nights with Jones, he remembered one night spectacularly well—what it felt like, the cramped quarters, the smell of old clothes and old boards and oil and the water, cramped quarters and cold feet, and Jones' skin next to his, which had somehow corrupted all his judgment and made him fool enough to risk her—

—to *have* her, which was altogether selfish and reprehensible, but Jones was like a force of nature, like the flooded Det itself, that just swept over his good sense and his objections and made him envy the people in those skips tonight—made him wish he had been born to that and not where he was, and that his enemies would let him do what Jones wanted and take to the water and live the way Jones wanted. No troubles. Just the problems of getting a few coins to keep going, enough food to fill out what the Det put on the hooks, and enough fuel to cook it; enough blankets to make the hidey warm, two sweaters and two pair of pants for days like this, when you worked wet and you wanted to sleep dry.

That was what he wanted. God, he wanted it.

Not—what Kalugin offered.

He stopped on the little Calliste bridge, just stopped a moment, leaning his elbows on the railing and looking out at the nightlights reflecting across the broad Grand, stood there above the swirl of Det-water under the wooden arch, looking at nothing, looking at everything, just breathing the smell of the city and letting the wind and the rain take the stink of Anastasi's presence off him.

Jones says the waterside stinks. She doesn't know what corruption smells like.

" 'Ware!" a kid's voice shouted, close, and muscles jumped, dropped him into a deep crouch and had his hand going for his sword as a cloaked figure rushed him, up the arch of the bridge, sword glittering.

He came up on guard, met the attack, flung his cloak out of the way, attacked and parried, pushing the cloaked man back and back, —*mad*, blind mad, and with an opponent who used plain steel. Attack and parry and attack, a scratch on his opponent, a second scratch, a third, and the man backing and backing.

But the kid was screaming murder, there was something else, *someone* else—

Diversion cost him a scratch of his own, blade slipping past the quillon and the half-guard, and he came back in quarte, back again and back again with a triple disengage and a plain feint to terce, then attack, straight in past the too-extreme reaction, hardly a shock as the point went in and the shocked opponent ran up on him, still trying to defend himself when Mondragon spun and freed his blade and kicked his opponent off the bank into the raging Grand.

—facing a second swordsman and a third, holding Denny Takahashi with a gun to his head.

"Drop the sword," the assassin said, and Denny wriggled and yelped in pain. "*Drop it.*"

Mondragon let his arm fall.

"*Drop* it."

As the kid struggled and came close to getting his brains blown out.

Mondragon slumped in an attitude of defeat, jerked

the cloak-tie at his throat, yelled, "*Boy!*" and flung the sword with all the strength in his arm as he hit the ground and rolled. A shot echoed off the walls, he parted company with the cloak, hung onto it and whipped it sidelong into the men's faces as he came up on his feet and kept going.

A blade came past it, scored his leg, and Denny was still yelling a warning as he carried his attack body-to-body with the first man he could get to, got a grip on him and sent him into the Det with an effort that tore his gut.

He was face to face with two sights then: Denny Takahashi flailing away at a man bringing his gun up dead-sighted at him; and a skip coming out of nowhere, boiling up the water toward him.

He dropped, the gun went off, the assassin hit a Calliste shop-front with a terrible impact and the boat scraped the bank with a splintering sound.

With, he saw as he rolled to his feet again, a terrified Raj Takahashi sitting in the well of that damaged skip holding a pole in both hands.

"Come *on!*" Jones yelled, and Thomas Mondragon, fool and catspaw for too many powerful, grabbed Denny by the arm and jumped for the skip as it grated past.

As Jones angled the tiller and sent the skip out into the Grand.

He fell, landed on his rump on the slats of the well with Denny panting in his arms, with Raj still sitting there in shock and the pole slanted over the side.

Skip-sterns whipped past. Pilings did, and shadow came over them, Fishmarket's underside.

"Ye all right?" Jones yelled at him.

He was holding onto somebody who was holding onto him. He remembered it was a scared twelve year old. He looked at Jones in shock.

"Ye make a damn lot of noise!" Jones yelled over

the engine-sound. They came into open night again, and the skip whipped into a turn. "Ye all *right*, f' Lord's sake?"

"I'm fine!" he yelled back, and shivered the way the kid was shivering, with the wind going over him.

The walls of old Foundry going past as the skip leveled out.

Not Anastasi, he told himself, no way that Anastasi had reason to set on him now. Just a little problem Anastasi could straighten out—dropping a few words into Boregy's ear.

He believed that. He believed it because he had to believe it, because Anastasi, by the evidences he had given, could more afford to believe him than he could the Boregys. Honor was only a commodity, in the circles of the powerful. Lives could be bought as well as sold.

And for the meanwhile, —by some miracle involving Jones or the Angel who loved fools, —he was going home.

A DAY IN THE LIFE

by Lynn Abbey

Greening: a celebration of the triumph of spring over winter. Its origins went deep into human history, seemed rooted in life itself, even in Merovingen where the only plants grew in pots. Budded branches from the nearby manor-estates and hothouse flowers from the Chattelen had been brought to the city, coaxed into bloom, and draped from every available window and banister. The pace of life palpably quickened. Friendships were renewed and social obligations, which had been ignored in the wretched months, were remembered with lavish entertainments.

As in all things, House Kamat put on a proper show for the season—not too ostentatious, but certainly not miserly either. The wainscotting in all the public rooms was nearly hidden behind living draperies. A profligate number of candles recreated the warm reflections of a summer's twilight. In the dining-room a mountain of marzipan flowers was the centerpiece for a buffet of gargantuan proportions. Lively music came down from the grand stairway where a hired orchestra provided entertainment. Two hundred people were dancing, eating, laughing, and celebrating the end of a salt-air winter.

Andromeda Casserer Garin, allied with Kamat

through a voluntary, exclusive marriage contract, and hostess of this affair, steered a course through the public rooms, exchanging pleasantries with her guests, and inspecting every detail with a commander's critical eye. She was radiant, gracious, and truly satisfied with the fruits of her labors. Everyone in Kamat had responsibilities, and she was *the* m'sera Kamat. Domestic regulation was her purview and evenings like this were the epitome of her achievement.

The orchestra began a ceremonial piece long associated with the Greening festival, and, more specifically, the consummation of the holiday feast. Guests migrated toward the atrium while liveried servants hastened to either side of the closed dining-room doors.

Like any other mercantile establishment of a certain size or reputation, the residence was riddled with private corridors. Members of the household and other initiates could move quickly and invisibly from one part to another, circumventing not only the public rooms, but also the shops, apartments and workrooms that did not participate in any of its rituals, but merely rented space. Thus the Kamats, who had been mingling with their guests, literally vanished into the woodwork in order to take their appropriate positions beside the candied violets, daffodils and baby-blue-eyes when the doors were opened.

Andromeda entered the by-ways from the parlor. Her path led over the atrium and past a dozen or more spyholes, each equipped with a focusing lens. Other, half-running footsteps echoed along side and above her, but she was the first to arrive and had a moment to contemplate her handiwork before other family members arrived.

It was an especial triumph. After twenty-five years of estrangement from the Garins and Casserers, her Nev Hettek families had accepted Kamat's invitation.

Nemesis Garin would never forgive her for a marriage which strengthened her husband's interest at the expense of her father's. But her mother and aunt, Folly and Dolor Casserer, had made the downriver journey. It was a token presence, yet it was also the vindication of Andromeda's adult life.

Richard and Marina arrived next. Richard was the image of her husband, and—perhaps because there was not room for two such men in her life—an enigma to her. Marina, though, could have passed for her younger sister. The girl had been a trial and a challenge, and confidant. Patrik Kamat, her husband's younger brother, and his three children were breathing hard as they emerged from the stairway. Finally, just as the orchestra was concluding the coda, Andromeda heard the sound of her beloved Nikolay's tread on the creaking boards.

The horns pealed the final chord. The glassware vibrated and the guests, on the far side still, broke into applause. Andromeda turned to face the doors, never for a instant doubting that her husband would manage to get to his place in time. It was the high point of her evening, of her year, of her life—and yet it was somehow terribly wrong.

The wide-eyed astonishment on her guests' faces did not focus on the sumptuous beauty of the feast, but on something well behind the laden tables. Andromeda turned slowly, feeling the movement of air against her face, the blood in her heart. Her eyes saw the tumbled-down shadow emerging from the private stairway.

Chaos erupted. Weights attached themselves to her arms. She struggled free and clawed her way into the dark wall between herself and her husband. The air itself called her name and held her back, but she was m'sera and her orders were finally obeyed.

The dark wall parted. A halo of painful brilliance

surrounded the doorway obscuring that which she wanted desperately to see, to join. Within her desperation, an absurdly calm voice spoke from the back of Andromeda's mind.

This cannot be. This is mine. I have planned it. I have lived it before; perfected it. But it is not right. . . . Her eyes became accustomed to the brilliance. There were three figures posed for a religious tableau—one recumbent, one kneeling, and one holding a sword; Nikolay, Folly and Dolor; her husband, her mother, and her aunt.

"Nikky!" She heard a shrill, hysterical voice, but did not recognize it for her own. "*Nikky!*" She lunged toward him, but her feet were rooted in the carpet and did not obey. *"Dear God, it's happening again! Let me through! I* must *join Nikky!"* It would be all right, if only she could reach his side before the steel descended. If she could . . . but she could not and the sword pierced his skin. Crimson cascaded from the wound, hiding her husband and her family until there was only herself, the blood, and Dolor's skeletal face.

"Wake up, m'sera!" Alpha Morgan threw back the bed curtains and grabbed her mistress's flailing arms. "It's a nightmare, m'sera!" She squeezed hard, hard enough, or so she hoped to rouse the sweat-drenched woman, but though Andromeda's eyes opened, they did not see beyond the dream.

Other servants bustled into the bedroom, awakened by screams that echoed throughout the upper stories of the house.

"Get cold water," someone commanded. "Get some brandy," came the immediate correction. "Get enough for us all." "And wake Doctor Jonathan—if he's not awake already."

Morgan heard, but did not listen. She had been

Andromeda's nurse long before she'd been her maid; she had no other children. She called Andromeda's name and slapped her hard enough that a bruise would rise. One could be dismissed for striking the dowager of a Merovingen House, but one's fate would be much worse if she sank into complete insanity.

A bowl of cold compresses appeared at Morgan's elbow. She laid one across Andromeda's forehead. The wide, black pupils contracted from the shock. Tears mixed with dribbles from the compress.

"It was not right," the widow sobbed as she became aware of her surroundings. "He should not have gone like that. Not with Dolor. Not with the sword. He should not have gone without me."

Morgan's lips whitened. She gathered her adult child to her breast and rocked her gently. "It was a nightmare m'sera, just a dream,"—though she had ample reason to suspect it was no such simple thing.

"How is she?" Andromeda's daughter, Marina, made room for herself at her mother's bedside.

There were some voices which must be both heard and listened to. "She's had a nightmare," the elderly woman whispered.

"Angel in heaven, I thought she'd gotten over them—"

"It's a year next week," Morgan snapped. "She remembers, even if you don't."

Marina gaped and the servants standing around the bed held their collective breath. The House heiress was not noted for her ability to withstand Morgan's acid scoldings with any grace at all. If there was a common thought in their minds, it was heartfelt regret that Richard was downcoast inspecting storm damage at one of the indigo estates and wasn't expected back for a week or more. Young, but solid, he would have brought peace to the room by his simple presence.

"How dare you . . . How dare you speak to me that way? How dare you say that I don't love and remember my father?"

Alpha Morgan said nothing further. What she'd said was largely true, though hardly fair to Marina or anyone else. To say more would acknowledge the unhealthiness of Andromeda's dreaming. The unhealthiness that had caused Richard to send his mother away last summer and which even Morgan had thought things of the past.

A young valet appeared carrying a crystal glass of brandy on a silver-gilt tray. Morgan transferred her ire to this new example of Merovingen's Revenantist moral decay. In Nev Hettek, virile youths did not, under any circumstances, enter a lady's bedchamber after dinner. But she took the brandy with her free hand and tilted it toward Andromeda's lips.

The room was shadowy with the light from a half dozen candles. Nothing showed its true color or texture, yet something made the old woman pause to examine the liquid more closely. She swirled it, sniffed it, sipped it—but spat it back rather than swallow.

"Where did this come from!"

Marina understood. "Deathangel!" she exploded at the expressionless valet, then froze. "You— You—" She threatened him with the glass she had wrested from Morgan's grasp.

The valet would bear her wrath in silence, but not Andromeda who caught her daughter's sleeve with a clawlike hand. "Please, Ree, Kidd gets it for me because it is what I want. It does me no harm . . . and it makes the nights bearable."

"Bearable!" Marina drew away from the bed as if they were all mad. "Bearable? How bearable when you wake screaming? Deathangel dreams become *real*, mother. You could have spent eternity in that nightmare!"

Andromeda shook her head as she tugged on the glass. "One nightmare. One nightmare—a small price to pay for all the other times we have been together. I have you, Dickon and my memories of your father, and if I must choose, I choose my memories. Love is stronger than family, you know that yourself."

Marina's fingers relaxed involuntarily, and her mother drained the glass in two swallows. Kidd caught her eye and it seemed that he smiled swiftly and slyly at her. Kidd, the stranger, the man who appeared and made himself invaluable . . . The servant who located Thomas Mondragon and who poled her boat each time she went trysting. She looked away and clutched her night-robe tight around her neck.

"I did not know," Morgan said quietly, though no one thought she had and no one—not even Marina—was blaming her.

The glass slipped from Andromeda's fingers. It rolled across the quilt without leaving a mark. A faint smile settled on her lips and she whispered her husband's name.

The room fell silent and remained that way until old doctor Jonathan appeared in the doorway. They made room for him gratefully and he began his examination, though it was clear what was wrong. He moved his candle in slow patterns before her eyes, and frowned as the wide pupils failed to move.

"How long has this been going on?" He demanded, but those who were willing to answer did not know, and the one who could had somehow disappeared.

"The brandy was here . . . in the room," a helpful, hesitant voice offered anonymously from the darkness.

"Get rid of it!" the doctor commanded, venting his frustration on the servants rather than Andromeda who had not yet acknowledged his presence. "And those who have no business here, back to your quarters."

The offending carafe was placed on the tray beside the empty glass and whisked from sight and temptation. Only Morgan, Marina and the doctor remained in the room, and both Marina and Morgan were wrapped in their own thoughts.

Doctor Jonathan sat on the mattress. Grimacing, he pressed his finger against the nerve-bundle above Andromeda's wrist. "Enough of this, m'sera Andi," he said with gruff friendliness. "Enough of drinking deathangel brandy and looking for Nikolay in your dreams. You've gotten nightmares—just as you knew you would, sooner or later, just as you did before. There's no excuse for this, m'sera."

Andromeda's tears flowed freely. "I *want* to die—don't you understand that?" She looked at the physician, but she spoke to the other women. "Don't you think I know what deathangel is? He's there in my dreams. We'll be together when I die."

Doctor Jonathan scraped his fingers over his stubbled chin. Not to put too fine a point on it, but the m'sera was talking both Revenantist and Adventist heresy. No one on Merovin was allowed a personal nostalgia; religious dogma of all kinds positively stipulated that the karmic wheel moved forward and away from this world, or it did not move at all. Not surprisingly, there were some neurotic patterns facing Doctor Jonathan and his contemporaries which had no precedent in their carefully preserved Pre-Scouring texts.

Deathangel deathwish was a problem for physicians and theologians alike. The drug had demonstrated paranormal properties. It provided evidence for reincarnation and prophecy which could withstand any doubts launched by Merovin's crippled scientific community. But could it, as Andromeda Kamat was claiming, weave an alternate, enduring reality—a private reality where the addict's ego set the limits of what could be and what was forbidden?

The theologians evaded the question beneath the umbrella of heresy; and the physicians lamented that their patients were invariably dead by the time the question could be answered.

"I don't want to come back, Jonathan." Her pupils were huge and throbbing. She dug her fingernails into his arm and shook it with unexpecting strength. "I love Nikolay. I have always loved him. I will always love him. Death *will* not keep us apart."

Doctor Jonathan—who had been with House Kamat far longer than she—listened, nodded, smiled, grumbled politely, and refused her. "We've been through this before. Hiding here behind your curtains, living for deathangel dreams isn't anything that Nikolay would have tolerated, and you know perfectly well that Nikolay—the real Nikolay—wouldn't be waiting in some drug addict's world. We are not going to let you slip away, m'sera. We will see that you get restful sleep, sunlight, and hard, healthy work."

The widow looked past them all, then buried her face against the pillow. "You have no right to do this," she whispered, then was silent.

Doctor Jonathan released her wrist, allowing her to slip into deathangel dreams again. "Send for milk with tryptoph powder. Rouse her as you've seen me do, and give her a glass every six hours. I'll send to the College for the extract in the morning, but we'll keep her asleep until the worst's over."

Morgan sniffed. She didn't approve of fighting one drug with another, but she'd do as she was told—and be secretly grateful that her mistress wasn't suffering the torture of withdrawal. The dysmutase extract was expensive and tightly controlled by the College. Acquiring it was an admission of addiction, which the cardinals took quite seriously (not that House Kamat would honestly admit *who* within its walls had succumbed), and they made certain the cure was as unpleasant as it was effective.

The doctor misunderstood her reaction. "Don't blame yourself," he assured her. "Andi has wanted dependence and dreams since the day he died. But I think something happened tonight that was terrifying enough that a part of her, at least, wants to be helped. We'll have her back on her feet before Richard gets back."

Morgan nodded. It would be just as well if Richard never learned what had precipitated the nightmare—never knew what had happened to his great aunt. Indeed, she would rather not know herself, but Andromeda had read her Nemesis Garin's letter the previous afternoon.

Marina's nightgown billowed furiously as she stomped out of the room. The doctor had no words of wisdom for her, no neat precription to tell her how to deal with the collapse of *her* ideals and fantasies. In her mind there could be only one explanation for the whole sordid mess; if Kidd was getting deathangel powder, he was getting it from her lover, Thomas Mondragon. How else could her mother have located the elusive Nev Hetteker?

"Children," the doctor muttered indulgently, unable to remember that he was already employed here when he'd turned twenty-five.

"Love," Morgan responded, well aware that the heiress was armpit deep in her first affair, though unaware of her lover's identity. The combination of Merovingen's loose morals and romantic novels imported from Nev Hettek were ruining the daughter as surely as they'd overwhelmed her mother.

* * *

The heavy draperies which had kept the sunlight from Andromeda's bedroom for very nearly a year were tied back by the time she woke up again of her own volition. Her first glance was to the serving table where the carafe should be. She was in a rage before her heart had beat twice.

Her feet were freezing, her hands trembled, and her mouth had the taste of swamp water in it. She *wanted* the brandy, even though she knew it wouldn't work even if she had it. The cardinals' extract left its victims with remarkably intact memories of their ordeal. Andromeda knew she had been cured, and knew, as well, that she would see her husband again. The extract would linger in her blood, ever ready to interact with deathangel toxin; ever ready to destroy it and her in dreamless agony.

She grabbed the bedpost, hauling herself upright with willpower alone and resisting the servant bell with the same strength. Her gut rolled. She took two staggering steps toward the washbasin as the acid rose in her throat. There was nothing in her stomach—nothing but the undigestable dregs of useless deathangel toxin. Little blue threads that would not dissolve in the water she poured from the pitcher.

Oh, Nikky, what do I do now?

Had the deathangel lingered in her brain, she would have heard an answer. As it was, she felt only his absence and the absence of anything joyous or meaningful. The embroidered bellpull dangled within reach . . . Kidd would come; Kidd would understand. She could tell him everything. It was too late for the deathangel, but there were other drugs . . .

Her fingers crumpled the embroidery. She was sober now—seedy, but sober as she had not been in memory's mornings when she found the carafe on her nightstand. Without the deathangel to taint her perceptions, the dreams—even the ones where she and Nikolay had lost themselves in erotic pleasures—were grotesque. Her hand fell to her side.

What do I do now—and caught herself before her husband's name formed in her thoughts. *What do* I *do now?*

The Signeury bells began the noontime peal, and despite her preoccupation with Nikolay—or perhaps because of it—she was shamefully aware that she was still in her nightgown. This was a merchant's city, a worker's city, unlike Nev Hettek where the ranking families lived well apart from the sources of their wealth. She'd grown up surrounded by art, novels, music and unspeakable boredom.

Nikolay had freed her from Nev Hettek. He'd make her part of House Kamat. Now he was dead. Without him, she had no place or purpose here, just as she'd never had any place or purpose in Nev Hettek. She went to the window. It was bolted, but glass was easily broken . . . She made a fist and imagined herself falling.

And imagined herself in the canal, and the scandal that would be her legacy to Nikolay's House. Kamat had never been tainted with scandal—not until now. Her fist opened and she pressed her fingers against her lips. Appearances were important on Merovin, and for the first time since Nikolay's death, Andromeda considered *her* appearance.

She stepped back from the window and made herself look in the mirror. What she saw was not enough to give her a new lease on life, but it did convince her that she had become an embarrassment to herself and her family: a mad, addicted wraith wearing a flimsy nightgown in the sunlight.

Once her mind found a focus, even the trivial focus of selecting a sweater from her wardrobe, the yawning emptiness receded a bit. It threatened to return when she looked at garment after garment and saw in each piece its history with *him*. Irony intervened: she had sought Nikolay in deathangel dreams, only to find him in her closet. And to be uncomfortable with the discovery; perhaps it was time to summon her tailor. Or, better yet, to visit her neglected atelier where the design and construction of hightown fashion had been her personal business.

No, no—the atelier was too great a physical and emotional challenge. It was too far away, and asked too much. Today, without the fantasy aid of deathangel dreams, she would get herself dressed. Today, that would be enough; she would not end her life in a nightgown.

She was staring at a pale green sweater, remembering the other times she had worn it, when the door to her bedroom suite closed quietly.

"M'sera?" Morgan inquired with an unmistakable note of concern in her voice. "M'sera, where are you?"

Hastily shoving the sweater back on its shelf and grabbing a heavy dressing robe instead, Andromeda faced her servant. "I'm here. Right here where you left me, the madwoman in the spire."

Morgan rolled her lip inward. "I've brought your lunch—"

Andromeda interrupted with a bitter laugh. "Tell the truth, Morgan. I haven't eaten anything solid in what . . . six days, a week? And I wasn't *eating* before that. You came to check up on me, and you feared the worst when you didn't see me lying in my bed."

Anyone else would have drawn from the bitter venom in Andromeda's voice—or from the gray pallor of her complexion. But not Alpha Morgan. "I brought your lunch," she averred with flat finality. "It's on the table. Doctor Jonathan said you'd be up and about today. Come, have a little of your prawn salad, and the chowder's still piping hot. You'll feel more like your old self when you've had something tasty to eat." She took Andromeda's hand and led her to a sun-bathed table.

Doctor Jonathan and the kitchen staff knew how to tempt her. These were among her favorite foods, carefully and attractively prepared with a sprig of dwarf cherry blossoms rising from an antique vase and the silver polished until the Kamat crest flashed in the light. Andromeda's mouth watered, but her stomach wasn't sure.

"You did me no favors, Morgan, letting them bring me back like this," she whispered, taking up the fork. "I'll never be my old self again. Nothing will ever be remotely the same again." She stabbed a prawn but did not bring it to her mouth.

"Nothing's ever the same as it was," Morgan replied with a pragmatism that owed nothing to any religion. "That's no reason to starve or drug yourself to a stupor."

"But I've nothing to live for. Nothing—"

"Your children—

"Are grown and don't need me."

"The household—"

"Has done very well without me."

"The business, your designs. Everyone misses your designs. I've heard them say so myself, and not just Kamat people."

Andromeda thought of the stacks of clothing in her wardrobe. She could remember whether Nikolay had liked each garment, but not whether she had designed it or not. "Marina has a flair for that, not I." The prawn fell onto the greens and was not retrieved. "There's nothing, Morgan, nothing at all. Maybe there wasn't very much to begin with. A marketable daughter sent downriver to seal an alliance for alum . . . and

I didn't even do that right. I gave myself to Kamat, but they never needed me, any more than the Garin or the Casserer did."

"Nikolay needed you," Morgan blurted out before common sense could censor her tongue.

The fork followed the prawn and silent tears were massing to follow the fork. "I'd be better off deathangel drunk and locked away in a spire! See what a mistake you made."

"*I* need you, m'sera, all of us who are not Kamat but live here need you. The others are afraid to admit how much they need you, but I'm not. Where would I go without you—back to Nev Hettek after all these years? You had many good years with your husband, m'sera, and now you owe for them."

A trace of a smile grew on Andromeda's face. "You sound like a Revenantist, Alpha Morgan. Next you'll tell me about karma and reincarnation."

Privately, Morgan conceded she'd talk about anything to fan that spark of vitality, so she made a show of her embarrassment. "Ain't no Revenant. I'm not coming back *here*, I'm not. No point to goin' through Merovin twice," she explained with great exaggeration. "If I'm owin', then I'm payin', too. Right now."

Andromeda's smile faded. The joke could not be sustained, and touched too close to the truth in any case. "If it were only that simple," the dowager said, picking up her fork again with a sigh. "I keep hoping for a sign . . . something that will tell me what Nikky would want me to do with my life . . . now that he's gone. That was the start of it—looking for a sign, that is—that led me to the deathangel in the first place. Now I don't even know what to wear."

Doctor Jonathan had warned them of the indeciveness and depression that was certain to follow Andromeda's cure; certain to follow because it was the underlying cause of the addiction in the first place. *Make decisions for her*, he'd advised Alpha Morgan who, having known her as a child, would be most able to deal with her childishness.

"Wear something comfortable," the older woman instructed. "And warm. Fresh air is what you need and you'll be going for a ride through the city later this afternoon—"

The flaccid muscles of Andromeda's face hardened. "No," she replied without explanation—for what was childishness but a mixture of stubbornness, rebellion and a denial of enlightened self-interest?

"Doctor's orders: fresh air, rest, good food—"

"I'm going upstairs to the atelier," Andi announced, though the decision was more of a surprise to her than it had been to Morgan. "I shall make my own clothes; new clothes. You said yourself that I should."

Morgan frowned; it had been a long time since she'd dealt with a child. She'd forgotten how they had an instinctive way of fastening on to the one thing that should not have been said. "That would not be wise, m'sera," she said reluctantly.

"I need something to do," Andromeda replied, not illogically. "Sitting in the back of a poleboat holding my parasol is not going to help me half so much as *doing* something."

Subtlety was useless; Morgan drew a deep breath and plunged to the core of the problem. "There would be a dreadful scene with Marina, m'sera. She has taken this all very hard. She thinks . . . She believes . . ." Morgan ran out of air and resolve. "This thing with Kidd," she said softly, "it was very poorly done, m'sera."

"What thing with Kidd?"

Morgan could not raise her eyes. "The deathangel,"

she whispered to her feet. "Getting the deathangel from . . ."

"Speak up! I can't understand a word you're saying."

"Mondragon, m'sera! Getting the deathangel from Mondragon, then sending Marina to his bed in payment!" Shame burned in Morgan's cheeks that the child she had raised could have done such a thing.

"Tom Mondragon?" It was patently unbelievable. "Where would Tom Mondragon get deathangel?" Ah, but where *had* Kidd gotten the deathangel he so regularly provided? She hadn't wanted to know, so she'd never asked. And he had known how to find Tom Mondragon who was as illicit and dangerous as deathangel.

Perhaps it wasn't patently unbelievable. Perhaps it was all too believable.

The wind went out of Andromeda's sails with a long sigh. "Mondragon . . ." She needed both hands to get the water goblet safely to her lips. A cascade of images paraded inevitably through her mind. Images that were strong enough to overshadow Nikolay's death. Deathangel, angel of death, angel with a sword, sword of God, Tom Mondragon, Nev Hettek, Mondragon, Karl Fon, Mondragon, Aunt Dolor, Mondragon, Marina . . .

"I must talk to her." She rose unsteadily to her feet. "Now. I'll go to the atelier—"

"No, m'sera, you mustn't."

"I will not be told what I can or cannot do."

Her first step was a stagger, but the second was stronger, and Morgan was filled with the sudden knowledge that m'sera Kamat was quite capable of climbing the seventy steps to the atelier and having a confrontation with her daughter. Anything would be better than that. *Anything*.

"But you should dress, m'sera. There's a package

on your writing table. A gift from Marina. Wouldn't it be wise to wear her gift when you see her?"

It would, of course, be extremely unwise—Morgan knew full well what the gift was—and, if she'd misjudged, there'd be no repairing the damage. Morgan offered up a silent prayer to the personal, unnamed god of all servants that she would not have misjudged and a second prayer that Richard would return home on the evening tide.

Andromeda snapped the string and ripped through the tissue paper. She yanked the gift from the wreckage of its package and shook it open. A piece of paper fluttered unnoticed to the floor.

It was an evening sweater; a first-bath sweater knit from gossamer merin wool, then padded and crusted with bead embroidery. It was a masterpiece . . . and it was a nightmare. Gold, silver, jet and garnet had been stitched into the shimmering likeness of a mature deathangel fish. Its dark blood eye was filled with evil and held Andromeda in thrall.

Guilt for what had been done; shame that she had been the one to do it became the halves of Andromeda's heartbeat. She did not faint because she would not allow herself to escape Marina's punishment.

"I must see her," Andi repeated tonelessly, though there could be no forgiving.

Morgan pried Andromeda's fingers open, allowing the sweater to fall. She'd loosed the whirlwind; there was no going back and no stopping halfway through. She put the note in her mistress' hand. It did not matter that Andromeda was still paralyzed by the gift, there were only two words written on the note.

I'm pregnant

The myriad implications burst forth like the ancient

Pallas Athena emerging from the skull of her father, Zeus. Heartfelt anguish became physical pain and Andromeda began a slow collapse to the floor.

Morgan had no trouble catching her and shoving her to an armchair. Her eyes were on the service bellpull before Andromeda's weight was gone from her arms.

"No," Andromeda pleaded. "Don't, please. No one else. Just leave me alone." Morgan shook her head, but she did not move toward the bellpull. "It's all my fault."

She expected loyal Morgan to disagree. She expected the arms she held to relax and comfort her, but they remained rigid and unforgiving. Mechanically, Andromeda unlocked the muscles in her fingers and set herself free. She was not stupid. She knew the condemnation in the older woman's eyes sprang from a misunderstanding over deathangel; she knew that condemnation was very different from the self-condemnation in her own heart. And she was not mad. The cardinals' cure had scrubbed every trace of deathangel toxin from her body and soul.

The serene clarity she felt, then, as her world crumbled around her was quite real, quite sane. It was, perhaps, more mythic and inevitable than rational, but that only enhanced its sense of truth. There was only one pathway out of this darkness, a sword-bridge of light across the abyss—and it must be walked alone.

"Does Mondragon know?" she asked calmly.

"No, no one except you and Marina know."

Andromeda nodded. There was no contradiction or inaccuracy in Morgan's words. Servants did not occur in myths; they were not real players in the unfolding drama.

"I know what I must do."

"Don't go to Marina, m'sera. Leave her alone. Let Richard handle this when he gets back tonight—"

Andromeda blinked. It had not occurred to her to include her son in this. He entered her mind's stage as a stranger, an unknown force who could not be allowed to act. "Tonight?" she repeated.

"He's expected on the incoming tide."

She had sunk so deep in deathangel madness that she no longer had an innate knowledge of moon and ocean. She could not let her mind go blank and feel the movement of the water against Kamat's foundations, so she did not know how much time she had—only that she would have to move quickly if she was not to drag everything into the abyss.

"Where are you going?" Morgan demanded as Andromeda strode resolutely out of the sitting room.

Clarity produces simplicity. "I'm getting dressed, and them I'm going out to meet with Thomas Mondragon."

Alpha Morgan was dumbfounded. "You can't," she stammered, following her mistress into the wardrobe where, without any trace of her former indecisiveness, Andromeda was assembling a serviceable stack of garments. "This is utter foolishness, m'sera. You've been ill. Even if it were a good idea, you don't have the strength to go to Mondragon—and it isn't a good idea."

Clothes chosen, Andromeda swept her servant aside. She shed her nightgown in the center of her bedroom. "I'm going, Morgan. I *will* speak to Mondragon. You can't stop me, so you might as well help me."

"This is madness, m'sera. A moment ago you could hardly stand— "

"I'm going, Morgan." She buttoned her trousers, then went to her vanity table where she selected one atomizer from many and gave it a tentative squeeze a few inches in front of her nose. It fit her mood and she began systematically spraying her pulse-points. "You can't stop me."

Morgan swallowed the truth in that. "But, m'sera, you don't even know where he *is.*"

The atomizer was silent as Andromeda considered that. "Kidd is gone, isn't he?" She didn't wait for confirmation. "Marina knows . . ."

"M'sera, don't ask Marina."

"Then you ask."

"Me?"

Andromeda slammed the atomizer against the vanity. "Morgan, someone in this House knows where he is—if you don't, in fact, know yourself. Both Marina and Richard have been dealing with him. Now, don't argue with me, just do as you're told."

For forty-five of her sixty years, Alpha Morgan had been doing just that, and she was too old to change. She grumbled and offered a few more feeble arguments, but in the end, she left the suite and found the information her mistress wanted. They met again in the hallway above Kamat's boat slip.

Andromeda had applied her cosmetics carefully. Her complexion was pleasantly blushed; her eyes had lost their bruised and sunken appearance. The muted colors of her sweater and collar led the eye away from the protruding bones of her face and neck. The uninformed might well believe she was healthy, but not Morgan.

"Please reconsider, m'sera. At least, content yourself with a note and trust me to deliver it—"

Andromeda shook her head. "This is something I must do myself. Trust *me*, instead. If all goes well, I shall have undone all that I have done; and if it goes badly—well, at least I shall have tried to undo it." She took Morgan's face between her hands and kissed the old woman lightly on the forehead. "Now, tell me where I shall find him."

* * *

Andromeda did not recognize the boatman who helped her into the family craft—and he did not seem to recognize her. He nodded when she told him their destination, then devoted his attention to getting out of the slip and into the stream of traffic moving toward the Grand Canal.

The sunlight was as refreshing as Doctor Jonathan might have hoped it would be. Andromeda closed her eyes and rested her head against the cushions, letting the warmth soak into her skin. It hadn't been that long since she had been outside; the cure had taken only a week, but it had been months since she'd faced the world without the intoxication of deathangel brandy.

She had been scrubbed clean by the cardinals' cure from the inside out. Everything was new, yet familiar at the same time. Each sound and smell called its name from her memory, and seemed very precious. She was content to savor everything as it flowed past and gave no thought to what she would do when she reached her destination.

A part of her saw the upcoming conversation with Thomas Mondragon as the karmic conclusion of her life; that having been given the opportunity to set things right, there would be nothing left for her to do. Yet she was not thinking of death in any literal way when the boatman hooked a dilapidated spar and brought the boat to rest in deeply shadowed slip off East Dike.

"Shall I wait?" he asked, looking down a line of less prestigious boats.

It was cold here, and would only get colder as the afternoon wore on. She hadn't brought a shawl or jacket, or money enough to hire a public boat. "Yes, wait for me," Andromeda murmured, ignoring the mask that descended over his face as he helped her to the dock.

Sometime during the winter—the exact day was

blurred, though the conversations were clear enough in her mind—Richard Kamat had conceived the idea of a private security force answering to the greater merchantry, rather than any of the Kalugins. It had not been a revolutionary idea, for it found backers quickly, but it had taken Richard places that no Kamat had been before.

He dined with Vega Boregy about once a week—Andromeda recalled from her drug-dazed memories of the recent past—and spent a good deal of time here among the warehouses. Richard could hold his own with the Boregys, but he was out of his depth when it had come time to actually hire his Samurai. And so, acting in part on her own advice and Marina's yearnings, Richard had hired Thomas Mondragon to help him. Thomas was at home with the subtle dangers of the Boregys and Kalugins, but he was even more at home in the company of thugs, thieves and traitors.

Andromeda ran her fingers along the dusty, chipped paneling until they touched a Kamat sigil etched almost invisibly into the wood. Glancing around to be certain no one was watching, she leaned against the mark and stepped into a secret passageway. It took a moment for her eyes to adjust. The phosphorus paint was old, dust-covered and gave only faint clues to the location of the next stairway. If she counted wrong it might be days before she found her way out—but she was in the grip of myth and karma, and she did not miscount.

The oiled hinges moved silently. Andromeda looked across a bare room to the obviously startled face of Thomas Mondragon. Though she had asked Kidd to find him several months before, and had listened to her daughter's accounts of their affair, Andromeda had not herself laid eyes on the young man since his arrival in Merovingen. Indeed, she had only seen him once before, shortly before she'd left Nev Hettek when he was still a beautiful, but horribly spoiled, child.

Yet there was no doubting he was a Mondragon. The family resemblance was there, and that childhood beauty had matured into a handsomeness that could easily get a young woman in trouble. But his eyes were harder than a man's eyes should ever be, and his moods were undoubtedly dangerous.

He spoke first: "M'sera Kamat?"

"I am glad you recognized me. It has been a long time since we've seen each other."

"You look very much like your daughter, m'sera, and only a Kamat would have been able to find this room—or so your son assures me. I do not remember you from . . . any other time."

"I shouldn't think that you would even try to remember," she said recklessly. "It was the hall of your father's house; the occasion of a nephew's birth, as I recall."

Mondragon's lips grew thin and firm. "Why have you come here, m'sera? I do not talk about the past."

Andromeda came closer to him. "I wanted to see for myself what a murderer looks like."

His fingers twitched a warning that his patience was dangerously frayed. "You should go home, m'sera. You do not belong here."

"After all I've done for you, I think I have the right to see you with my own eyes."

"You're m'sera. You do not, I hope, know what you are saying."

"Would you deny that you are, or have been, a cold blooded murderer?"

"Your daughter accused me of the same thing. The fact that you are here yourself should answer that question. I do not know Mick Kidd; and I did not supply him with deathangel—as you well know."

Andromeda hadn't expected that Marina had already confronted him. The knowledge shook her complacency a bit, as if her reasons for being here were no longer so correct and full of karma. "Is that all Marina said?" she asked in a smaller voice.

"Aside from telling me that she never wanted to see me again, that was all. She wasn't interested in anything I might have to say on the matter."

"Nothing about herself—about the child?"

The words were out before Andromeda had a chance to reconsider them. She hadn't meant to tell Tom about his unborn child, but then she hadn't planned anything in any conscious sense. Tom blinked and moistened his lips, but he gave nothing else away.

"My child?" he inquired, as one might ask "my turn?" in a card game.

"You are a dangerous man, Thomas Mondragon. You always seem to survive, but no one else seems to. What could you feel for a child that you did not feel for your family."

His eyes grew very intense. "It is all lies, m'sera. I thought I could protect them, and I was wrong. If that makes me a murderer in your eyes, so be it, but I was not there when it happened and I would have died myself to prevent it."

Andromeda measured the sincerity behind his words. He wanted her to believe; she thought he wanted to believe himself. She dug into her trouser pocket and pulled out a letter. "That would not be enough," she said, handing the paper to him.

Nemesis Garin had clear, bold handwriting as befitted any househead in any city. His note was a concise and unemotional two paragraph statement of facts. Paragraph one said that Dolor Casserer was dead—starved to death in Karl Fon's dungeons. No one knew quite how she had offended the mercurial young man who held all the power in Nev Hettek and who was also a cousin by marriage contract. The offense had probably been trivial, still, Andromeda should know that her aunt was dead. Paragraph two advised that word of the Samurai had reached Nev Hettek and that it was his personal opinion that it was a very poor idea for merchants to get mixed up in security.

Mondragon folded the note and returned it to her. "My condolences," he said, without betraying any emotion.

"Is that *all?*" Andromeda demanded, feeling the blood rise to her cheeks. "You read that and offer *condolences*!"

"I've been in Karl Fon's dungeon's, m'sera. I know them better than you can imagine. Your aunt died a horrible death, no doubt, but it's hardly my fault or my concern."

Andromeda grabbed his wrist. "Marina's child is your child. He or she will be heir to Kamat . . . and heir to Mondragon. Perhaps you have forgotten what that means, Thomas Mondragon, but I do not think that your Sword of God friends will forget."

"You're overwrought, m'sera. I think you should go home." The coldness in Mondragon's voice was endless, but he did not call her a liar.

"I came here with many debts, m'ser Mondragon, the debt I must pay for mourning my husband too long, for hiring Mick Kidd and his deathangel, for enabling my daughter to meet with you. These are mine, but I came with one other for you.

"This is a Revenantist city, m'ser and woe betide the lonely Adventist who forgets it. Karma debts are collected with interest in Merovingen and, will you or nil you, Marina's child will be your debt."

A bitter, malicious laugh escaped through Tom's

lips. "Are you suggesting that I contract a marriage with your daughter, m'sera?"

"I'm suggesting that you stay the hell out of her life and the hell away from Kamat. But I'm telling you that whatever happens, whatever you do from now on, that there's karma between you and all of us, and what happens to us will lie, in part, on your soul."

He laughed again. "You are indeed mad, m'sera, if you think I care about karma or my soul."

"I've made you aware of your debt, and that discharges a part of mine."

She turned and left the room.

FAIR GAME

by Leslie Fish

"Oh, who's the slaver in our town?
Something's burning.
What's the way to bring him down?
Something's burning.
Who's the one we can do without,
Unprotected, beyond a doubt?
Where will they go when they're down and out?
Something's burning—
Burning . . . down."

By the third chorus, everyone in the front room of Ho's tavern was singing along. Visiting river sailors liked the bold marching tune, the joyful-fierce way the two women sang it, and the general sentiment—without any detailed knowledge of the local references. The canalers took it as a fitting anthem for their grim and lasting outrage; Megarys, the slavers, had never before dared—but now had—to touch one of theirs, one of the Trade, and that did not slide well on the water. Others—clients, shippers, small merchants, folk of more esoteric and less describable trades, all of whom relied on the canalers for their transport—found it politic, not to mention enjoyable, to express enthusiastic support for their canaler allies. Combined voices thundered echoes from the walls.

Hoh smiled and opened another keg. Singing dried the throat, and such enthusiasm guaranteed good sales. He briefly considered using up the cheap brew—this crowd might be too thirsty to notice—but then decided that such abundant feeling might overflow onto the nearest target, and that might easily be himself if the crowd noticed the taste. Best play safe.

Rattail and Rif finished the last thundering chorus, ending with the sharp whoop that signaled the finish and brought the audience up in cheers and howls of applause. They tossed their heads back and whipped their instrument-straps off their shoulders in a single practiced gesture, bowed just low enough for gratitude without fawning, then up again, a flash of a bright smile, and a quick leap off the stage while the applause still rolled. A good finish to a successful set; now for a half-hour's break before last performance and away for the night.

Rattail ducked off after a particular admirer she'd been playing on the line for the last half moon, but Rif went straight to the bar to collect booze and news. She particularly wanted to know what that last song might have dredged up.

Sure enough; three canalers, a boatwright and a rag-dealer offered to buy her drinks. Rif accepted them all, one after the other, canalers first, carefully doling out the minutes spent on each: just enough to be polite and keep the customer hopeful, no longer than necessary to learn if he had any valuable gossip. The last song provided the obvious topic, and the customers were more than willing, witting or not, to play the game.

"Y'hear, Megarys got burned again last night," offered a poleboatman. "Put a good hole in their roof-tiles, she did. Enough to let the rain in, up top floor."

"They keep most o' their folk up nights, now,"

another canaler noted. "Up all night, watchin'. Must sleep by day. Ye don't see no trade comin' near there by day."

"Precious little by night, too," said the third, one of the sprawling Deiter clan who owned four skips among them. "Damn few on the water these days'll take Megary coin, but there's lotsa eyes watchin' ter see who does."

"Won't many folks buy nothin' from 'em," commented the boatwright, "nor sell to 'em, neither. Had a canaler come up ter my shop t' other night, wantin' 'er bow fixed. I looked close at the poler, and 'e wasn't no one I knew, and I meet most onter water."

"Hey, no bilge?" Rif prodded him, wanting first-hand details.

"S'truth, 'e weren't no canal-rat. Wore shoes, if ye please, an' handled the pole like she were a shovel. All hog-fat an' muscle in the wrong places." The boatwright leaned back on the bar and warmed to his tale. "Used ter orderin' folk about, too. No House-colors on 'em, but I had me guesses. So I looks over 'is boat by candle, an I see she's new, good wood an' no rot, but 'er front's all charred unaccountable. So I says ter me, an' likewise ter him, 'I can't tell how bad she is in this light. Ye'll have ter bring 'er back come daylight.' "

He paused to take a long pull of his beer, waiting (Rif could tell, with skill of long practice in just such ploys) for his audience to clamor for more. Sure enough, the rag-dealer and the second canaler urged him on.

"Hey, but 'e raises a stink: 'Can't take 'er back undone,' says 'e. 'Fix 'er now.' 'Can't,' says I. 'If ye can't bring 'er back, then leave 'er 'til morning and I'll look at 'er then.' Well, he spits an' stews, but there ain't much else ter do, so 'e leaves 'er an' heads fer some tavern. I has my guesses he'll be back sooner nor dawn, so I hauls the boat under main dock, drags her bow up under my best lights, an' takes a good look. Now what d'yer think I finds?"

"A lot o' charred wood?" Rif suggested mildly: In her opinion the boatwright was a good storyteller, but not a great storyteller: he tended to draw out suspense a hair too long.

"Charred wood? Oh, aye, but charred in a pattern like, say, an oil-spill." The boatwright picked up speed. "Looked fer all the world like someone went an' threw lit chugger all over 'er bow."

Rif smiled to herself. "Chugger" was the common and spreading canalers' term for fuel-alcohol, that marvelously cheap and plentiful canalside undrinkable that could make any engine chug. Oh, yes, she knew chugger.

"Now why should anyone be throwin' burnin' chugger about, I wonders. No one with sense ter live would do that out on the water, am I right?"

"Oh, right," the boatman agreed, looking soberer than their drinks in truth allowed. "Lord, no; she might splash anywhere."

"So this had ter happen at tie-up, I figures. But what tie-up? Where've I heard o' fires lately? Like, just the night before?"

The crowd at the bar laughed knowingly in their beers.

"Now I wants ter be hundred-percent sure, so I looks close inside 'er, and what does I see all along 'er bilge centerline, an' all along under 'er gunwhales?"

"What?" demanded the Deiter boatman, whose clan weren't known for their patience.

"Why, I sees big iron rings bolted right inter the wood, *Big* rings, mind; bigger nor ye'd need ter pass lines fer holdin' any ordinary cargo. Bigger 'n my arm."

He paused once more for a gulp of beer and Dramatic Effect.

"Big enough ter pass shackles through." The boatwright looked around him, as if daring anyone to contradict. "Weren't no use fer them things 'cept holdin' chained prisoners. Slaves. An' some of 'em, like I said, were down in the bilges. Now would yer need ter ask any more?"

The crowd at the bar allowed that no, they wouldn't. That was, yes, m'ser, pretty damned convincing evidence.

"So what'jer do?" the Deiter man insisted, hooked.

"Why, I improved on them burns." The boatwright smiled and took another swig, emptying his glass. "Eh, this 'un's gone dry."

The Deiter man hurriedly bought him another, to Rif's amusement.

"Ye know I keeps jugs of acid fer makin' mordant-paste," the boatwright went on, "and she didn't take me but a minute ter fetch a jug and pour some of 'er all over that bow, right where the burns were, one burn lookin' much like another. Then I sets that poleboat right back where the Megary-man left 'er, tied up right and proper, bein' real careful not ter get no acid on the tie-rope. Then I goes back inside and goes ter bed so'd I'd be ready and fresh come dawn."

"When'd the Megary-man come back?" the smaller Canaler wanted to know.

"Dunno when he come back, but he was poundin' on my door come dawn, lookin' like he'd spent half the night sleepin' on the dock, and no sweeter-tempered fer it. So I gets up and dressed, and we goes down ter look at the poler, innercent as ye please."

"A pretty sight she must o' been, by then," the rag-dealer chuckled.

"Oh, aye, she were. Down by the bow, low in the water and 'er bilges sloshin' full. 'She's taken water!'

says he, like ye'd say the sky were fallin' in. 'That she's done,' says I. 'Must o' crept in by the charred wood down at the waterline, and worked 'er way up from there."

The canalers chuckled, having seen charcoal float often enough.

" 'We'd best dry-dock 'er,' I says, 'and have a good look at 'er. Gimme a hand on this winch.' "

"Bet ye made him do all the work," Rif guessed.

"Oh, aye," the boatwright grinned. "We took 'er up by the bow tie-line and starts haulin' 'er in—him doin' most o' the pullin' while I guides 'er. And soon as 'er bottom starts scrapin' up on the dry-dock, soon as she starts puttin' a little more pull on the rope, what d'ye think happens?"

Rif could guess, but she didn't want to spoil the story.

"What?" everyone else asked, thoroughly caught.

"Why, 'er whole bow splits and falls off," the boatwright grinned. "In pieces. Right down ter the waterline."

"Ho!" the audience breathed in awed delight.

"Aye," the boatwright delivered the punchline. "And o' course the line's tie comes off with it. Ye should o' seen that Megary-man's face as he watched that slaver-boat slide back down the slip and inter the water—where she sank."

The crowd at the bar exploded in whoops of laughter, crowings of victory, great pattings on the back and orders of more beer for the boatwright.

Rif laughed too, salute for a tale well told and encouragement for a clever piece of sabotage. She'd have a good bit to tell Sister Rowan tonight, including the point that lowtowners were quite ingenious at practical chemistry.

"M'sera," piped a diffident voice at her elbow.

Rif turned to see Denny, crouched over to look smaller, face set to look dutiful and a little bewildered, nothing to attract attention—sure sign that he had important news.

"Hey, I'll be right back," Rif promised her admirers, setting her empty glass on the bar. She followed the boy to the storeroom in the back, where Rattail was already thumbing through the music sheets in preparation for the next set. "What's the word, Denny?"

"Megary's is wide open, and don't know it." The boy grinned wide enough to show most of his teeth. "Just tonight. Here's yer saw-wire back." He handed over his borrowed tools.

"Ye did 'er!" Rif crowed, hands stuffing the tools into her own pockets. "Which window?"

"Tell us the whole thing," said Rat, coming over to catch the details. "Don't leave anything out, but be quick; we've got to go on again soon."

Expanding in the glow of their admiration, Denny gave his report.

Rattail waited until the door on their apartment at Fife Isle was safely locked before turning to her partner. "It's perfect," she said. "Bolts sawn nearly through, and up near the top, under the eaves. It's a golden opportunity, Rif! We'll never see a better one."

"Not good enough by 'erself," Rif insisted, sliding out of her songbook-bag and cloak. "They got their guards up on the roof, and Jane knows where else, lookin' out fer fires."

"So, that many on the roof means less inside the house."

"Less is still too many. We ought ter have a diversion er two. Lemme think on 'er."

"Don't think too long, or the Megs'll discover those cut bolts and we'll lose our chance."

"Ney, not too long." Rif paused a moment, considering. "By work-time t'morrer night, I'll have 'er."

"Him, you mean," Rattail smirked. "You planning to get your friend in on this deal, or just get info out of him?"

Rif glared at her partner. "Not a word, Rat. Not one word about him, ter anyone. I mean it."

"Not a word," Rat agreed. "Hell and Retribution, don't you think I know where my bread's buttered by now?"

Easy it was, in the normal course of daylight business, to drop word here and there along the canals. Easy to answer hails and hellos from customers who knew them from Hoh's, with bits of gossip about Megary's. Easy to stir already-troubled waters.

"Hey, d'ye know Megary's short on boats? Losin' another hurt 'em good. Oh, aye, they're watchin' their roof fer fires ternight, but they ain't watching their boat-dock so well, ney? No moon ternight, is she? Ye knows where Megary's boat-dock is. Ye knows how well chugger burns. Ye knows how easy clay bottles break. Now s'pose 'er cork's made o' rag, and the rag's burnin' when the bottle breaks . . . Fine fun, hey?"

The word spread fast and well through the canals, until Rif and Rat could guarantee everything but exact numbers and timing. It would be a night full of distractions for Megary's, but the particular distraction they wanted the partners would have to manufacture for themselves.

By dinnertime they'd collected about five liters worth of that.

Black Cal stared up at the plastered ceiling, green eyes unfocused and dreamy, contemplating the feel of heat-stirred air moving on his skin, pulse beating slower now but still so heavy he could feel it all the way to his toes, gentle fingers meandering up to his jawline and down to navel in an ever-varying pattern.

Ah, Rif . . .

He couldn't believe how she made him feel.

. . . So of course I have to keep trying . . . A smile crinkled the corners of his mouth.

Rif trailed a fingertip over the shy laugh-lines. "Ye look so different when ye smile," she murmured. "Like sunlight on the water . . ."

He glanced at her, touched, and noted that in fact her eyes were elsewhere, abstracted. Only part of her thought was on him. He felt absurdly jealous. "What's troubling you?"

Rif looked back, startled. Oh, he was quick, Black Cal. No sense lying to him, either. "Yer job and mine," she said. "Ye know I do other things than sing."

"How well do the Janes pay?" he asked, eyes wandering back to the ceiling.

"Fine when they got 'er," Rif said quickly, wondering if she should deflect him from this train of thought or not. "O' course, that's not too often."

Black Cal said nothing, sorry he'd gotten Rif off onto the subject of money.

She misread his silence. "Ye know I don't work fer 'em only fer the money! But, dammit, I've gotter make a livin' too."

"I know that." He paused, looking for the words to describe the whole difficult balance of personal honor where love had taken him. He wasn't used to explaining himself, and the pause stretched long.

"Look . . ." Rif propped herself up on her elbows and finger-combed her hair out of her eyes. "I won't ask ye ter go 'gainst the law fer me. I try ter keep my . . . games outter yer sight, so's ye won't hafter choose."

"I know that!" Damn, she'd laid it out so clearly, so simply, and he was still struggling with words. She had the advantage, being a singer, a poet, words her common tools.

Rif looked off into some indefinable distance, chewing over a possibility. "I'll even warn ye when not ter look."

"Better I shouldn't know."

Rif thought on that awhile. "What if . . . what if I tell ye about other things goin' on, things that don't do nobody good, folk that really need bustin', for everybody's safety. Will that balance 'er out?"

Black Cal shut his eyes in relief. Balance: yes, she understood. "Yes," he said.

"*You* know, none better, there's lots worse nor squeezin' around dumb regulations an' trimmin' a little fat off the rich."

"I know that."

"Would ye agree," Rif smiled grimly, "that slavin' is worse?"

Black Cal snapped his eyes open, seeing bits and pieces fall into a pattern. "Oh, yes."

Rif paused for a moment, calculating fast. "Ternight," she said, "right about three bells,, do ye stroll past Megary's, ye might see some good evidence ter bust Megarys for slavin'. Ye game fer it?"

A slow, wide smile spread across Black Cal's face as he saw the pattern unfold. *Lord, what a team we make!* "Fair game," he said.

"Will you quit checking that timepiece?" Rattail whispered, easing her way up the thick bracing-timber. "Pay out the rope."

"Aye." Rif reeled out another yard of line. No more words now, they were close to the target. She counted timbers once more, making absolutely sure this was the window Denny meant. Then she inched after her partner in total and elaborate silence.

Most of their caution was wasted; the shouting, cursing and crackle of flames down by the boat-dock would have covered the noise of a dozen burglars. There lay all three of Megary's boats, burning merrily down to the waterline in bluish flames that smelled strongly of alcohol. Other burning splashes crawled up the dock and the nearest wall, showing where bad aim or enthusiasm had scored other targets.

Megary retainers, a good two dozen of them, were running back and forth to the water, filling buckets and flinging their contents on the flames. They made headway slowly; fuel alcohol burned even when diluted, and there was an impressive amount of it soaking the wood.

Boats, dock and walls were spotted with black char marks, some still wet and steaming, showing that this was by no means the first fire of the night.

Farther up the narrow water, hidden from the light of the troublesome fires, canalers watched and laughed. This wouldn't be the last fire of the night, either.

Rattail paused, just under the window, to study the scene a moment longer while Rif climbed up beside her. "Blacklegs?" she whispered.

"Bought off," Rif whispered back. "Canalers. Didn't take much."

Rattail chuckled, understanding. Megarys paid the blacklegs regularly to not investigate rumors of slave-dealing, but this current rash of raids had eaten into the budget a good bit. House Megary had not thought to pay the blacklegs extra to come and guard the house, or else had chosen not to spend the money. It didn't cost much at all to persuade the blacklegs to keep on keeping away from Megary's, especially at night.

All blacklegs but one, anyway.

Rif suppressed an urge to check the time again. Not now: just get in, do the work, let the "evidence" loose at just the right time . . . Sweet Jane, but this was going to take precision, and she didn't yet know exactly what they'd find inside.

Rattail reached the window, staying carefully below the ledge, and eased a listening-tube over the sill, through the bars, against the glass. Now patience: listen for a good five minutes at least, make damn sure there was nobody awake and waiting on the other side of the glass.

Rif crouched in the shadows on the timber, waiting for her partner's report and keeping an eye toward the water below.

Five minutes passed, no boats came by, and no sound came from behind the glass. Below and off-starboard, the boats still burned and the house-guards still labored. Rattail nodded, and Rif passed up one end of a short, heavy-hauling line. Rattail quick-tied the end to the nearest of the window bolts while Rif ran the other end through a pulley on a hook and strong-tied the hook to the timber. Another quick glance around for witnesses, and Rif handed up her end of the line. Rattail took it, hauled in the slack, looped the excess over her shoulder, put slow but serious muscle into the line. The pulley tuned silently, the hook's anchoring tie stretched taut, and the bolt on the window began to bend.

Slowly, quietly, the aged metal bent outward, then down. When it pointed so near to straight down that the line was in danger of slipping off, Rat slacked off the pressure. "Easy," she whispered, untying the line and reaching for the next bolt.

"Shh," Rif warned, reaching up to put a cautious ear to the listening-tube. A moment's checking revealed no sound. Rif signaled go-ahead.

Rattail tied the line to the next bolt and applied pressure again.

It took almost exactly a quarter of an hour to get the screen down. By that time most of the boat-fires had been put out, but the Megarys staff was busy examining the boats—and dock, and walls—for damage and leftover embers. They'd stay busy for awhile. Rif made some more silent calculations, then sent a note-perfect birdcall toward the nearest rooftop across the canal. Denny's whistle came back: ready and waiting for orders. Good.

Rattail took out a suction cup and pressed it tight to the glass. A light tug proved it was firm. Rif took up the glass cutter and ran it slowly, carefully, over the glass as close as possible to the frame. Twice around she went, making sure the cuts were deep.

They stopped again to listen, making sure the Megary folk were busy, and noisy. Rif tapped experimentally at the glass.

Tink.

No, too loud. Too much noise to tap the pane free.

Rif sighed, then whistled again to the other building. A different bird-call acknowledged. The partners waited, motionless.

Across the canal, a stone dropped to the water. A soft splash, then a laugh. A small flame winked briefly.

Out of nowhere a bottle came flying across the canal, its neck trailing a flaming wick, tumbling end over end, smack toward the front of Megary's Island.

Howls of outrage followed its course, and guns began firing into the dark even before the bottle hit, but there was no further sign of the unknown arsonist. The bottle, a good-sized jug, smashed gloriously on the wall above Megary's front door, splashing its contents far and wide. An instant later, the splash caught fire.

An irregular star of blue flame spread across the wall, lighting up the building front, the docks and the water below. The Megary staff shouted, swore, and ran for the buckets.

On the other side of the tall isle, Rif broke the glass free and scaled it away across the water. It struck and sank somewhere in the dark, unnoticed in the noise about the fire. Thirty seconds later, both partners were through the open window and inside.

For long moments they sat still, eyes shut, listening for any sign of another presence. Hearing none, they took out two small dark-lanterns and lit them, using the flare of the matches to look at the room around them.

"Sweet Jane," Rif breathed, even as her hands closed down the shutter of the dark-lantern. "It's their record-room!"

Paper: boxes, shelves, cupboards and file cabinets stuffed with papers filled the room from floor to ceiling. There was scarcely room to walk between the piles.

"Years' worth," Rat agreed. "Retribution, what dirt we could dig up here!"

"No time. Maybe we could move it out, look at it later . . ."

No, Rat didn't need to answer that. Clearly, there was too much paper here to shift. A moment's thought showed that they couldn't just pitch it out the window, either. The splashing would be noticeable. The partners looked at each other, sighed in regret, fetched their gear in through the window, then got up and pulled out their bottles of chugger.

Setting the fire properly took up nearly all their fuel, leaving barely enough for the leader-trail running out the door. Rif took point-position this time, spying out the corridor and checking rooms on either side.

Most of them were locked, the only open one revealing a spartan, rumpled bedroom—probably used by the house guards between shifts. A key-ring hung from a hook near the door. Rif grabbed the keys, listened a moment for approaching footsteps, heard none, and unlocked the nearest closed door.

Inside were four women, wearing plain coarse shirts and trousers, huddled in sleep on the floor. Rif smiled, left the door open, and padded silently away.

In the next room lay a burly man, bruised about the face and clearly unconscious. Rif left him lying, and the door open, and went to the last room.

This one was full of children, maybe a dozen of them, curled together like puppies. One, a girl of maybe twelve at most, stirred and looked up. Her eyes widened and her mouth dropped open.

Rif smiled and held a warning finger to her lips. The little girl shut her mouth and watched. "Wait," Rif whispered, and backed out the open door. She ran on tiptoe back down the corridor, knowing her admonition wouldn't hold the child for long. Back to the room with the women, signaling fast to Rattail in passing, inside and down beside the nearest sleeper: Rif pressed a hand over the woman's mouth and added a quick shake to waken her. The woman didn't move, but her eyes snapped open.

"Get the others up quick and quiet," Rif whispered. "Get the man next door, and the kids beyond 'im. When we tell ye, everybody run, scatter and get out. Ye got that?"

The woman nodded quickly, staring. Rif left her, looked down the corridor once more, then hurried back to Rattail. Already she could hear small feet pattering about in the last room.

"Check out the corridor," she said. "I'll light 'er."

Rat nodded, got up and hurried down the hall,

eased around the left corner and disappeared in the dark. Rif checked the time again, made a few calculations, took a sliver of wood to the dark-lantern and lit off the trail of chugger.

Blue flames leaped to life on the floor, grew, and wandered off into the soaked and waiting record-room.

Rif ran back down the corridor, stopped for a moment at the roomful of now-awake women, and told them: "Now. Every'body, up and out. Let loose every other slavey y'can find here." She tossed them the guard's key-ring, then followed Rattail around the corner.

"Shh!" Rat whipped out a hand to stop her. "Watch feet."

Rif looked down and saw a pair of feet sticking out of a doorway.

"Help me haul him the rest of the way in," Rat explained. "I caught him coming out, but he'd heavy."

"Aye." Rif took the feet, which turned out to be attached to a burly lout with a beltful of weapons. Rat took the arms, and they toted the massive body back into the room that was clearly the man's own, to judge by the clutter.

Back down the corridor and around the corner came sounds of running and dragging feet—and the smell of burning.

Rat lugged the body to the bed, removed the weapons-belt and settled it around her own waist.

"Find the cuffs and keys," Rif whispered, searching the man's pockets, turning up coins, assorted keys, dice and a penknife.

"Here." Rat found a sturdy set of cuffs on the belt and handed them over. Rif, smiling unprettily, handcuffed the man to his bedstead and resumed her search of his pockets.

"Just leave him here?" Rat asked, casting a worried look toward the door.

"Aye. Let's go."

"Which way?"

"Upstairs. Everyone else'll be runnin' down."

"Ah."

They took their usual care examining the rest of this hallway and its rooms, finding no more than empty cells and servants' quarters, before proceeding upstairs. Now they eased along the walls, listening constantly, keeping track of the shoutings and thumpings both above and far below. With altitude came the wealthier apartments, better loot but more chance of meeting guards. At the first sound of close voices, they pulled their weapons out.

Ah, voices right behind the wall, here: two men, arguing.

"Hell and bad water, this is *your* fault! It started with that grab of yours, and I've had nothing but trouble since. Damn it, Magruder, you owe me!"

The reply was unintelligible, but sounded like a grumbling snarl.

Rat and Rif looked at each other. "Who?" Rat mouthed.

Magruder. Rif remembered the name. A wicked smile spread slowly across her face. She reached into a seldom-used pocket and brought out a particular tool, held it up where Rat could see. Rat looked at the odd-shaped tool, looked at the door, shrugged and grinned. Rif bent to the lock and got busy.

It took less than ten seconds' work to jam the lock solid.

As the partners ran away on tiptoe, giggling silently, the first sounds of alarm came echoing up from the floor directly below. So did a new, strong smell of smoke. Rat and Rif took to feeling the walls and doors for telltale heat, as well as listening for voices and watching for approaching staff in the hallways.

Once a woman who looked like a clerk came hurrying out of a door right ahead of them. Rif and Rat, gear carefully hidden under their loose shirts, put on respectable, preoccupied expressions and marched past her as if on their way to important tasks. The woman didn't bother looking at them as she passed. Rat and Rif turned back to check the room the clerk had just exited, but heard voices behind the door and turned away from it.

At the end of the hall they found a locked room with neither heat nor voices behind the door, got into it quickly and found a nicely-appointed luxury suite. Fine pickings here: Rat and Rif loaded their bags with assorted jewelry (some of it cut roughly off collars and cuffs), decorative gewgaws in fine metal and crystal, fistfuls of cash found in a drawer and a few expensive items of clothing. It was quite sufficient pay for the night's work.

Howls of dismay and alarm grew louder in the corridor outside. Rif looked again at the time. "Let's go," she whispered.

Rat nodded, tied up her stash-bag and headed for the window.

Getting out was much easier than getting in, since the window-grills on this level unlatched on the inside. Projecting beams below the window on the outside made ropes and pulleys unnecessary. The only possible problem lay in their position; this window was on the side of the building and near the front. Rat and Rif prudently kept in the shadows under the beams as they worked their way downward.

A puff of offshore wind brought heavy smoke, sounds of firefighting and evacuation gloriously muddled, and the ominous crackling of flames.

Rif thought a moment, then started working her way toward the front of Megary Isle.

"Where you going?" Rat hissed.

"Front-row seat." Rif whispered back, wriggling into the angle of a corner beam and its brace.

Rat chuckled and followed her.

The argument between Chance Magruder and Old Man Megary came to a full stop with a shifting of wind. Both of them smelled the smoke and heard the noise at the same instant. Both of them stopped in mid-word and stared at each other, eyes widening with all-too-likely surmise.

In that moment's pause they clearly heard the house majordomo bellowing: "Everybody out! Fire on the second floor, west! Everybody—"

Megary shrieked a curse and ran to the window, threw open sash and grill and shutters, and peered out to see where the flames had reached.

Magruder only ran for the door.

"The records!" Megary screamed, recognizing that particular window where flames were climbing out and upward. "They threw one into the records-room! Lord, Lord, the files—"

"Open this door!" Magruder bellowed. "Unlock this damned door, you fool! Where's the key?"

"Locked? I didn't lock it."

Magruder swore incoherently and threw himself against the door.

Megary's construction was unusually sturdy, even for burglary-conscious Merovingen. The door barely echoed with the impact. Magruder rebounded with a sore shoulder, and tried an experimental kick. The door barely quivered.

Old Megary fumbled a keyring from his pocket, hurried to the door and fussed with the lock. "Damnation!" he squeaked. "It won't even go in! Someone's jammed it!"

A puff of visible smoke rolled in through the window. Megary's mumbling broke off in a fit of coughing.

"Is there another way out?" Magruder howled.

Old Man Megary only shook his head, then began pounding feebly on the door.

Magruder snapped a broken fragment of a Nev Hettek curse and ran for the open window. Below lay the water, three stories down.

Behind him, Old Megary began screaming thinly for help.

Magruder swung his legs over the sill, balanced a moment, took a deep breath, raised his arms over his head, and dived out.

Megary stopped screeching, smiled from ear to ear, and waited for the splash.

Sploot!

Old Megary frowned, annoyed. A sharp, clean impact: the bastard must have dived right and landed well, was probably still alive. Hope he swallowed half the canal before coming up. Ah, well.

Megary shrugged, went to a full-length mirror on the right-hand wall, tugged at a concealed catch on the frame. The mirror—and the hidden door behind it—swung smoothly outward. Old Megary stepped through the narrow doorway and into the next room, opened the obvious door into the corridor, and walked unhurriedly toward the stairs.

Black Cal stood at the foot of the bridge, leaning casually into a patch of shadow. His little quartet of rookies obligingly did the same, even having the sense to keep their voices down to a near-inaudible whisper as they speculated on the fire, its sources, and Black Cal's reasons for waiting here so long. "Observe carefully," he'd told them. "Watch for details, and wait for my signal." Oh yes, they'd do that; nobody wanted to argue with a legend, especially when his last such sortie had won two of them a good, solid bust and much prestige. Work right with Black Cal and you'd climb far and fast. Besides, everyone knew about Megarys. Lord and Ancestors, what a fine big bust this could be!

Black Cal watched the bridge and waited. Megarys' boats were charred useless and the nearby walkways were loaded with small crowds of . . . innocently . . . loitering canalers (observe Rif's fine hand at work there), so this was the likeliest way for any escapees from the fire to take. Judging from the noise, flames, confusion and speed of the scampering silhouettes on the island, the commotion would come this way soon.

Aha! There: a small scurrying figure in rags, ducking from minimal cover to cover, heading this way. Right.

Black Cal signaled the other blacklegs to stay put, crouched in his patch of shadow and waited for the right instant.

The runner—identifiable now as a long-haired child—came pelting down the bridge, going all out.

Wait, wait . . . Lunge!

Black Cal sprang out like a loosed arrow, grabbed the child around the body, swung her in a neat half-circle and dumped her—stunned, unharmed and gulping—on her feet, pinned against the railing by his immovable arm.

"Who are you, and what were you doing in Megary?" Black Cal asked, as calm and polite as if he were inquiring about the time of day.

"T-T-Tilda," the girl stammered. " 'N' I'm tryin' ter get away from 'em! They had me locked up there. Please, m'ser, I just wanter go home."

"How did you come to be in there?"

"A man grabbed me off Slaney's dock," Tilda whimpered, tears spilling out of her eyes. "He threw a bag over my head an' grabbed me up. I was goin' home. My Ma doesn' know where I am . . ."

"You were kidnapped and taken to Megarys?" Black Cal asked quietly, very precisely.

"Yey. Was." the child blubbered. "I cried at 'em ter lemme go home, but they wouldn' lissen . . ."

"I'll take you home, But first, do you want to get back at the slavers?"

"Y-yey . . ." Tilda stopped crying and looked up, hope dawning on her smudged face. "Ye goin' ter get 'em?"

"Slavery and abduction are crimes," said Black Cal. "You stay here behind me and identify the slavers for me as they came down the bridge. You understand?"

"Oh, yey." Tilda's face split in a wide, gap-toothed grin. "Hey ye're Black Cal, ain't'cha?"

Black Cal smiled, nodded, patted the girl's thin shoulder and stood up to look at the bridge. Oh yes, here came another batch of runners, two kids and a woman dressed like the girl, running maybe three fathoms ahead of a burly lout in a jangling belt full of keys and small weapons. The woman and kids were running all-out and wild-eyed. The man was well-dressed, and had a good-sized padded mace in his hand.

"I know him!" Tilda squeaked, pointing. "He snatched me!"

Black Cal signaled silently to his waiting squad, and pulled out a short truncheon of his own.

The woman and kids reached the foot of the bridge, ran right past Black Cal and his team without seeing them. The man came pounding into reach.

Black Cal swung his truncheon in a fast, high, roundhouse arc that caught the slave-chaser neatly across the forehead. The satisfying *thunk* was muffled by the noise of the fire, as was the meaty *thud* of the man hitting the boards face-first.

A little farther down the walkway, the lattermost of Black Cal's squad caught the running woman by the arm, spun her around—not quite as neatly as Black Cal had done it, well enough—blocked her panicky swat at his head, and announced: "Blacklegs! Stand still; we need you t'identify this perp."

At a quick signal from Black Cal, two more of the rookies came up to the unconscious slaver, clapped the cuffs on his wrists and dragged him around a corner of the railing, sufficiently out of the way and out of sight.

Tilda giggled in delight.

The woman came tottering up to Black Cal, dizzy at the speed of her change in fortunes. "More," she panted. "There's more of 'em."

"Stand here, keep quiet and point them out," said Black Cal, watching the bridge. Soon enough, he guessed, others would come along.

"Hey, someone jumped!" Rattail paused in her downward climb, noting the splash three stories down. "There."

Rif looked, saw the foam and the surfacing body. Hmm, close to the front wall. From the amount of splash, he'd jumped a fair long way. She glanced up the building and made a few good guesses. "He was in that," she said, hardly whispering now that the other noise was so loud. "That's either Old Megary himself or that Magruder fella."

"He still alive?" Rattail grunted, roping down from the beam above.

"Yey. Pity. Hmm." Rif paused where she was, stuck two fingers in her mouth and threw a shrill, complicated series of night-bird whistles toward the building across the canal. She hoped Denny could make out the description and instructions in all this noise. Too bad she didn't dare use one of her pistols, this close to so many ears. Ah, well.

Ah, there! Faint above the racket came the short whoop of acknowledgment. Right, Denny alerted.

"Perch here," she laughed up at Rattail. "Let's watch the fun."

Denny leaned out perilously far above the roof-gutter, peering down at the water. Yes, he could see it now—the faint splashing wake of a man swimming slowly, laboriously, across the canal . . . and away from Megarys. Yes, slowly enough to allow plenty of time for good aim.

He pulled back onto the roof proper, selected a previously loosened roof-tile, hefted it to judge its weight and likely flight path. Then once more to the gutter, pinpointing the target. Right. Perfect. A good ways out, but very possible.

Denny scaled the tile out into the air, and watched it sail gracefully down into the canal.

Magruder gulped another lungful of air, clamped his eyes and mouth shut and wished he could close his nose and ears as well. The canals down here in the tidewater of Merovingen were open sewers, raw and stinking with unguessable pollution. When he got out . . . (if he got out . . . No, mustn't think that way, or he'd never get out) he'd have to take a dozen different treatments for contamination. Lord, keep the lips pressed tight; don't swallow even a drop of the water. Might as well be swimming in a huge vat of mixed poison, and it was so far to safety.

No, not really so far, he kept telling himself. *Just a few dozen meters across, farside of West . . . Stroke, stroke . . .*

But the water was so cold, and sludge thick, and reeking. His wrenched shoulders ached, and the throbbing in his hands warned that at least a few fingers were broken—and what could he expect, diving three stories straight down into the canal? Lucky he hadn't hit bottom, had arched his back properly to come up in a good, shallow arc—and Lord, his back hurt too, probably strained up and down. No, forget that; he was alive, and his injuries were curable. Stroke, stroke. He'd trained for years to deal with just such ordeals as this. Stoke, stroke, use mainly the legs . . .

Something large splashed into the water beside him, breaking his concentration.

For a moment Magruder floundered and splashed, making no headway, while he grappled with the question of what the hell had just missed him. Body? Missile? Wreckage? Should he dive, or change course?

But there was no further sound or motion. Inanimate object, probably a piece of wreckage off Megary Isle. Maybe a chunk of the old man still trapped in that locked room, and serve him right. More trouble than he was worth: let him burn. Probably some ambitious heir had locked him in . . .

No, never mind that now. Keep swimming. Aim toward the far edge of the canal, get clear of the crowds, keep himself hard to locate in this damned pitch dark. Filthy, degenerate city: not even decent lighting. Stoke, stroke, stroke. Lord, this stinking water was *cold.*

The second tile came plummeting down bullet-fast, and hit Magruder squarely on the right leg, just above the knee.

The impact knocked the wind out of him in an explosive grunt, and thrust him down deep into the water. His leg went numb from the knee on down.

Magruder flailed weakly with his feeble arms and

one good leg, dizzily trying to reach the surface and not—please, Lord, *not*—swallow any of that poisonous water. And where the hell was the surface? His lungs were screaming for air.

A sudden splash and he was up, head free of the water. Magruder floated for a long moment, gulping blessed air, trying to collect his sluggish wits. His lower right leg was still numb, useless.

Far bank . . . Where?

There it lay, visibly in the firelight, not five meters off. Magruder kicked out, lopsidedly, pawed with his barely workable arms, crawled toward that mockingly close edge of the canal. The sluggish but steady tug of the Det's seaward current teased at him. Closer now. Four meters. Three . . .

Another huge tile smacked the water, right behind him. The turbulence of its impact shoved Magruder sideways down the current.

At that point he realized that the missiles were deliberately thrown.

Megarys? he thought, letting the river drag him downstream, closer to the cover of a large bridge. Oh, that would make sense; whoever had locked him in with Old Megary was trying to cover his tracks, eliminate the last witness. Treacherous Merovingian bastards. Magruder cursed wearily and lashed hard with his good leg, made his aching arms move. Two meters—and now the shadow of a bridge fell over him. One more meter . . .

There was no landing here. The masonry wall of an isle rose a good meter and more above him, studded with boat-tie rings, but offering no easy stairs.

Magruder clutched a ring and floated there, panting. How to climb up? His abused shoulders wouldn't lift him. Somewhere on this island there had to be a flight of water-stairs he could climb. But where? How could he get there, injured and exhausted like this? And the cold of the filthy water was eating into his bones.

Wait: voices up there, by the foot of the bridge—cursing, crying snapping grim replies. People up there, drawn by the fire, had spotted him, Magruder caught at a boat-ring, wondered how many there were. Lord, they'd want money for helping him. How much? More to the point, seeing how his sore arms shook and his numb leg dragged, how much to hire a boat and take him to safety? He'd need good medical treatment, fast. *Tatiana* . . . The Rock. Other end of town. Canal-rats might not go that far, without the promise of good money. Well, he had that: a good ten dece,—still in his buttoned pockets— He'd make it.

"Now who's this?" said a soft voice, as long arms reached down to take Magruder's wrists. "And what're you doing down there?" The rescuing hands pulled.

As his body was dragged up from the water, the sudden weight on his arm made Magruder's wrenched shoulders flare with pain. His bruised ribs stretched, adding to the anguish. A screech jumped out of him, leaving swirling dizziness in its wake. More hands pulled him up onto the walkway, then patted over him as he lay gasping in a growing puddle.

Too late he realized that the searching hands had found his pistol. Magruder tried to roll on his side to protect his coin-pocket, and found that his strength was totally gone.

"Hmm, so how did you wind up in the canal?" the soft voice insisted. "Jumped?"

"Uhuh," Magruder grunted, trying to get his wind back. " 'M hurt. Take me home. I'll pay well."

"Hmm, and where's home?"

Tatiana. Medical supplies . . . "The Rock. I'll pay . . ."

"My, my, my," purred the soft voice, taking on a

slight edge. "And what would a nice hightown m'ser—from the Rock, no less—have been doing down here at Megarys, so late at night?"

Magruder turned his aching head enough to look up at his questioner. He saw a very tall, slender man in the characteristic all-black livery of the city guard. A blackleg, no doubt fishing for a bribe. Lord, not a dickering-session now, not now when he could barely think, let along move.

"Business," he mumbled. "Just get me home. No questions . . . and I'll pay extra."

"Extra, hmm? And what were you paying for there? A pretty bed-girl? Or boy?"

"Girl!" Magruder snapped. Hell, let the man think it was a simple case of whoring, good for blackmail. Offer enough money to make him reckless. Eliminate him when he came back for more. "Five dece, gold. Get me home, no questions . . ." That should do it.

"Witness!" the soft voice growled, utterly cold. "Confession of whoring and attempted bribing of an officer,"

What? Magruder struggled to make sense of this sudden reversal.

"I heard it!"said a gleefully voice nearby. "I did, too!" claimed another.

Somewhere farther off, a child giggled.

"You," said the soft-voiced blackleg, "are under arrest."

Makes no sense. . . . Magruder tried to shake his head clear. Was this a set-up? But he'd made sure no one knew he was coming here, no one but his own men. Had one of them turned? How? And why hadn't they left him in the canal, then? What was the game here?

Magruder opened his eyes again, and found himself looking into the muzzle of the biggest pistol he'd ever seen. The tall blackleg holding it smiled, smiled like a sherk, his eyes showing green in the firelight.

"Got 'im," Rif purred, watching from the beam. "A fine haul tonight."

"An interesting love-gift, anyway," Rattail agreed. "He ought to be grateful."

"Enough," Rif snapped her a warning look. "Time ter go. Fun's over."

Rattail shrugged, glanced across the canal and whistled three notes of a night-bird's song. A single chirp acknowledged.

The partners climbed downward, listening for the almost-inaudible swishing sound of a small pole-boat coming toward them through the darkness across the water.

From walkways, from the tie-ups, from a dozen shadowed vantages, canaler eyes watched the delightful troubles of Megarys' Isle. Pity that the fire seemed to be contained, if a long way from out. And what fun to see the house emptied, captives running to freedom, Megary's goons getting caught and pummeled well—and, of course, all the House's boats burning. A fine night's work, altogether. And there would be other nights.

"What in hell were you doing?"

Tatiana Kalugin had waited hours for enough privacy to ask Magruder just that question. She couldn't resist adding: "You don't know what it's costing me to keep this quiet. Lord, a scandal this juicy: 'Nev Hettek Trade Delegate Caught Dealing in Sex-slaves.' Think what the scandal-sheets would have done with that!"

Magruder suppressed a groan as he rolled over on his uninjured side. His whole body ached, throbbed and stung, —not least from the multiple antibiotics shots from his own kit—and he knew he'd be spending days and days moving like this. "I was following up a lead," he said shortly. "That Deems business."

"To *Megary*? Not with Gallandry involved."

"Not that they knew," he said shortly, trying not to sound impatient. Woman was dense. He ached. He wanted sleep. "But the link exists."

"On whose information?"

"One of *my* sources. I don't want it disturbed."

"*You* don't want. *You* don't choose. *I* know something in this city, m'ser outsider, I can tell you Megary is applying to high connections *outside* my control, I can tell you Megary's running scared and they're doubting their safety right now. They're afraid and they're just liable to talk in the wrong ears—"

"It'll be handled."

"Handled." Tatiana studied her lover's puffy and sickly-looking face. He looked miserable, totally unappetizing, probably too dull with pain to invent specific evasions. "Why in *hell* did you say you were consorting with prostitutes?"

"He suggested it; I just agreed. God, what did you want me to say? I was shopping for a bolt of silk? A side of beef? Aw, hell, pass me the water, will you?"

Frowning, Tatiana handed him a glass of water, saying nothing.

Yes, everyone knew that her city militia could be bought. It was part of the system, from time out of reach—and nonetheless, that system worked. The well-understood, unwritten schedule of payoffs and patronage formed a pattern whereby people could live, Kalugins could hold power, trade could flourish, the city could run efficiently—but how was she to explain that life-learned system to an outsider?

And he *was* an outsider, as she could see very

clearly this morning. For all his charm and cleverness, he didn't really know her city as well as he thought. He didn't even know all the unspoken rules, let alone the exceptions thereto.

In this case, he'd had the bad luck to encounter Black Cal, the one unbuyable blackleg in the city. She tried to imagine the meeting. And the consequences.

Had Black Cal bought the story? Or would he take the warning, if he discovered his commander's money had bailed Magruder out?

"God," Magruder was groaning, "I won't be able to tend to business for a week. —Or anything else." He patted her leg. "My apologies."

Tatiana's smile remained fixed. *Fool*, she thought, not questioning the real source of her distaste. Did he think he looked seductive right now, between bandages, his foreign-pale skin spotted with purple bruises and clashing orange disinfectant? A truly impressive picture.

He was woefully ignorant—of her, her city, his limitations. He took her for incompetent in intrigue—and in managing her office. Perhaps he mistook her interest in him for infatuation and her ambitions limited to the bedroom. *Fool.*

It occurred to her that it would betray too much to inform him of her reactions, betray too much even to hint at this stage. Let him come to the conclusion, by himself, that she knew this city better than he ever would. Let him convince himself, by sharply-learned lessons, that he needed her more than she needed him—

And thereby—that his future, in several senses, was more profitable in *her* service than Karl Fon's.

Seeing that she *would* rule the southern course of the Det—and that she was not, like her father, content with that; and not, like her elder brother Mikhail, a fool and a puppet; and not, like her younger brother Anastasi, a spoiler intent on war only as a mechanism for him to seize (and thereby damage) the power that would merely fall, intact, into her lap when her father died.

She would not proceed by war. She had other uses for the weapon that was Chance Magruder.

And all the clandestine apparatus he managed.

A brief vision of her father's face, rigid with disapproval, flickered through her mind—

—quickly, with a wince—dismissed.

At his spy-post in the corridor, the blackleg listened silently to the conversation inside, and took detailed notes.

The crowd at Hoh's was packed to the walls, bright-eyed and wild, but all laughing, grinning, drinking as if there were no tomorrow, singing along raucously with the performers on stage. Hoh himself worked the bar, all his regular staff not enough for such a huge and thirsty mob, smiling from ear to ear as he filled the cups and collected the silverbits. Oh yes, those singers were money in the bank; look at the trade they brought in, more every night, draining the barrels like a victory celebration—and never mind what war. A few more nights like this, and he could expand business.

The customers, mostly canalers with a few shopmen, drank merrily, bought more rounds for their friends, gossiped quickly during the songs' verses and joined merrily on the choruses—giving respectful room only to the table in the corner, where a legend sat smiling gently and nursing a beer as if he were almost one of them. Oh, it was that good a night at Hoh's.

Black Cal sat relaxed, almost sprawled, in the barely lamplit corner, fingers tapping time on his cup of

Hoh's best. He no longer even bothered to track his glance occasionally across the crowded barroom, but only watched one of the singers. He couldn't remember ever having felt this good in a public place. This was magic, true magic, and all her doing. Lord, what art.

On the stage, Rif could feel that warm green stare clean across the room. Yes, yes, let him see; last night had been work, done for many interlocking reasons, but tonight—this place and this celebration, and their time together afterwards—was her private gift to him.

Let him see it, hear it, take his own message out of this song that so many were singing tonight. Rif tossed back her tangled cloak of dark hair, vamped two beats coming off the instrumental break, and plunged into the new last verse.

"Slavers crying in their beer.
Something's burning.
Poor things get no pity here.
Something's burning.
Fire, clean this trash away:
Clear the karma yet to pay—
Give us back the stars someday.
Something's burning—
Burning . . . down.
All our chains are
Burning down!"

APPENDIX

MEROVINGIAN FOLKLORE 101
OR
ALARUMS, EXCURSIONS, AND RUMORS

Mercedes R. Lackey

Certain folktales dating back to pre-spaceflight days seem to crop up wherever humankind plants its roots, whether or not the immediate ancestors of those settlers ever heard of those tales in their lives. The following archetypical stories may be heard all over Merovin in one form or another, and are told to this day from hightown to canalside throughout Merovingen. And the teller will undoubtedly aver that although *he* didn't witness this, he has a brother (cousin, aunt, friend) who knows someone who *did*, so you can be certain that it is *true*.

THE CHILD ON THE BRIDGE

It is a dark and foggy night, usually just after Festival Moon. A lone woman is making her way homeward, and takes a shortcut across Hanging Bridge. Just beneath the statue of the Angel, she sees a child huddled, crying. Being kindhearted, she stops to ask the child what is wrong.

When the child emerges from the shadows, she can see that it is well-dressed (and, in some versions, dripping wet), so it is no half-orphaned bridge-brat.

The child tells her that it is lost, and gives a middling hightown address as its home. The woman now sees the prospect of a reward, as well as incurring the karmic debt of someone in a position to do her well, and so offers to take the child where it belongs. She generally offers the child the protection of her cloak, which the child accepts gratefully.

But the moment they step off the bridge, the woman notices that the warm little body pressed against her side is gone—nor is there any sign of the child, on the bridge or off it.

It is not until the next day, relating the story to another, that she learns that a child of that description and Family fell to its death from Hanging Bridge exactly one year before.

THE PHANTOM PASSENGER

It is very late at night; a poleboatman is making one last tour of canalside hoping to attract a final fare. And much to his surprise, he is hailed from Ventani by a very attractive young hightown woman.

He picks her up; she is looking something the worse for wear on close inspection. She explains to him that she was out with a party of young people when she became separated from them and robbed. She promises him that although she has no money he will be able to collect his fare from her father if he will just take her home. She offers him a very expensive scarf (or in some versions, a piece of jewelry, usually a ring) as a pledge to hold.

He acquiesces and takes her to the water-door of one of the Families. But when he arrives there and turns to assist her from the boat, she is gone, and so is the pledge.

He then usually goes to the doorman and tells him

the tale. The doorman tells him that the girl he described was the eldest daughter of the House, and that she was murdered by robbers on this very night just outside Moghi's Tavern.

In another version, the girl will not give her name, but asks to be taken to House Hannon and says that she was attacked by a man named "Chud." When the boatman arrives, she is gone, and her description matches that of the murdered Teryl Hannon who was drowned during Festival by an unknown assassin in the pay of the Gregoris. The man calling himself "Chud," disguised as a poleboatman, is wanted for the murder.

THE DEMON LOVER

A canaler (male or female) is out on the Rim fishing, and sees what appears to be a fellow canaler of incredible physical beauty out on a Rim sandspit by a small fire. If the canaler is paying attention, he (or she) may notice that the other casts no shadow, and that the bottom of his (her) breeches are always muddy and dripping with water, no matter how dry the air is. The charisma of this stranger is always so great that the canaler nevertheless throws all caution to the wind, and asks the stranger to sleep-up.

The stranger agrees, and steps aboard the canaler's skip. But at that moment any one several things may happen. In some versions, the canaler mentions the Dead Fleet. In others, the light from the fire falls upon a religious icon. In still others, they make it as far as Hanging Bridge, where the shadow of the Angel falls upon the stranger. In all cases, the stranger vanishes, proving to be a Dead Fleet ghost.

THE DEMON LOVER, PART TWO

In this case the canaler in question is vowed to be a no-good, rotten (exclusively male) bastard. He is out on the Rim for No Good Purpose. He discovers a very beautiful and very battered young woman on a sandspit, who begs him for help, saying she has just escaped from the Megarys. He, being a no-good, rotten bastard, agrees to help her—but is planning on raping her, then selling her back to the Megarys. In most versions he meets an acquaintance with whom he had a meeting, and tells of his changed plans for the evening. He intends to head for Dead Harbor again, it being unlikely that anyone will heed the girl's cries for help there.

He (of course) then vanishes, and his boat is found the next day floating at anchor in Dead Harbor just above the location of the sunken Ghost Fleet. The decks are stained with incredible amounts of blood, scored with what looks like claw marks, and there is usually something (a medallion, a very ancient coin, a bit of ship's insignia) identifying one of the ships known to have gone down with the Fleet on the halfdeck of the skip.

THE CATS OF JANE

A young mother is at her wits' end; there is no money, no prospect for any, her children have eaten the last crust and the rent is due. She goes out begging with no luck whatsoever; she even tries to sell herself, but has no takers.

She is about ready to kill herself on the steps of the College so that the priests will have the karmic obligation to take in her children, when an old canaler woman stops her and tells her to trust in the Good Goddess Jane Morgoth and not in the priests.

The woman laughs at her and says that Jane never helped her before, so why should she help her now. The canaler woman tells her that if she really wants help she must ask for it from one of Jane's special messengers—the black cats of Merovingen.

The woman, in despair, supposes she has nothing to lose and looks for a cat. It is very late when she finally finds one, and strangely, it does not run from her, but seems to listen until she has told her whole sad story, and only then leaves, heading straight for the roof.

The woman goes home and falls asleep in utter exhaustion.

In the morning she awakens to find a bag of silverbits beside each of her children's heads, or, in one version, a black kitten wearing a solid silver collar with a gold medallion of Jane at the foot of her bed.

THE SHARRH OF NAYAB

This story is always set at Nayab.

A gang of bridge-toughs is stalking a child; the presumed reason for the attack is to sell it to Megarys. The child runs injudiciously down to the waterline and begins trying to make an escape by using the narrow and treacherous walkways that edge the isle, most of them partially under water. The child is at length cornered after several narrow escapes. Just when all seems lost, there is a roar and a hideous manlike monster emerges from a hole in the foundations and attacks the toughs; killing at least half of them, and sending the rest into the canal. It turns to the child, and the child sees its face and faints.

The child wakes up on one of the walkways, with no

recollection of how it got there, and clutching a silver medallion inscribed with the strange characters of the sharrh. The child can no longer properly recall the face it saw, only that it was so alien as to make the eyes hurt. A hunt under Nayab reveals nothing except another silver medallion like the one the child found, and what appears to be an underwater escape tunnel that no one wishes to follow.

GOLDEN RULE

Lyrics by Mercedes Lackey

Lady from the hightown come a-walkin' down below—
Lady lookin' down 'er nose an' thinkin' we don't know—
If that lady lose 'er purse soon as 'er back be turned,
Figure, hightown lady, it's the price fer what ye've learned.

Duelist on the bridge lookin' mighty high an' proud,
Duelist reckons that 'e's better nor th' whole damn crowd.
If that fancy man should miss a coin or two or three,
Reckon that's the cost 'e pays that looks but doesn't see.

College priest a-strollin' thinkin' 'e's so pure an' fine.
College priest a-countin' sins an' layin' out his line,
Maybe some 'un's seen 'im with 'is lovers an' 'is toys—
Maybe soon 'e'll pay summat t' see there be no noise.

Merchant man with rooms all full of things 'e doesn't use
Merchant man, if some 'un begs yer help, why ye'd refuse.
Merchant man, walk through yer rooms, an' tally with
yer pen
Ye'll find yer house be lighter by a trinket now an' then.

Me, I ain't a-sayin' who did what, nor where they be
Figure that there ain't no profit in morality—
Not unless ye be the feller that kin fleece th' fools.
Reckon them as got the gold is them as makes the rules.

THE CATS OF JANE

Lyrics by Mercedes Lackey

In a one-room apartment in Ventani Gut
A mother weeps in hopeless fright,
For her children are hungry, the rent money's gone
And her man vanished into the night,
Tomorrow the hightowner landlord will come—
Tomorrow he'll drive them away.
But then in the darkness of night she awakes
And recalls what the old legends say—

Chorus:
"Tell your troubles to cats, the nightwalking cats,
The black cats of Althea Jane,
Tell your trouble to cats, Her messenger-cats,
For She cures the poor folk of their pain."

So she creeps out the doorway in search of a cat
And what should she find on the stair,
But a bright-eyed black tomcat, as bold and as proud
As if he had awaited her there.
She told him her woes, and he listened, it seemed,
With his eyes gold, unwinking, and bright,
And then when she had finished, he ran to the roof
And the shadows soon hid him from sight.
Now when she had turned homeward, it just might have
been

That a shadow moved where none should be,
And a shadow cat-footed, moved silent away—
But of course there was no one to see.
And it could be this shadow danced off on the roofs
With a shadowy cat-wise-like guile,
And it could be this shadow slipped soundlessly in
By a window of Ventani Isle.

Come next morning, the mother awoke to the sound
Of a kitten that purred at her feet,
And a second and third were curled up by the sides
Of her children that slept sound and sweet.
They say great was her wonder and great her surprise
And still greater her joy and delight,
For the kittens were black and each bore round its neck
A fat pouch full of silverbits bright!

LADIES OF THE HIGHTOWN

Lyrics by Mercedes Lackey

Oh the ladies of the hightown
Dressed in silk and lace so fine,
As they stroll along the bridges
You can see their jewels shine.
But the ladies of the hightown
To canalside never go,
And they'll never see the hunger
Of their sisters here below.

Oh the ladies of the hightown
With their perfumed hair so sweet,
Never smell the stinking water
That's so far below their feet.
But the women of canalside
And the women of the Trade
Know the worst of daily living—
Know that every debt gets paid.

Oh the ladies of the hightown
With their hands so soft and white,
Hands that never held a boathook,
Hands that never had to fight,
Hands that never nursed a fever,
Hands that never sewed a seam—

See the ladies of the hightown
Walking in their waking dream?

Oh the ladies of the hightown
Ladies of the town above—
They have never learned to suffer,
So they don't know how to love.
In their hearts can be no passion—
There is only room for pride.
Look down, ladies of the hightown,
Come and see the other side!

Come you ladies of the hightown
To canalside down below.
Come see dying and see living
Come where nothing is for show.
Can you brave the dark and danger?
Can you bear to learn to feel?
Come you ladies of the hightown,
Come and see what's true and real!

DARK LOVER

Lyrics by Mercedes Lackey

Young Moll was known to all the trade.
The River Det flows free.
She was a wild and proud young maid.
Down to the Sundance Sea.

It was the season of the cold
And hunger made our Molly bold.

She poled out to the Rim to see
If there might some good fishing be.

The night it took her unaware
She saw a sight to make her stare.

A handsome lad stood on the Rim
And Molly boldly said to him,

"No crazy do ye look to me—
So why not spend the night with me?"

"Fair Molly I will partner you
If you can read my riddles true.

Say what is darker than the night

And what is wilder than delight,

And what is worse than any hell
And what will never women sell,

And what is sharper than a thorn
And what will never be reborn?"

"Now sin is darker than the night,
Deathangel wilder than delight,

Canalside's worse than any hell,
Her heart will never woman sell,

And hunger's sharper than a thorn—
A Dead Marsh ghost can't be reborn—"

And as she named the lad aright,
    The River Det flows free,
He disappeared into the night
    Down to the Sundance Sea.

FALKEN LOVER

Lyrics by Mercedes Lackey

Come all you forsaken, take warning by me
And don't take a lover who lives by the sea.
They only hold true to their crewmates and ships
And nothing but lies ever passes their lips.

I once had a Falken-love, fair-skinned and fine
He swore that he loved me, he vowed he was mine.
But soon as the tide turned, my idol turned clay
As soon as the wind rose, my love sailed away.

I once had a Falkenaer, blue were his eyes,
And all of the vows that he made me were lies.
He came with the winter, he left with the spring,
As hard to hold down as a bird on the wing.

I once had a Falken-love, gold was his hair,
So handsome a man that the Angel would stare,
So handsome without and so hollow within,
The vows that he made me might never have been.

The sea was his true love, no other he had.
I was just diversion to my Falken-lad.
So all you forsaken, take warning by me,
No mortal love can ever rival the sea.

CANALERS' LOVE SONG

Lyrics by Mercedes Lackey

I won't ask you for a promise you can't make,
I won't tie you to a bargain that you'll break,
Love is just another counter in the Trade—
Like a coin that's easy spent, but dearly made.

Chorus:
So the old Det, he runs slow, but he runs deep
And the rising tide will rock us both to sleep.
Like the river Det my love runs deep and slow
And it's with you, love, wherever you may go.

I won't ask you for forever—just tonight,
Just the time between now and the morning light.
I won't tie my karma to you, that's not fair
And that's not the way to prove how much I care.

I won't beg you for the things you may not feel,
Just the little time together we can steal.
I won't ask you to say things you know are lies,
For I know that tears are all that lying buys.

But if you decide to stay here by my side
Then I'll show you all my feelings that I hide
And I'll try to make you happy that you stayed
And we'll show the world just how the game is played.

INDEX TO CITY MAPS

INDEX OF ISLES AND BUILDINGS BY REGIONS

THE ROCK:
(ELITE RESIDENTIAL)
LAGOONSIDE

1. The Rock
2. Exeter
3. Rodrigues
4. Navale
5. Columbo
6. McAllister
7. Basargin
8. Kalugin (governor's relatives)
9. Tremaine
10. Dundee
11. Kuzmin
12. Rajwade
13. Kuminski
14. Ito
15. Krobo
16. Lindsey
17. Cromwell
18. Vance
19. Smith
20. Cham
21. Spraker
22. Yucel
23. Deems
24. Ortega
25. Bois
26. Mansur

GOVERNMENT CENTER
THE TEN ISLES
(ELITE RESIDENCE)

27. Spur (militia)
28. Justiciary
29. College (Revenant)
30. Signeury
31. Carswell
32. Kistna
33. Elgin
34. Narain
35. Zorya
36. Eshkol
37. Romney
38. Rosenblum
39. Boregy
40. Dorjan

THE SOUTH BANK

Second rank of elite
41. White
42. Eber
43. Chavez
44. Bucher
45. St. John
46. Malvino (Adventist)
47. Mendelev
48. Sofia
49. Kamat
50. Tyler

THE RESIDENCIES

Mostly wealthy or government
51. North
52. Spellbridge
53. Kass
54. Borg
55. Bent
56. French
57. Cantry
58. Porfirio
59. Wex

WEST END

Upper middle class
60. Novgorod
61. Ciro
62. Bolado
63. diNero
64. Mars
65. Ventura
66. Gallandry (Advent.)
67. Martel
68. Salazar
69. Williams
70. Pardee
71. Calliste
72. Spiller
73. Yan

PORTSIDE

Middle Class
74. Ventani
75, Turk
76. Princeton
77. Dunham
78. Golden
79. Pauley
80. Eick
81. Torrence
82. Yesudian
83. Capone
84. Deva
85. Bruder
86. Mohan
87. Deniz

88. Hendricks
89. Racawski
90. Hofmeyr
91. Petri
92. Rohan
93. Herschell
94. Bierbauer
95. Godwin
96. Arden
97. Aswad

TIDEWATER (SLUM)

---

98. Hafiz (brewery)
99. Rostov
100. Ravi
101. Greely
102. Megary (slaver)
103. Ulger
104. Mendex
105. Amparo
106. Calder
107. Fife
108. Salvatore

FOUNDRY DISTRICT

109. Spellman
110. Foundry
111. Vaitan
112. Sarojin
113. Nayab
114. Petrescu
115. Hagen

EASTSIDE
(LOWER MID.)

---

116. Fishmarket
117. Masud
118. Knowles
119. Gossan (Adventist)
120. Bogar
121. Mantovan (Advent.) (wealthy)
122. Salem
123. Delaree

RIMMON ISLE
(ELITE/MERCANTILE)

124. Khan
125. Raza
126. Takezawa
127. Yakunin
128. Balaci
129. Martushev
130. Nikolaev

① **MEROVIN**

(first quarter — frontispiece map)

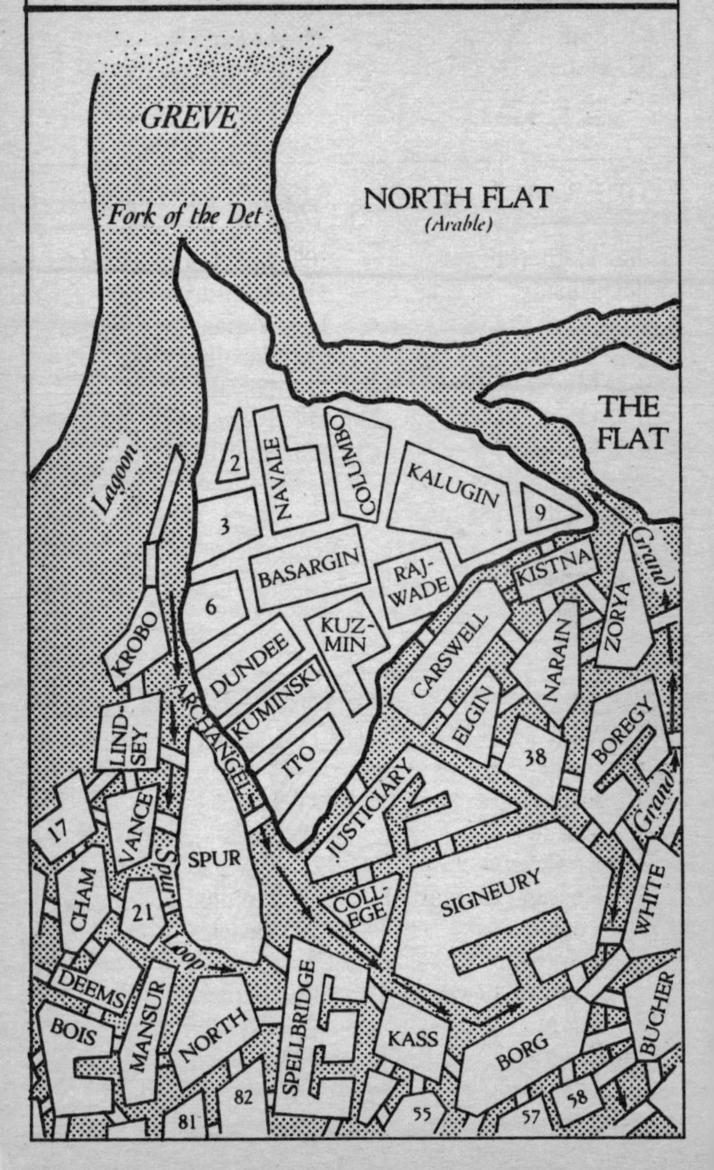

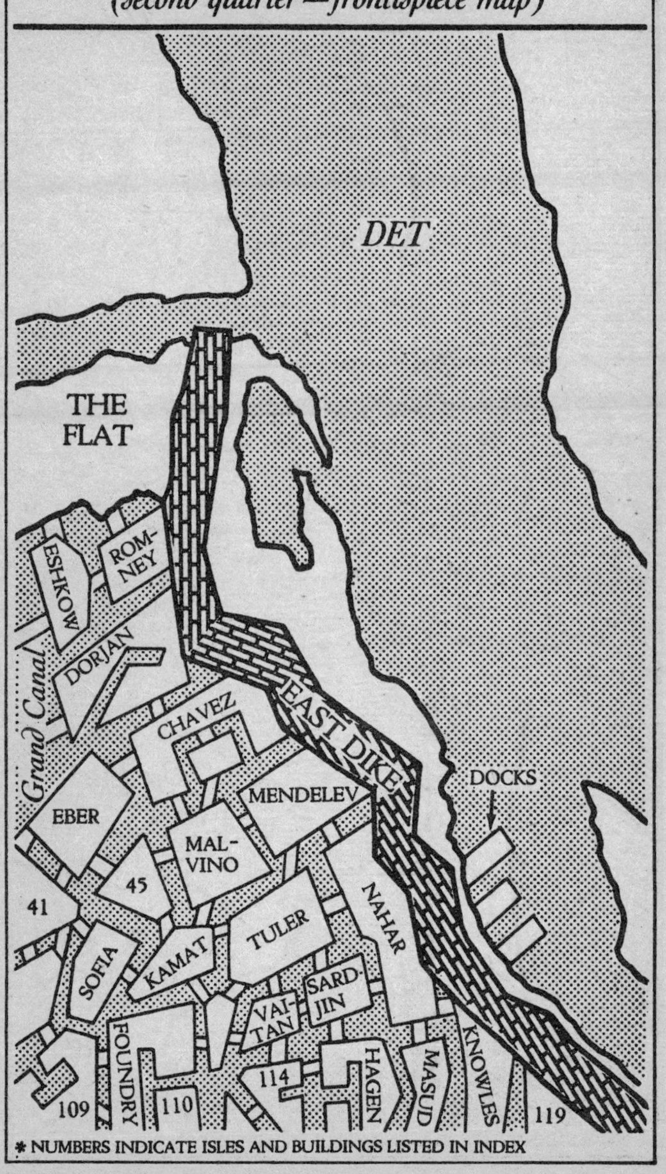
2
MEROVIN
(second quarter—frontispiece map)
DET
THE FLAT
ROMNEY
ESHKOW
DORJAN
Grand Canal
CHAVEZ
EAST DIKE
DOCKS
MENDELEV
EBER
MALVINO
45
41
NAHAR
TULER
SOFIA
KAMAT
SARDJIN
VAITAN
FOUNDRY
HAGEN
MASUD
KNOWLES
114
109
110
119
* NUMBERS INDICATE ISLES AND BUILDINGS LISTED IN INDEX

③

MEROVIN

(third quarter—frontispiece map)

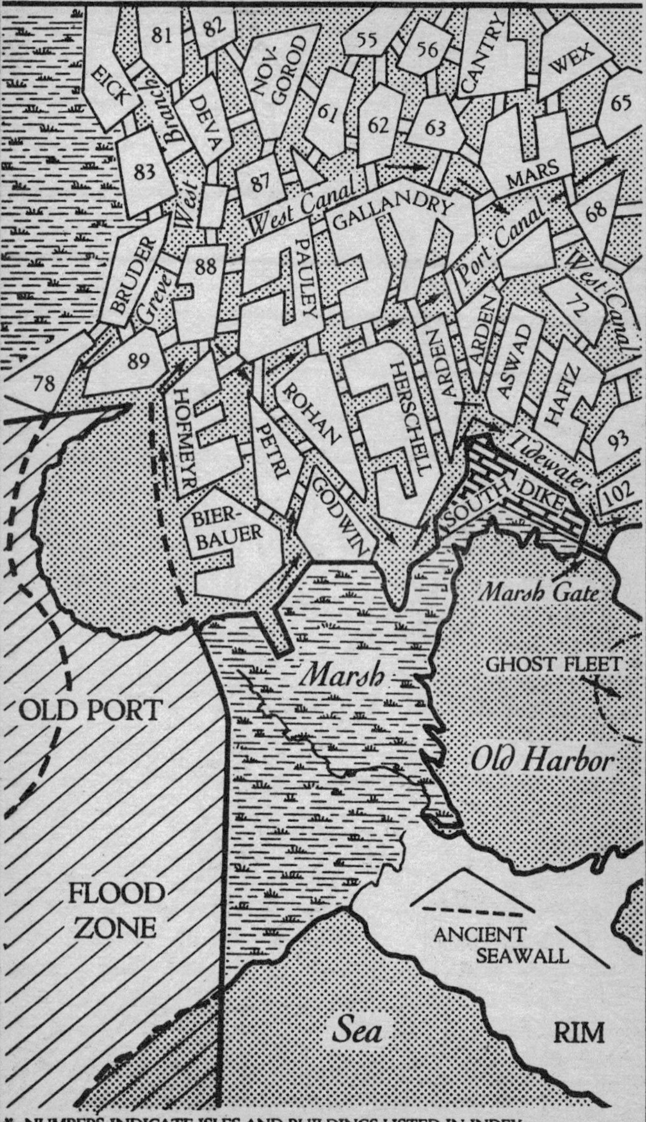

81 82 NOV-GOROD 55 56 CANTRY WEX
EICK Branch DEVA 61 62 63 65
83 87 MARS
West West Canal GALLANDRY
Port Canal 68
BRUDER Greve 88 PAULEY
West Canal 72
ARDEN ARDEN ASWAD
89 HERSCHELL
78 HOFMEYR ROHAN HAFIZ
PETRI 93
Tidewater
GODWIN SOUTH DIKE 102
BIER-BAUER
Marsh Gate
Marsh
GHOST FLEET
OLD PORT
Old Harbor
FLOOD ZONE
ANCIENT SEAWALL
Sea
RIM

* NUMBERS INDICATE ISLES AND BUILDINGS LISTED IN INDEX

MEROVIN

(fourth quarter—frontispiece map)

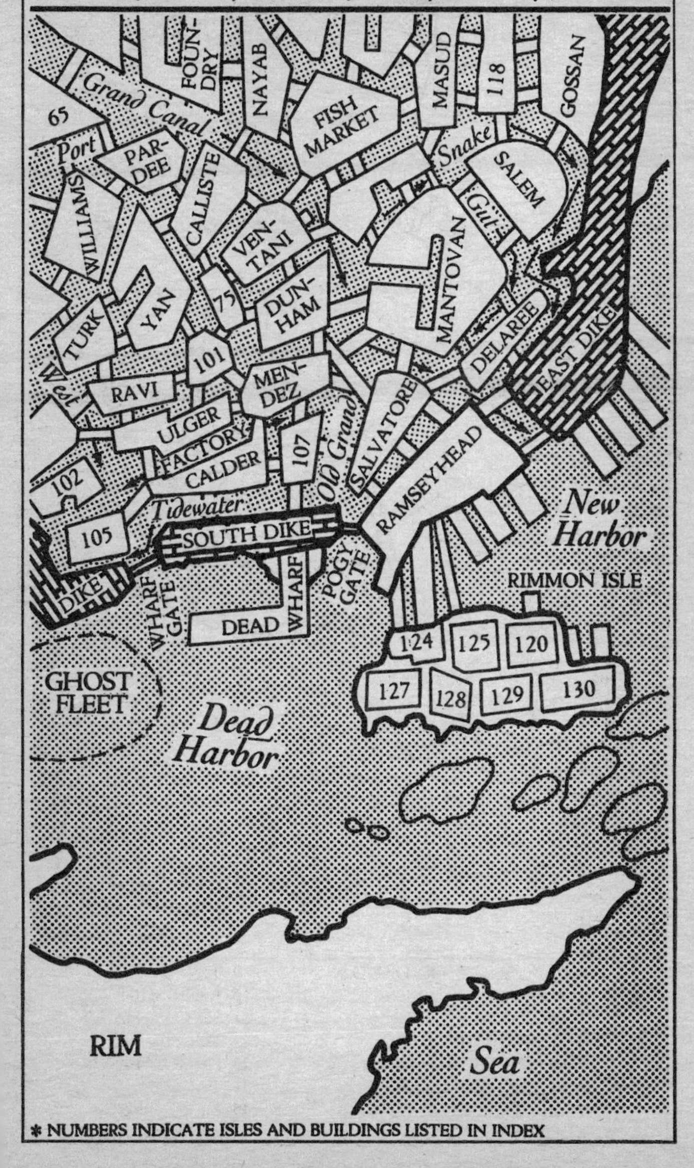

* NUMBERS INDICATE ISLES AND BUILDINGS LISTED IN INDEX

VENTANI ISLE

(Canalside Level showing Moghi's Tavern)

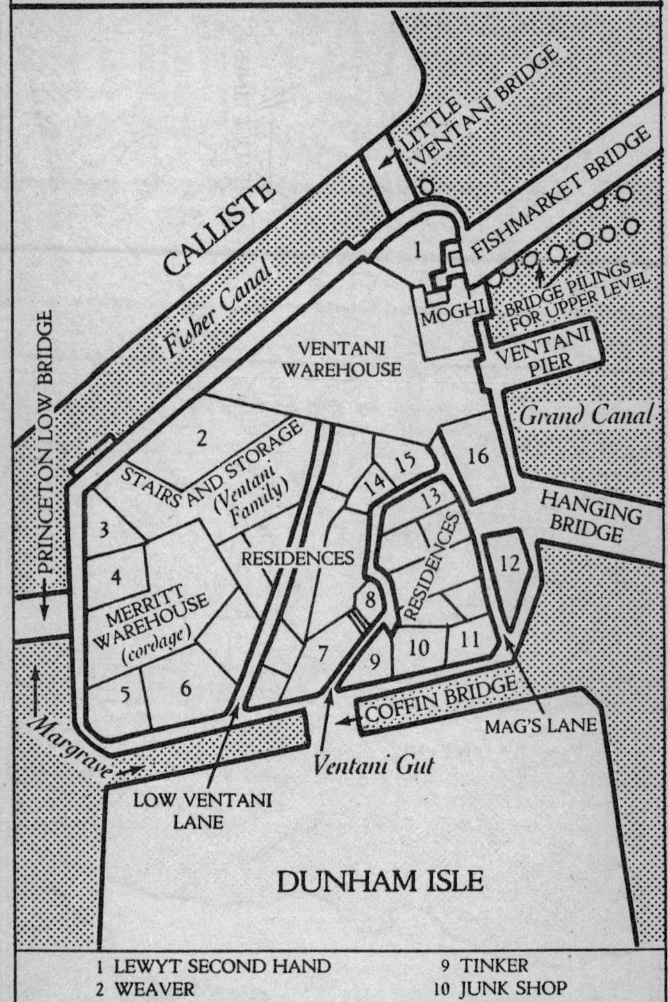

1 LEWYT SECOND HAND
2 WEAVER
3 DRUG
4 DOCTOR
5 CHANDLER
6 FURNITURE MAKER
7 KILIM'S USED CLOTHES
8 JONES
9 TINKER
10 JUNK SHOP
11 SECOND HAND
12 SPICERY
13 LIBERTY PAWN
14 TACKLE
15 MAG'S DRUG
16 ASSAN BAKERY

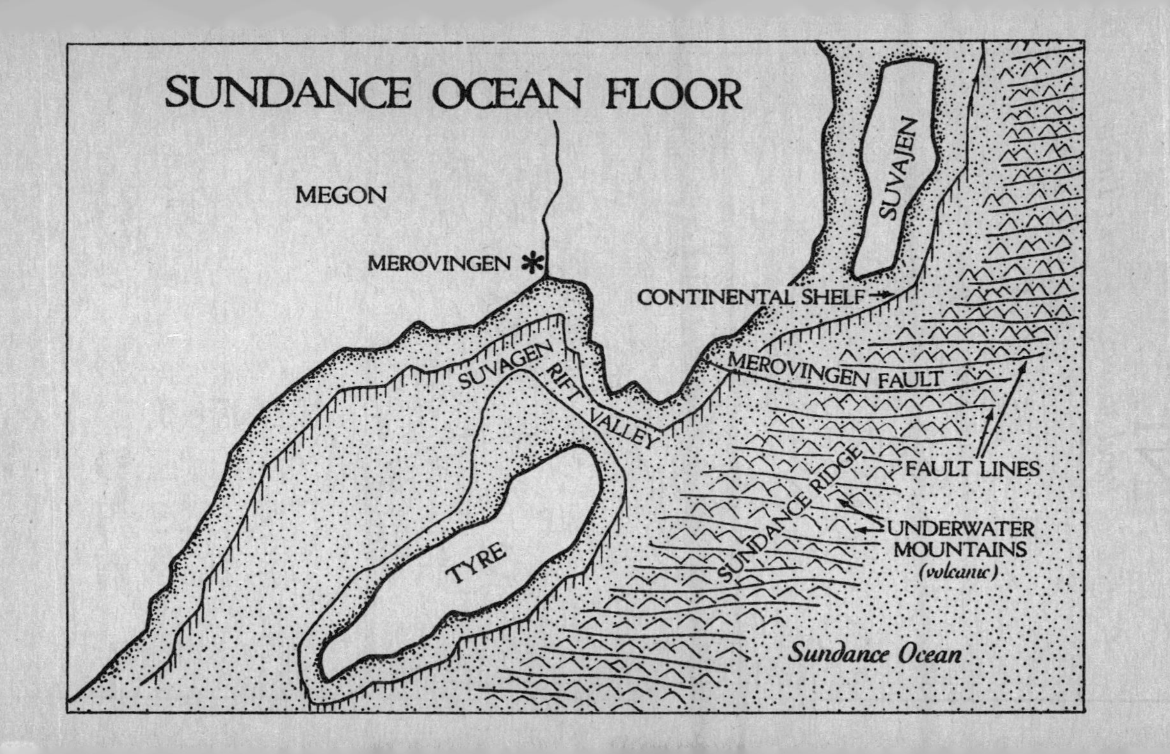
SUNDANCE OCEAN FLOOR
MEGON
MEROVINGEN
SUVAJEN
CONTINENTAL SHELF
SUVAGEN RIFT VALLEY
MEROVINGEN FAULT
TYRE
SUNDANCE RIDGE
FAULT LINES
UNDERWATER MOUNTAINS
(volcanic)
Sundance Ocean

MAJOR EASTERN OCEANIC CURRENTS

(affecting climate)

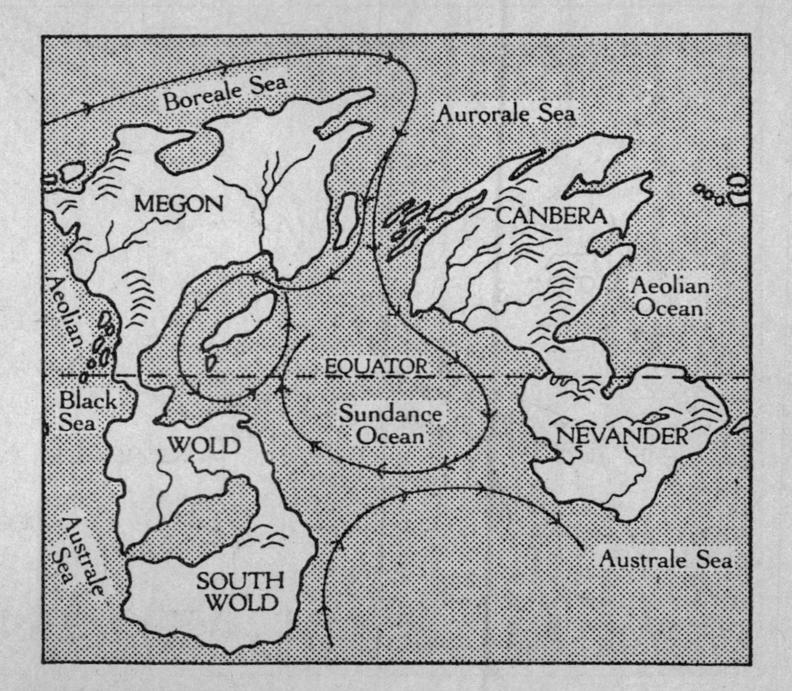

WESTERN

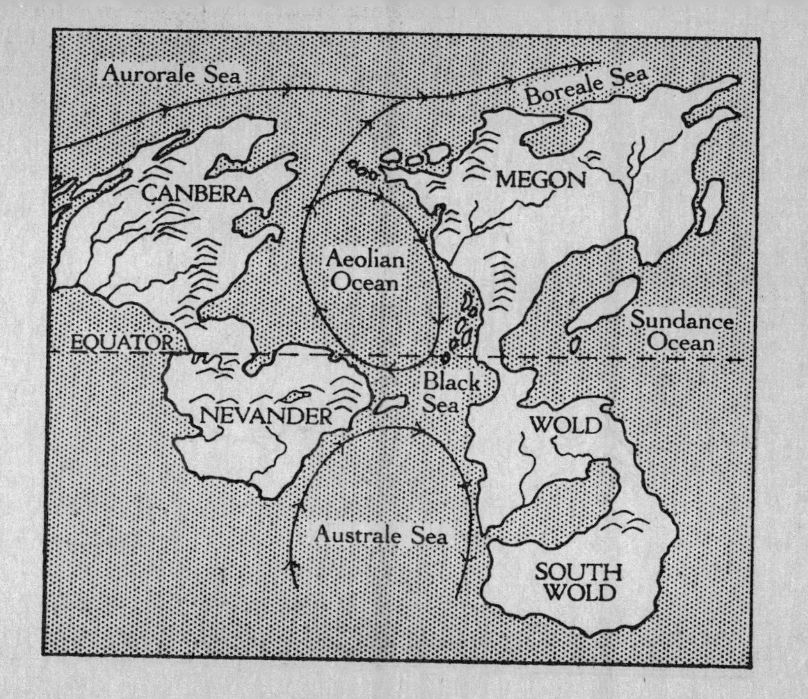
Aurorale Sea
Boreale Sea
CANBERA
MEGON
Aeolian Ocean
Sundance Ocean
EQUATOR
Black Sea
NEVANDER
WOLD
Australe Sea
SOUTH WOLD

WESTERN HEMISPHERE

BOB SHAW
has also written:

ONE MILLION TOMORROWS
OTHER DAYS, OTHER EYES
ORBITSVILLE
MEDUSA'S CHILDREN
PALACE OF ETERNITY
A BETTER MANTRAP

and many more.

''There's a minor planet in this system, name of Ceres, with a diameter of about seven hundred kilometres. I presume you've heard about its disappearance?''

''Yes, but . . . What has that to do with the Moon?''

''We put a bank of mass displacement units on Ceres and drove it out of orbit. It's on its way to the Moon right now, accelerating all the way, and in two days from now there's going to be one hell of a collision!''